WORKING FOR MR. EDWARDS

By Warren Allen

Published by Allen Literary Works, LLC

ISBN 978-0-9962394-0-0

For more information, visit:

www.iamwarrenallen.com

Editor: Tricia Scott

Cover Design: Matthew Morran

DEDICATION

My journey in life thus far has not been traveled alone. Indeed GOD has blessed me with the right people to help me along the way. I dedicate this book to two very important people; my loving parents Bruce and Lori Allen.

In the loving memory of my father, Bruce Allen I say this: I thank GOD for you and for the sixteen years he allowed me to spend with you. I thank you for the gift of your presence and for modeling manhood in front of me every day. I thank you for bestowing on me the honor of carrying your name. I cherish your memory and will forever hold you in my heart.

To my loving mother Lori Allen, the words thank you don't really seem to suffice when addressing the person who helped give me life. So my gratitude to you shall be in that of a different form. My thank you to you shall be in me reaching my full potential. As I ascend to new heights, I'll say thank you. In the pursuit and obtainment of my greatness, I'll say thank you. As I become the full embodiment of the man that GOD has called me to be, I'll say thank you. So, for now I say I love you...

Again to my loving parents I dedicate this book to you both. It truly is an honor and a privilege to be called your son.

Love always, Warren

TABLE OF CONTENTS

CHAPTER ONE
HUMBLE BEGINNINGS

It was Thursday night on the Winterville Community College Campus; however it wasn't the typical Thursday night antics. Not this Thursday night because tonight was the eve of graduation for this small class of one-hundred and twenty-five. Normally one would expect to find a campus filled with keg parties and beer pong tournaments on the night before its graduates were about to be sent off to fend for themselves in the uncertainty of the American workforce. However, on this night not one beer was sipped nor one pong tossed. Instead, all the seniors were huddled together at the Campus' not-so-state of the art auditorium. The atmosphere itself was a mixed breed, filled with the thoughts and memories of those who cherished the small town and its even smaller campus as well as the dismal opportunities it had to offer. Versus those who had a bright gleam in the eye of their minds caused by an overtaking euphoria of what the future might bring. However, there was one young man whose ambitions were set to full speed with no signs of slowing down. A young man, whose mind was made up that he was going to put the small town as well as its small minded people in his rearview mirror---a young man by the name of Jonathan Cross.

"Dude can you believe this is it?" "Kiss Winterville goodbye," David whispered to his friend in an excited tone. Jonathan turning his head to look his friend in the eyes and replied, "If you're referring to the end of this reoccurring four year nightmare then yes, I can most definitely believe it." said Jonathan in a sarcastic yet direct tone, "Man whatever, you act like this place is SO horrible", said David. "That's because it is", said Jonathan.

As they both rolled their eyes in a joking manner, they both turned to face the center of the auditorium where Dean Morgan was giving his classic pep talk he gives every senior class on the eve of graduation. "You have all done well and I'm very proud of all of you but I won't go into my big speech, I'll save that for tomorrow" said the Dean, with a sense of pride as if he raised all of the young adults seated before him. "Thank GOD", said Jonathan. As the Dean continued to speak, the students were beginning to get a little worn out from the Dean's long winded commentary. While Dean Morgan was still rambling on, a voice shouted out among the small mass of students. "All right now Dean, time to wrap it up!!" Laughter immediately began bursting out of the mouths of everyone in the auditorium; everyone except Dean Morgan. "All right who said that?!" shouted the Dean, his eyes scanning the rows of students looking for the random voice who interrupted him. As the students' laughter subsided, the Dean began his closing remarks. He had a look of forced sternness plastered on his face, giving breath to the illusion that he was closing with his speech of his own free will and not that of an unidentifiable voice that embarrassed him just a few moments ago. Jonathan sat there, stiffly unamused at the whole display of mediocrity as he fidgeted in his seat, his body expressing its discomfort of the environment.

"I think that moment summed up his entire life", said David with a cunning grin on his face. "And that might have been the most clever thing I've ever heard you say in yours", replied Jonathan. David smiled to himself and nodded his head in agreement, while Jonathan glanced down at his watch trying to figure out exactly how many minutes of his life had been lost. But suddenly he found his focus broken as he heard Dean Morgan say, "You are now dismissed!" As those joyous words passed from Dean Morgan's lips, the students started busting out of their seats and wasted no time stampeding to the exit doors of the auditorium.

"Hallelujah", he whispered to himself as Jonathan began to

rise from his seat while watching his fellow classmates rush through the doors as if their favorite celebrity was awaiting them on the other side.

As the crowd began to subside, Jonathan and David made their way into the aisle and headed out the door. As they exited the building they could feel the cold sharp air almost cut through their faces. "Dang!" "Did it drop thirty degrees while we were inside?" asked Jonathan. "Feels more like fifty but don't worry news said it's supposed to be eighty-five tomorrow. So everybody will be able to see those pearly whites when you walk across that stage", said David with a slight smirk. "Well I'll have to make sure I floss and brush real good in the back then won't I?" replied Jonathan. "You getting smart with me Mr. Cross?" "Cause if so, I'll have to call your momma." said David; as the two were walking through the crisp air of the night on the campus' ill kept sidewalks. Jonathan felt a sudden tingle on his leg. Jonathan looking down at his right leg pocket noticed a dim light shining through his jeans. He reached in his pocket and pulled out his cell phone, the name on the caller ID read *Mom*. "Ahh looks like she beat you to the punch Dave", said Jonathan. As Jonathan grabbed the phone, he saw David wave goodbye as they both began to head their separate ways. Jonathan now directing his attention to his phone pushed the answer button. "Hey, Hey", said Jonathan. His mother responding back in a high pitch and excited voice almost to the point of yelling said, "Hey Johnny! How's my handsome graduate doing?" Jonathan, with a look of both disbelief and embarrassment on his face shook his head while thinking to himself, "Did she really just say that?" "I'm doing pretty good mom, no complaints just ready to get this whole thing over with, ya know?" replied Jonathan.

"Oh, Johnny!!!", said Ms. Cross. Now her voice returning to a normal decibel level, "You really shouldn't say things like that because I'll tell you now, you're gonna be begging to have these days back when you get to be my age", advised Ms. Cross with a certain hint of reflection and nostalgia riddled within her voice. Jonathan allowing his mother's words to swiftly enter one ear and out the other promptly quipped, " Well I promise you this, if you ever hear me refer to these last four years as the best time of my life then I would have officially failed as a human being." Ms. Cross not sounding too receptive of Jonathan's display of jaded sentiment responded, "Sometimes I just don't know what I'm going to do with you." Jonathan began to smile to himself, "Well, hopefully you'll continue to love me because I heard that's what mothers do." "Well, look at you, getting ready to graduate and your already sassin your momma!" retorted Ms. Cross. As Jonathan heard his mother's remark he couldn't help but laugh. "Well, you know I'm just messing with ya." "Oh I know honey I just wish that you wouldn't." pleaded Ms. Cross in a joking manner. "Good One", said Jonathan with sarcasm grabbing his vocal cords with a strong grip. In fear of getting trapped in a two hour sappy phone call, Jonathan began to wrap up the conversation. "Well alright, I'm getting ready to head in I'll see you tomorrow." "Oh please, you're just trying to get off the phone with your Mother", replied Ms. Cross. Jonathan now rolling his eyes to the fact that his mother caught on to what he was doing. "I wrote the book on cutting conversations short, I used to do that to your grandmother all the time when I was in school", confessed Ms. Cross. "Alright then, so I guess you know how this works", said Jonathan. "You know what?" asked Ms. Cross. "Remind me to pop you when I get there tomorrow", she quipped. "Will do", said Jonathan with sarcasm still having that firm grip. "Well alright honey, I'll see you tomorrow around eleven o'clock, wanna make sure I get there early", said Ms. Cross. "Alright, sounds good", confirmed Jonathan. "Oh, and Jonathan one more thing", as Jonathan heard his mother say this he began to think to himself, "What is it now?" But to his surprise the next words that came out of his mother's mouth wasn't another lecture or anymore nagging questions. She simply said, "I love you Johnny and I'm very proud of you."

Upon hearing this, Jonathan took a moment to think about what his mother was saying about enjoying the moment and to soak in these college graduation memories. Perhaps she had a point, hearing her say she loved him made him think about that but only for a moment. Then he thought about how ready he was to move forward with his life and what it had in store for him outside the confines of the infamous Winterville mentality. He also began to think about how much he loved the woman on the other end of the phone. How much she had sacrificed for him over the years and what it would mean for her to have her only son graduate from college to begin his own quest through life. It was odd at first but Jonathan never stopped to think about the fact that this graduation was more than just about him, perhaps for her sake maybe he would attempt to put on a happy face. With all of that in mind Jonathan simply replied, "I love you too."

As Jonathan hung up the phone, he looked around the campus. His eyes scanning the scattered groups of students who were still lingering around the campus yard after enduring Dean Morgan's recycled and less than mediocre speech no longer than ten minutes ago. Jonathan stood still in the chill of the night's breeze as he watched his fellow classmates laugh and interact with one another. He noticed that one group of students seemed to be playing what could only be described as a miserable attempt of charades. He then directed his attention to two couples who were apparently engaged in a serious game of hacky sack. His line of sight then shifted toward two jocks who were seated at one of the worn down wooded tables outside. The duo were competing in a good old fashion arm wrestling match, while being surrounded by some of their fellow teammates shouting and egging each other on to see who would win. As Jonathan continued to look around, he began to wonder what some of these youthful faces would do with themselves and their lives. He wondered how many of them aspired to be something once they would receive that diploma tomorrow afternoon. He imagined if any of them would be successful at their craft or even stand out in their profession. He also contemplated if he was in the midst of any future doctors, engineers, lawyers, or any future big wig politicians. He simply wondered if any of his fellow classmates from the Winterville *Wildcats* would change the world. Unfortunately, it only took Jonathan about half of a millisecond to come up with the answer to that question and the answer NO echoed from the depths of his belly. Jonathan had a mental and emotional grudge against *W.C.C* and all of its residents. The reason for his emotional hostility could be summed up in one word, that word was **_small_**. Jonathan didn't like the fact that Winterville was a relatively small town or that the campus itself was a small campus. Neither did he like the fact that the student population was around 1,300 students and that was before almost half of the senior class dropped out. He had grown disgusted with Winterville. In fact, the only reason he went to College in Winterville is because he wasn't able to secure a scholarship to one of the schools he *really* wanted to attend. There was just no way he would've been able to afford that school without a scholarship. So, he got stuck with attending the less expensive and much smaller community college. He also felt that even most of the people of Winterville were small minded. He would often test out his theory by striking up conversations with his fellow classmates to see what their plans were for post college life. Many times to his constant disappointment the answers were never surprising, either they planned on working on the family farm or they were going to be working for a relative in one of their small local businesses. This frame of mind just didn't go over well with Jonathan because Jonathan was a young man with vision, high goals, and the ever present force of self-motivation to not become like one of his Winterville counter parts. Jonathan wasn't the type of person to take pride in humble beginnings; on the contrary, he was the type who took pride in bettering himself and achieving his goals so that he could have a successful future. With this in mind he stood there in the cool of the night as he thought to himself that he would be different. He would do everything within his power to make sure that he broke free from the confines and limitations of what this small town prison had constructed. He made a mental pact with himself that he would not settle for less in life and that he wouldn't be afraid to venture out and take chances.

While Jonathan's mind was still engaged in deep thought his eyes continued to peruse the students who were spread throughout the campus yard. It was then when he noticed a small group of three students who seemed to be wrapped in deep thoughts of their own. He stopped for a moment to make sure what he was seeing was indeed what he thought he was seeing and not just some illusion. As Jonathan began to intently stare at these unfamiliar faces, his mind immediately started to go through its memory files to see if he knew these students. However, to Jonathan's surprise his mind came up blank.

Given the fact that the graduating class was only one hundred and twenty-five people, their faces at the very least should've looked familiar. This definitely sparked Jonathan's interest and without hesitation, he began to make his way over to the three students. Wanting to avoid looking overtly obvious, Jonathan started to slowly walk in the direction of the three students. As he made his way over to the mystery trio, he noticed that they were all seated on the ground by a thick tree. Closest to the tree, with their backs turned were two young guys seated near each other and facing in front of them was a young woman. As Jonathan made his way closer he pretended to be looking around, so that the three of them wouldn't realize that he was trying to listen to their conversation. As he got closer he was able to start making out some words, however he made sure that he walked passed them and stood somewhat close so he could hear what they were saying. As he stood about a foot away he began to listen to their conversation in an attempt to figure out what they were talking about. He heard the girl say that she just couldn't believe what was going on. The two guys nodded their heads and said that they felt the same way. As Jonathan heard this, he wondered what they were really talking about. Could it be that something actually worthwhile was taking place in Winterville? Perhaps they knew something important that he didn't, that involved the school or maybe there were some new policies that the school was adopting? The possibilities seemed endless and at this point Jonathan was definitely intrigued. As he continued to listen, he heard the young girl clearly say, "I just can't believe she broke up with him, they've been together since season one!" Once those words hit Jonathan's ears and traveled to his brain it registered to him that these three were sitting around a tree and talking about a DAMN T.V. SHOW!! He immediately lost focus and respect for the mystery trio and all hope was deflated. Without thinking Jonathan instinctively responded with a bewildered look on his face, "Are you serious?" As he said this he thought to himself that he did not mean to say that out loud. However the three students all turned their heads and looked directly at him. Thinking that he was trying to join in on the conversation the young woman replied "Oh my God, you watch the show too?!" As she said this, she turned her body to the left and it was then that Jonathan quickly directed his attention to the girl's neon orange shirt that read *"Class of 2018"*. As the girl sat there awaiting Jonathan's reply he just shook his head and walked away. *"Freshman"*, Jonathan said under his breath as he walked away in slight disgust at what just happened. Although that moment was very disappointing to Jonathan, due to the fact that for a brief moment, he thought that there might have been some others like him on Campus. He also took the time to reflect on the slight silver lining of this present dark cloud, because this incident did nothing more than offer more proof that Jonathan did indeed need to leave this place and never look back.

At this point Jonathan made up in his mind that he has had

enough disappointment for one night and decided to head back to his dorm room. He continued to walk across the campus yard, however this time he didn't bother to look at what the other students were doing. This time he kept his eyes forward and his legs moved with a swifter urgency, as if he was running from something. Contrary to Jonathan's mind that's exactly what he was doing; running from something. Except this something, wasn't visible to the human eye yet its presence was still felt and posed a very real threat to Jonathan. It harbored the threat of failure and mediocrity within in its veins. Jonathan felt that it was like the very spirit of Winterville was piercing his mind and body so that he would remain in the small town just like the rest of its victims. This was what the people of Winterville were in Jonathan's eyes, victims of mediocrity and failure. As he continued to walk through the campus, Jonathan quickly began to realize that he didn't need to be afraid because he knew that after tomorrow it would be all over. Still walking swiftly he glanced upward and noticed that his dorm building was in sight and he was only two minutes away from arriving at its front door.

As he continued to walk to the dorm he managed to look around at some of the campus and thought that this would be the last time he would see this place and walk on its worn down grass. It would be the last time that he would have to wait in long lines in the cafeteria just to eat what looked like grey slop. It would be the last time that he would have to sit through an hour long lecture led by his verbally bland professor.

As he smiled at this realization, he also noticed that he was approaching the front door of his building. Jonathan walked toward the door, and reached in his pocket for his keys. He grabbed his keys out of his right pocket, put them in the doorknob and opened the door. Jonathan walked into the entry way only to be greeted by several of the seniors running around the small lobby in their underwear. They were all singing *"We-are-the-Champions"* entirely out of sync. Jonathan paid them no attention as he made his way to the stairs, he knew he only had to travel up three short flights of stairs and he would be in his room. As he made his way up the stairs he saw more and more guys living up their last night as college kids. Some took to a game of cards; others were in their rooms with the door opened conducting Madden tournaments. Jonathan just simply wanted to get back to his room, maybe watch a movie and hit the sack. As he traveled up the last flight of stairs he could see his room at the end of the hallway. He remembered that out of all the things he didn't like about the campus, his room was the one thing that he actually <u>did</u> enjoy. His old roommate, Jerry who was about a hundred pounds overweight and never stopped talking, had to move out last semester.

It turned out that Jerry's dad needed him to start working at the family meat packing company a lot sooner than the both of them expected. So off Jerry went, and left Jonathan with the dorm room all to himself with no one there to annoy him with their snoring or late night snacking on bacon double cheeseburgers. Jonathan unlocked the door to the room and stood in the doorway for a brief moment. He reached around with his right hand to turn on the light; he did a quick scan of the room and took a big sigh of relief. He thought to himself that it had been a long day and an even longer night and he was ready to do nothing more than relax and unwind. Jonathan walked in the room and closed the door behind him. He walked to his bed and sat down on the edge. Jonathan always thought that the mattress was pretty comfortable for a cheap college one. He slid off his shoes and laid down on the bed staring at the ceiling. At this point he thought to himself that the movie was out and he was heading straight to bed. He figured that the faster he went to sleep, the faster the next day would come. So with this in mind he got up and changed his clothes and got ready for bed. He cut on the lamp next to his bed and then walked toward the door to shut off the main light. The room was now dimly lit and he walked back to his bed and stood at its side for a moment.

He thought to himself that this would be the last time that he would sleep in this room and this bed. He then got under the covers and once again he began to stare at the ceiling.

His thoughts still very much focused on how after tomorrow he would begin a whole new journey in life. Actually; in Jonathan's eyes the first day of his life would start tomorrow and everything up until then was just practice. Just like when they show previews when you go to see a movie, it's just something to occupy you before the main event starts. Winterville was nothing more than a preview of a movie that Jonathan would never attempt to go see. After he walked across that stage tomorrow it would be as if the lights in the theater were dimming, signifying the real movie was about to begin. This thought fresh in his mind Jonathan turned to his right side and turned off the lamp. As Jonathan laid there in the dark, he thought to himself that the previews were definitely over and that the real movie was about to start.

CHAPTER TWO
GRADUATION

The next morning Jonathan laid in the bed still sound asleep. The room was full with a calm and peaceful silence hovering over the atmosphere. Jonathan was still submerged in a deep sleep until the sound of his alarm clock cut through the air like a high powered chain saw. Jonathan's eyes sprang open as his body instinctively rose up; dazed for a moment he paused to collect his thoughts. He was experiencing that initial moment in the morning when someone first wakes up, before their memories come rushing toward their brain. Nevertheless, the moment quickly passed and Jonathan definitely remembered where he was and what today was. Today was the day that he would remember for the rest of his life. He even might go as far as to say that this is the day he was actually re-born. Today was the day that life became life and had some excitement and meaning to it and if he was lucky maybe a little adventure too! However, before any of this was going to happen, Jonathan needed to shut off that alarm clock. Still screeching, the clock continued to blast its high pitched sound that somewhat resembles a cross between a rooster and nails going down on a chalk board. Jonathan swung his legs across the bed onto the floor. Sitting upward, he reached for the alarm clock that was on the left night stand next to his bed and using his fingers to feel its way towards the snooze button, he was startled at a sudden loud knock at the door. He quickly looked over to the door to see it shaking from someone pounding their fist on it from the other side. Jonathan yelled out, "Who is it?!" With the alarm clock still going off, the voice on the other side of the door yelled back, "Hey, shut that crap off!!"

Jonathan shook his head in the same way someone would if

they just witnessed something disappointing. He reached his hand behind the night stand and yanked the cord out from the wall. The room was silent again and Jonathan could tell that the person at the door had left because he didn't see a shadow underneath the door. Still seated at the side of his bed he got up and walked over to his jeans that were across the room crumpled up in a ball. He had thrown them there last night because he was ready to go to sleep and didn't feel like hanging them up. He also knew that he had left his cell phone in those jeans; he would be able to see what time it was from the clock on the phone. He bent down to unfold his jeans and grab the phone from out of his pocket. The time on the phone said **9:15 A.M.**; the graduation ceremony was scheduled to begin at 12 noon. He also noticed that his phone was left on vibrate and he missed two calls from his mother, as well as a text from his friend David. He pressed the enter button on the text message icon and read the message. It read "Sup bro!!! We made it man, try not to trip out there today LOL!" Jonathan stood up as he read the text message and had a slight smirk on his face after he finished reading it. He knew his mother would be at the school around eleven, so he looked around his room to make sure that everything was in order. Despite a few clothes on the floor and his bed unmade the room was actually in pretty good shape. However, just to be on the safe side he swept the floor neatly and began to pick up his few clothes that were on the floor. After he was done with that he made up his bed and headed to the bathroom to take a shower. As he walked into the bathroom his feet touched the cold tile, which made him think of the times Jerry would shave his overly hairy gorilla like chest and leave the hair on the floor. He also thought about that fact Jerry was no longer there and within a couple of hours he too wouldn't be there either. He hopped in the shower to give himself a jolt of energy and really wake himself up. Jonathan would rarely start his day off without a shower; some people get up and work out, others grab a big breakfast or a hot cup of coffee on their way to work. This wasn't the case for Jonathan; all he needed was some warm water on his body to get him going. After he finished, he grabbed the towel from off the rack and dried off. With his towel now wrapped around his waist he walked over to the sink and ran his hands across the mirror to clear the steam off, so he could brush his teeth.

Now that he had his normal daily grooming out of the way, he opened the bathroom door and headed toward the small closet that was tucked away toward the right side of his room. Jonathan slid the closet door back and saw his light blue dress shirt and khaki pants that he had ironed three days ago, in anticipation for this very day. To make sure that he wouldn't forget anything he already had his brown belt neatly wrapped around the waist of his pants, as well as he his brown loafers with the dress socks already inside the shoe nestled away on the closet floor. In the corner of his eye he could see a green light shining, grabbing his attention. He turned his head slightly to the left and in there hanging up was his cap and gown. The school had made some poor decisions and decided to wait until the last minute to order the cap and gowns for the students. The result of this lack of preparation was that the school was only able to get these neon green gowns that weren't very flattering and weren't even close to the school colors. Who knew that they even made graduation gowns in neon green? Jonathan thought that it was absolutely ridiculous and he'd probably look like a giant green skittle walking across the stage, but at the same time he didn't care, just as long as he got his diploma. He stood there for a second trying to soak in the fact that it was all about to be over in a few hours. Fantasizing about this day was one thing but to be actually experiencing it was a completely different scenario. Jonathan couldn't help but let out a small but satisfying laugh. He grabbed his clothes and got dressed, as he was tying his shoes he heard a faint buzzing sound from his cell phone vibrating on the hardwood floor. He could feel the small sound waves traveling through the floorboards. He took two quick steps   toward his phone and picked it up; the screen displayed the name "*David Nickels*". David was Jonathan's closest and only <u>real</u> friend on campus as well as the only person Jonathan would miss from Winterville. He tapped the answer button on his phone, "You ready to start that next chapter of your life?" asked Jonathan with a slight dose of excitement in his voice. "Unlike you Johnny, I kinda like the chapter I'm on."   "Hell, I might even flip back a couple of pages and read it again", said David in a joking manner. "Well, I tell you what." "Read it again   and let me know if it ends differently from the first time you read it", replied Jonathan. "Hey, look here funnyman, my folks are here and they wanted to know if you and your Mom wanted to join us for dinner after the graduation ceremony?" Jonathan knew that after today, he wouldn't see David for a while so he thought that this might be a good way to spend more time with his friend before he left. "Yeah man, that sounds like a plan." "I'll let my Mom know when she gets here", replied Jonathan. "Well look, that's later, you wanna go grab some breakfast from the cafeteria real quick?" asked David. "Like right now?" asked Jonathan. "No, I was thinking more on the lines of next Tuesday." "Yeah, Cross right now!" replied David in a joking manner. "Ha-ha alright, you wanna just meet me there?" asked Jonathan. "Well actually I'm right outside your door now." said David. Right as David finished saying this; Jonathan heard a knock at the door. He hung up the phone and headed toward the door with a grin across his face. He hollered out "Who is it!" "It's your fairy godmother with a bottle of tequila, open up." said David.

As Jonathan opened up the door he saw David standing there in a neatly pressed pink dress shirt with dark brown khakis which had been over loaded with starch. Before Jonathan could open his mouth to speak David looks at him and says "Well aren't you a sight for sore eyes." "Yea, but I think your actually making my eyes sore just by looking at you." said Jonathan, while David stood there standing in the doorway leaning on the doorframe with his left shoulder. "Well you ready to go princess or what?," asked David. Jonathan taking his hand off the door knob and turned around to start making his way toward the nightstand. "Yea just let me grab my wallet and we can roll", replied Jonathan as he headed back toward the door. When he walked out of the room, he grabbed the door handle and shut the door behind him. Both of them now walking down the hall with David predicting how the day was going to play out, "Aight so here's the plan, we go grab some breakfast, head back to our rooms, do the whole graduation thing, go grab some dinner with my parents then it's PARTY TIME!!"

As Jonathan listened to David he knew that he probably wasn't going to want to go to some graduation party that would be filled with some of the very people he was trying to leave behind. Knowing this Jonathan just nodded his head in agreement, knowing that he would probably tell David later that he wouldn't be joining the festivities. The two continued their journey down the stairs and made their way to the entrance of the dorm. As they approached the door Jonathan could see the sunshine running through the glass windows at the front of the building. He could see some people already celebrating outside and walking around in those ugly cap and gowns. At this point David was still talking to Jonathan but Jonathan was in somewhat of a trance in thinking about how he was going to feel once he could finally be free from the bondage of Winterville. As the two of them walked outside he began to hear David's voice more clearly, like how when a blurry picture begins to come into focus. Then suddenly he heard David say "You hearing me Cross?" "Yea man I hear ya," retorted Jonathan even though he had stopped listening to David a few sentences back. As the two walked out of the dorm they were greeted with the sounds of laughter and raw excitement from some of the seniors who were more than ready to graduate. Similar to last night they were all scattered around the campus yard, in the same way marbles are scattered after being tossed on the floor. David and Jonathan continued to walk through the campus yard. The cafeteria was a small separate building located in the middle of the campus, Jonathan always thought that it was entirely too small, even for the amount of people that attended the school. Jonathan could feel the back of his neck starting to build up sweat from all the heat outside. He remembered that the forecast predicted that it was going to be 85° today and to make matters worse he was wearing his dress shirt. Not wanting to risk the chance of him sweating up the back of his shirt, he started to unbutton his top button as they were walking. David noticed what he was doing looked and over to him and said, "Tryna look good for the ladies, huh?" Jonathan looking straight ahead as he was walking responded, "Nah, just trying not to sweat so I don't look like Aquaman by this afternoon."

As the two soon-to-be-graduates continued to walk through what now seemed like a parade of students out on the campus yard, they finally made it to the front doors of the cafeteria. David opened up the door and allowed Jonathan to go in but not without announcing, "Lady's first" as Jonathan entered the room. The aroma of cheap and overcooked cafeteria food flooded Jonathan's nostrils almost immediately like a violent intruder. For once the cafeteria was full, no doubt due to it being graduation day. "Dang, it's packed in here!" said David entering behind Jonathan. "Yea like pigs to the slaughter," replied Jonathan under his breath." "Huh?" questioned David. "I said it looks like there are no seats", countered Jonathan.

Looking over the room they noticed that it was a lot of families that were eating with their soon to be graduates, which explained the cafeteria's apparent popularity spike. "Well, look how bout we just hop in line and see if we can find a seat by the time we get our food," suggested David. Jonathan could already feel himself starting to get annoyed at the situation and felt an almost possessive urge to just leave and head back to his room. That was until he saw that David had already headed toward the line and he didn't want to just leave him there, despite the fact that it was a very tempting proposition. Jonathan said his excuse me's as he passed through the crowd of people to get in line. Once he got there he grabbed one of the classic red trays that all schools seem to have no matter the grade level. Although Jonathan enjoyed hanging out with David, he was feeling as if it would have been better if he stayed in his room until the graduation ceremony. As the two of them made their way through the line Jonathan was now able to get a clear view of what he was about to digest, or at least attempt to anyway. Behind the glass panels were three trays, one was full of oatmeal, the other was scrambled eggs, and the one on the far right was filled with waffles. However, to Jonathan it appeared to be light brown slop, a block of yellow slop, and individual squared slop. As he slid his tray across the metal railing he told the lady behind the counter he would just take a bowl of oatmeal. As he paid for his bowl of slop he tried to look at the bright side of things and thought to himself that at least this was the last bowl of slop the would ever eat from this kitchen. The two of them got out of line and walked over to the side of one of the vending machines near the food line. The cafeteria tables were like the ones you mostly see in middle school and even some elementary schools. The tables were long and already had the benches attached to them like one piece of furniture. Jonathan never liked these tables because it always meant that you were going to be seated next to someone you didn't know, or in his case didn't like. David spotted a table that had enough room on the end for two people. They made their way over to the table and sat down; Jonathan wanted to make sure that he sat on the end that way he didn't have to sit next to anyone besides David. As the two grabbed their seat they began to discuss what they wanted to do next with their lives after graduation. Although they've had this conversation before, Jonathan was hoping that David might have changed his mind in regards to taking over his family's local grocery store.

"So have you thought about what you wanna do when you

leave?" asked Jonathan. David lifting his head up in pride looked over to Jonathan and said "You already know what time it is man, you're looking at the future manager slash owner of Stop-N-Shop, which is now proudly located in two counties I might add", David said. Jonathan always thought that David had hidden potential but if left unattended to could fade away along with any dream of a better life outside of Winterville. The only problem with that was it wasn't David's dream it was Jonathan's dream for him. As Jonathan heard his answer he took a deep mental sigh that was strong enough to seep through his face and form a facial expression of disapproval. However, Jonathan didn't even realize that his facial tick had even occurred, but David did. Jonathan had his head down toward the bowl as he continued to pick through his oatmeal, unaware of the storm that was brewing right next to him. David paused in his seat, his body not moving a muscle, all the while his eyes intensely focused on Jonathan. "What's that supposed to mean Cross?" asked David. Jonathan turned his head to look at David. As their eyes meet Jonathan could see that David was upset however Jonathan was still oblivious as to what was going on. "What do you mean?" Jonathan asked. David now staring at him with an intent look on his face said, "What is it about this place you hate so bad, huh?" "You think your better than me or something because you have these big shot plans to leave town and try to land some fancy job." said David. Jonathan was trying to interject but was cut off by David's rising tone of voice. "See, that's your problem, you think you're better than everybody!" snapped David. At this point, people around the table were starting to direct their attention toward David and Jonathan's heated discussion. Jonathan began to adjust himself slightly in his seat, as he continued to attempt to calm David down. "Dave, I didn't say anything", said Jonathan. "Oh no, you said something alright, loud and clear!" shouted David.

Jonathan was now embarrassed at the scene the two of them were causing and looked at David with a blank expression. "Look man I didn't mean too…" but before he could finish David cut him off again. "Let me guess, you didn't mean anything by it." David continued, "You know I'm so sick of you always talking about how you're gonna leave and never look back!" "Well I'm sorry we all held you back, sorry we can't all be superficial and self absorbed like you!" David yelled.

Jonathan was stunned by this sudden onslaught of verbal arrows that were being hurled by one of his best friends although Jonathan was unsure as to whether or not David would still want to carry that title after this conversation. Jonathan didn't know what to do. On one hand, he felt that David was blowing this thing way out of proportion and on the other hand, he knew what David was accusing him of wasn't really too far from the truth. One could even say it wasn't far at all. Jonathan took a moment to pause, his head slightly down as if he was searching for the words to say. As if the words were some how on the floor squirming around. Meanwhile, David's frustration wedged between Jonathan and himself all the while his eyes stayed in tuned to Jonathan's every tick. Jonathan now slightly lifting his head and looking David back in the face, he could feel the eyes of those who were near the table looking at him, to see what was going to happen next. Jonathan opened his mouth but paused before speaking, the same way one would hesitate before taking a big leap. "I'm sorry man" said Jonathan; while thinking about the various different occasions that he would often take to express his bleak opinion about Winterville.

The words left his lips and momentarily took flight into the air only to land on deaf ears. David was not moved by what he felt coming from Jonathan, was a lackluster apology. David shook his head and swung his legs out from underneath the cramped table and rose to his feet. Jonathan sighed because he knew that David was upset and didn't plan on listening to anything he had to say. Jonathan continued to watch David as he started to walk away from the table and headed toward the front door. As Jonathan sat there at the table, his oatmeal now resembling a hard block of brown rigid ice, his mind entertained swirling thoughts of how maybe he had made too many comments in the past. Jonathan's eyes continued watching David's back as he stomped his way toward the front door he seemed to swiftly disappear into the midst of the crowd and faded out of Jonathan's sight. Although Jonathan was remorseful for giving David the impression that he didn't approve of his plans of working at the Stop-N-Shop, it still didn't erase his drive and longing for something more out of life. That was one thing that Jonathan refused to feel guilty or apologize for, even if it came at the expense of his friend's feelings. Jonathan continued to stay glued to his seat as he turned his attention back toward his breakfast of champions, which had appeared to evolve into something else over the course of him and David's unpleasant conversation. He glared at the small white bowl that sat before him, grabbed his plastic spoon, jammed it in the oatmeal and slid the bowl away from him toward the middle of the table. Some of the students seated at Jonathan's table continued to stare as Jonathan excused himself from the table while leaving the bowl of oatmeal behind. He noticed the cafeteria had gotten even more crammed with students and parents. He sucked his teeth when he realized that he was going to have to make his way through the crowd of people. Jonathan could see that the double doors at the front were filled with people constantly walking in. He always thought that the school should've given the cafeteria another set of doors for people to exit from. However, this current inconvenience was just further proof to him that the school was ill equipped and that he was definitely doing the right thing by leaving and not looking back. Jonathan continued to make his way to the front as he rubbed against what seemed to be a never ending supply of people. The cafeteria was humid from all the body heat and the smell of sweat began to blend together with the aroma of the cheap cafeteria food. This profane combination started to creep its way up Jonathan's nostrils and traveled down through the pit of his stomach which made him feel nauseous. He quickly put his hand over his mouth with a tight grip to prevent him from both breathing in the air as well as keeping him from vomiting on someone. His legs picked up the pace while the rest of his body followed suit. He saw that he was approaching the front door and not a minute too soon before he reached the doorway and before his last few steps, he took his hands off his mouth. He collected himself and thought that he was ready to push the fast forward button on today so he could skip right to graduation. He did a good once over on the campus yard to see if he saw David but there were too many people out at the same time.

Everyone was all dressed up ready for the big event that they all seemed to just merge together like one big blob of people. Jonathan remained where he was when he heard his phone ringing. He thought it might have been David calling to smooth things over; after all they were best friends. However, it wasn't David's name that showed up on the caller ID, it was his mother. He answered the phone, "Hey" he said. "Hey Johnny!!" shouted Ms. Cross. "I'm pulling up to your dorm now!" she said. Not only could Jonathan hear the eagerness in her voice but he could clearly envision her with a wide bright smile on her face as she said this. "You're here early," said Jonathan in a tone that suggested a question more than a statement. "Well you could sound a little bit more excited to see your mom," said a sarcastic Ms. Cross. "And besides its 10:45; now where are you so I can hug your face and embarrass you in front of your friends", teased Ms. Cross. Upon hearing this, Jonathan moved the phone away from his ear almost in disbelieve that the time had flown by like that. It seemed like only a few minutes ago that he and David were making their way to the cafeteria. He looked at the screen and now the time read 10:47 AM, as he read the time he could hear his mother's muffled voice coming from the phone. He quickly put the phone back to his ear. "Hello, Johnny are you there?" asked Ms. Cross. "Yea, I'm here" replied Jonathan. "I'm headed back to the dorm now", said Jonathan as he began to make his way toward that direction. The campus courtyard was packed full of family members visiting and students basking in their success of how they made it through their four year academic trek. In order to avoid a repeat of being caught in a large mass of people, Jonathan quickly began to move through the crowd. "Well hey, listen I'm on my way back now so I'll see you in a minute" said Jonathan. "Alright honey, I'll see you in a few", said Ms. Cross Jonathan continued to quickly move through the crowd almost to the point of jogging. As he got closer he began looking around to see if he would see his mother in front of the dorm holding some corny graduation poster that she worked on the night before.

There was a small parking lot to the left side of the building, even though it was more like just ten spaces that the maintenance crew painted a few months back. He scanned it thinking he would see his mother's car and sure enough it was parked two spaces from the right. He walked over to the car with a smirk on his face with hopes of one day getting his mother a new set of wheels. He could see her face through the windshield as she stared back at him with a huge grin on her face. She opened the car door and quickly made her way to the front of the car. He could see his mother standing in front of the car. She was considered a tall woman by her family's standards, standing at 5' 10" with light brown hair with golden highlights throughout her hair which appeared lazy as it draped down her neck and rested on her shoulders. She stood there as Jonathan made his way toward her. She smiled with pure joy in seeing her little boy now appearing as a young man before her eyes. "Hey you!" exclaimed Ms. Cross, as she met her son with a warm embrace wrapping her arms around him and tightly squeezing him as if he were going off to war. "Hey!" said Jonathan. They released from their embrace as Ms. Cross looked up toward her son. "It's good to see you again kiddo!" said Ms. Cross. "It'll be even better to see me when I've got that diploma in my hand" replied Jonathan. Ms. Cross still holding him tightly, "I wish you would stop rushing toward the future so hard and just learn how to live in today." They loosened their grip from each other as Jonathan gave thought to what his mother said. "Well how 'bout this, I need to go upstairs real quick and grab my cap and gown", asked Jonathan. "How's that for staying in the moment?" teased Jonathan. "Oh you mean that God awful green blanket they have you guys wearing?" asked Ms. Cross. Jonathan nodding his head in agreement, "Yea, that would be the one," affirmed Jonathan. "I already got it, it's in the car, I had one of the nice young men who lives on your dorm open up your room for me" said Ms. Cross.

Jonathan's face somewhat frowning as he thought about who that could have been, then suddenly he remembered that the residential advisors have keys to everyone's room. Jonathan stepped to the side to look in the car to see if he saw the gown and sure enough it was folded neatly across the front seat. While looking through the window he noticed that the rest of his stuff including the two duffle bags he packed earlier was piled up behind the second row seats. Jonathan looked back at his mother as she smiled. "This is what us mothers do", said Ms. Cross. "I'll have to admit you do it well" replied Jonathan. Ms. Cross now looking down at her watch, "Oh, well we better get going Mr. Graduate it's already 11:15 so we can make sure you get yourself situated and everything." Jonathan relished in the thought that it was all about to be over. He had been working for this moment more than just the last four years but really ever since he was old enough to realize that he wanted more out of life, which was at a pretty young age. Jonathan opened the car door and slid the gown over his head and let it drape down over his body. He then reached for the cap and snuggled it down on his head till it felt nice and firm on top of his head. Although Jonathan wasn't very proud of wearing the neon green get up, he was more than proud to grab his paper written freedom that stood on the other side of the ceremony. All that was left for him to do was to simply walk across that stage and claim his prize when he heard his name being called. Ms. Cross stood to the side watching her son with a sense of fulfillment and great joy that his big day had finally come.

"Well, you ready?" asked Ms. Cross. Jonathan looking back at his mother with a mischievous look plastered on his face replied, "I was born ready." The two hopped in the car and headed over to the school's football field where the graduation ceremony was being held. It was a quick ride to the field, about three minutes by car. Jonathan looked out of the window as he drove by the campus and its old buildings that would no longer matter because after today Winterville Community College would cease to exist.

As they approached the parking lot of the football field it was already full due to the fact that the school was never use to so many people there at once. Jonathan looked across the cracked pavement of the old parking lot and saw that there were no spots left. "Hey just pull in on the grass over there", directed Jonathan to his Mom and pointed to the grassy spot where the parking lot ended and the grass near the field began. They got out of the car and made their way to the field and as they walked closer Jonathan could see the rest of the students seated in the upper middle part of the field. They were separated into two sections; half on the left and half on the right with a good gap separating them in the middle. It was the original field from when the school was built back in 1985 which put it just shy of being three decades old. Sadly it had very few renovations done to it since then and it definitely showed. There were worn down brown spots scattered throughout the field. The bleachers were only one of the few things that were "new" since they were renovated about 10 years ago. Jonathan and Ms. Cross continued walking onto the field and as they approached the bleachers Ms. Cross turned toward Jonathan and said, "Well this is my stop." As she looked at Jonathan, she gently touched him on the side of his face, holding her hand on his cheek. "Your father would be proud of you", said Ms. Cross as the tears began to swell up from the bottom of her eyes. Jonathan leaned over and kissed his mother on the head and headed toward his seat. Jonathan took his seat and directed his attention to the metal stage that the school assembled earlier that day. He saw Dean Morgan along with some of the other faculty all dressed up in that hideous green gown. Jonathan was ready to grab his life and leave but before he could do that, he would have to sit through the entire graduation ceremony. However, Jonathan wasn't going to do that, he wasn't going to give this school anymore of his attention so he figured he would cheat the system and close his eyes for a nap. Besides, he was only there to see himself graduate anyway and there was no need to watch anyone else, so he slid back in his chair and closed his eyes. It wasn't long before he fell asleep, his plan had worked and the time seemed to have just flown by. When he finally opened his eyes again he could hear that they were already at the "C" names and Jonathan knew he would be up next. He blinked his eyes hard in order to brush off the mid-day slumber. He then heard his name being called from the microphone and as the music played, he got up from his seat and stepped out into the grassy aisle. He didn't look back to see his mother but he knew she was standing up calling his name. He approached the steps to the stage and saw Dean Morgan looking at him square in the eye. The Dean had on his cheesy face of approval, the same one he wore every year but Jonathan didn't care because this was *his* moment. He walked across the stage and saw his target in the right hand of Dean Morgan. Jonathan reached for the diploma as the Dean handed it to him. Jonathan shook his hand briefly and walked off the stage and in that very moment; Jonathan could feel his inner being coming alive and felt as though he was a new born baby breathing air for the first time. Although tempted to leave, he managed to keep himself together as he headed back toward his seat to finish watching the rest of the ceremony. Once it was over the graduates all stood and threw their caps into the air. The students all disbursed to their families including

Jonathan, he could see his mother standing by the bleachers waiting on him with anticipation. Her eyes were red and he could clearly tell that she had been crying.

"I'm so proud of you Johnny." Ms. Cross stared at Jonathan intently and as she spoke Jonathan looked down at his diploma for a moment then looked back at her. "Thanks mom", replied Jonathan. "You ready to get out of here?" asked Jonathan as he put his arm around his mother.

They made their way back to the car, once they arrived Jonathan stopped in front of the passenger side door, took off his gown and threw it in the back seat. When he got in the car and closed the door, he stretched out in the seat and let out a big sigh of relief. He could hear the car keys jingling as Ms. Cross put them in the ignition. "I'm not gonna lie, it's gonna feel good getting back into my own bed", said Jonathan. "Well don't worry I'll have you there soon enough", assured Ms. Cross; knowing that their trip would be a short one since they lived a little less than an hour away. As Ms. Cross pulled out of the parking lot, Jonathan took one last look at the school as well as some of the faces that were out and about around the parking lot. As he gazed upon both the school and its occupants he felt nothing but pure joy to rid himself of this place. As he continued to look out of the window it came to his attention that there was only one person that he would regret not seeing and that was David. As they drove away from the campus he thought that perhaps he would give David a call later on that night or sometime tomorrow to see if he would talk to him. One thing was for sure, even though David was his friend it was irrelevant to whether or not he would participate in Jonathan's future. The only thing Jonathan knew for an absolute fact was that Winterville was now officially a part of his past and there was nothing anyone could do to change that.

CHAPTER THREE
EXODUS

A few days had passed since Jonathan's glorious day of transition into the real world. Although he hadn't actually entered it yet he was merely back at his mom's house, nevertheless it was a start. It was a quiet home on a one level ranch with an old wooden porch in the front equipped with two equally old rocking chairs that had seen better days. The house's white paint had faded over the years and now had somewhat of a brownish tint to its color, which now appeared to be more of a rusted bone color than actual white. Inside was more of the same, the floor boards were weak and often told you so if you walked on them too heavily. The walls were covered in a mixture of cheap paintings purchased from the local Mom & Pop Hardware store along with some old family photos hung up by Ms. Cross. With all its history and shortcomings it was still the same home that Jonathan grew up in. Jonathan was seated at the kitchen table flipping through a small collection of travel brochures that he picked up from one of the gas stations in Winterville. Jonathan's mission for a more fulfilling life was far from over and graduating was only the first step. His next move was to move out of Winterville all together and with the $8,000 he had managed to save up over the past two years from working various odd jobs, it was going to help him do just that. He sat still for a moment and stared at the open brochures that were laid across the table and envisioned himself and what life would be like in each one of the places the brochures talked about. They all seemed agreeable with Jonathan's ambition and all offered a fast paced lifestyle that Jonathan had been searching for. However, they all appeared to be just ok, none of them really had that WOW factor that made his heart jump.

There *was* one place that Jonathan did have in mind that wasn't on any of the brochures that he purchased. This place was a long way from home and worlds apart from anything Jonathan had ever experienced during his 22 years of living in Winterville.

Its reputation had indeed made its way to Jonathan's ears on a few occasions and had managed to be the topic of discussion from some of the local business men every now and again. This intriguing land of possibility was known as Silver Edge City; Jonathan would often hear people refer to it as Edge City for short. It was often regarded as being a place that would make or break you. Edge City was something that Jonathan was looking for, not to mention that it was about eight hundred miles away from all things to do with Winterville. The fact that it was quite a distance and if Jonathan were to move up there, then he would be forced to adapt or die so to speak, posed for an intriguing challenge and held a promise of uncertainty. All of these things peaked Jonathan's interest. After all, this was the kind of thing that he was looking for. Something that would challenge him in a way the he could never experience while living in Winterville. Jonathan began to quickly grab the brochures that were on the table and piled them on top of one another. He grabbed the stack and threw it in the trash; knowing good and well that he had already made his decision. It was the one place that truly fit both his desires and his needs and he knew that Edge City would be the place to help take him where he wanted to go in life. All that was left for him to do was to get the rest of his things together and take the first step toward embarking on his intrepid quest. Jonathan stood up from the kitchen table and stretched out his arms, yawned and looked out of the kitchen window that was over the sink. He could see the road out in front of his house and the seemingly endless woods that stood towering over the road like some sort of overprotective lover. There was nothing out there for Jonathan, nothing that offered any sense of purpose, belonging, or fulfillment. He knew that he had to leave and there was no other way around it;

simply put it was time to move forward. He continued to look out the window when he heard his mother's voice arise from behind him.

"Have you thought about what you wanted to do?", standing there still in her pajamas as Jonathan continued to look out of the window. "Yea", he replied turning his head to the left as if he were looking over his shoulder. The rest of his body soon followed as he turned to fully face her. "Yea", he answered again knowing that this time he was going to need to elaborate on his first response. "I'm going to Edge City", Jonathan affirmed with his arms folded as a signal to his mother that he would not be swayed out of his decision. Ms. Cross stood there as she took a breath and ran her hand through her hair, squeezing it as she reached the back of her head. "Goodness Johnny", she said while conveying a steep undertone of both disappointment and concern. She was standing in the door way of the kitchen as she started to walk toward the kitchen table. She pulled out the chair closest to her as it made a screeching sound as it dragged across the lifeless tile floor. Ironically, there was a loud silence that entered the room for a moment that seemed to last longer than necessary.

Jonathan now leaning with his back against the sink waited to hear the rest of his mother's response. Instead he heard nothing, which didn't catch him entirely off guard because he already knew what she was thinking. "I can take care of myself", Jonathan assured her. "That's just not the kind of place for a boy who's still wet behind the ears, Johnny" replied Ms. Cross. "You know I swear sometimes you act just like your father", said Ms. Cross. "Why do you have to bring him up?" asked Jonathan. "Because you act just like him sometimes!" shouted Ms. Cross as she slammed her hand down on the table. "I can't blame him for wanting a better life for us" Jonathan pointed out. "Yea well look where *that* got him" said Ms. Cross not quite shouting this time but still speaking in a firm tone of voice. "I have to do this", "I need to do this" he continued.

Ms. Cross still seated at the table, "I just don't want to see you become consumed and obsessed like he did", as a small tear rolled down her face and onto the floor below her. Jonathan taking his back off the sink, walked over toward his mother, and placed his hand on her shoulder. She looked up toward him and placed her hand on his. "It's just such a big place Johnny and there's just too much to get into and too much that can get into *YOU*", said Ms. Cross. "I'll be fine, I promise." "Besides, it's not like you'll never see me again" Jonathan assured his Mother. "I'll just be…" "Twelve hours away" interrupted Ms. Cross. Jonathan paused for a moment. "Yea, something like that" he said.

Ms. Cross wiped her face with her other hand as she began to stand up to give Jonathan a long and embracing hug, "You watch yourself Jonathan Cross, you hear me." she said. She then squeezed her son's sides until she felt his ribs alongside her own arms. Jonathan stood there and began smiling because he knew that he now had her blessing, no matter how reluctant she might have been. "I will" said Jonathan as he began to loosen his grip but Ms. Cross continued to cling to him as if he had just been diagnosed with a terminal illness.

Jonathan knew that it would be in his as well as his mother's best interest if he didn't try to cut their heart to heart moment short. So he continued to hold onto her in the middle of the kitchen as she stood there silently while being accompanied by her steady stream of unyielding tears. After a few moments, Ms. Cross eventually loosened her grip both physically and mentally, accepting the fact that Jonathan was making his own decision and doing what he felt was right for him. As she let go of Jonathan her eyes were now swollen and red from crying. Ms. Cross then looked up at Jonathan and said, "I only want the best for you." Jonathan looking back at his mother replied, "That's what I'm gonna go get, the *best* for <u>me</u>." "And when I get it I'll be sure to put some in the mail for you", he said.

Ms. Cross placed her hand on Jonathan's shoulder and slowly patted him as she walked by him exiting the kitchen. It wasn't easy but Ms. Cross knew she had to let him leave or watch him settle for less which was something she knew that Jonathan wouldn't be able to live with nor would she want him too. Jonathan watched as she turned the corner to head to her room. He stood alone there in the kitchen while feeling the dichotomy of his emotions pressing against him in a self-conflicting war. One part of him felt sorrowful for his mother's discomfort while the other felt great joy in knowing that he was about to embark on the voyage of his own destiny. Jonathan walked out of the kitchen and stepped outside onto the front porch and sat down on the steps and rested his arms on the top of his knees sitting slightly hunched over. Jonathan rarely ever sat on one of the rocking chairs from fear that he would appear to be like the rest of the locals who would spend countless hours out on their front porches chewing tobacco or just simply staring at the road in front of them. It was the middle of the afternoon and Jonathan could feel the sun hitting his body and its warmth lying against his skin. He closed his eyes and thought about where he was going to go from here; he knew there would be no turning back once he left.

Jonathan had made up his mind that there would be no in between and either he moved forward or he would be joining his friend David at the Stop-N-Shop. He closed his eyes and with his brain actively open he could feel the protrusion of another thought rising from the depths of his consciousness making its way to the front of his mind in full view for him to mentally see. Jonathan flinched in trying to recognize what the thought was as it appeared to be foggy but quickly began to come into focus. It was the memory of Jonathan's father, Daniel Cross. There was no question that it was aroused from the conversation that he just had with his mother. Jonathan often acknowledged the memory of his father but never really openly spoke much of him because he preferred to think of his father as the man he should've been today as opposed to the man he was the last time Jonathan saw him. With his eyes still closed, he wondered what his father would have said about his decision to leave Winterville and move to, of all places….Edge City. As his thoughts still lingered to the possibility of his father's reaction, he felt a hand lightly touch his shoulder; Jonathan opened his eyes and his mind snapped back to the present moment. His concentration had been broken and his train of thought derailed as he looked up and saw Ms. Cross standing over him. She dropped a pair of keys in his lap. "Well, if you're going to drive to Edge City you're going to need these", she said. She had given him the keys to his Father's old pickup truck. It was a 1979 Chevy Silverado that had just been collecting dust in their garage. Jonathan stared at the keys for a moment before grabbing them, "You're giving me ole' Beatty?" "Unless you intend to walk your way to Edge City, you're going to need some form of transportation" Ms. Cross quipped in a sarcastic tone.

Jonathan knew that it was a good thing to hear his mother joking around with him, as he knew this was a sign that she was coming around to the idea of him leaving. Jonathan stood to his feet and looked his mother in the eyes and could tell that she was trying to put on a good face so he wouldn't notice. He could tell that she was still being plagued by the thought of him being alone in what she thought to be a massive concrete jungle. "Thanks", said Jonathan. Trying to avoid another tear jerk conversation, Ms. Cross looked back at Jonathan with a calm toned voice and said, "You're Welcome". Jonathan turned and stepped down one step and skipped the last one, as he headed toward the garage to claim his prize. His mother stood back on the porch and watched Jonathan as he walked his way to the garage door. Their driveway wasn't exactly one at all. There was never actual concrete that was laid down but just some old dirt and grass. The only evidence that someone would park their car there at all were from the tire tracks in the ground. Jonathan made his way past his mom's old station wagon that was parked in the driveway and stopped at the garage door. The garage door itself was old and dirty, as he bent down and grabbed the rusty handle. He gave it a solid pull upward and as the door went up, he could hear it screeching loudly reminiscent of some wailing banshee taking its last breath. He winced as the door continued to go up; once it reached the top of his head he gave it one final push upward for the door to lock in place. Jonathan stood barefooted in the doorway of the garage, he could feel the dirt between his toes, there was no light in the garage but since it was daytime the sun served as the light bulb. The truck sat there, in the middle of the garage like a caged beast taking up most of the space. It was in fairly good condition with no major problems besides the fact that it was in need of a good paint job to revive its crimson skin. Ms. Cross kept up the car as best she could, it also didn't hurt that one of the local mechanics had a crush on her and would do things for free from time to time. Jonathan walked along the side of the car and slid his fingers on the door, until he got to the front of the car and stopped. He could see the black leather seats through the front windshield. Jonathan looked at the truck with approval knowing that it would be his companion in this new journey that he was about to embark on. He walked outside jingling the keys in his hands toward the garage door and reached for the door handle. Once his hand had a good grip on the handle he pulled it down until it was at the level of his chest, then he yanked it down hard and watched it slide down to the ground. Jonathan always liked to do that because the door wouldn't screech when someone was closing it, only when it was being opened. He made his way back toward the porch, his mother still standing there watching him as he approached the front steps. As Jonathan reached the top of the steps he looked at Ms. Cross, "I'll take good care of her", he said. "Make sure you take good care of yourself", said Ms. Cross with her finger pointed at Jonathan. Jonathan nodded his head in agreement but in silence, "Well, I guess I better get packing" said Jonathan. Ms. Cross' face immediately began to frown, her eyebrows squeezing tightly together while forming a look of confusion on her face. "You're leaving today?" she asked; dreading that the answer would be yes. Jonathan smiled lightly. "Nooo, I'm gonna head out tomorrow but I wanna go ahead and get the rest of my stuff together", said Jonathan. Ms. Cross not really liking that answer any better shook her head. "Goodness Johnny, you grew up on me overnight". As Ms. Cross said this, she turned and walked alongside Jonathan as the two of them went back inside. There was a brief moment of silence as they entered the house, neither one not really knowing how to address the moment, "Are you hungry?" asked Ms. Cross. "I'm ok, I'm just gonna head to my room and get a jump on this packing", said Jonathan as he walked through the living room and headed toward his bedroom. He walked into his room and stopped in the doorway, he saw his bags he had packed from school still lying on the bed. He never bothered to unpack them because he knew he would be leaving. The walls were bare; he never took the time to hang up any posters of movies or pictures of his favorite athlete. None of the usual stuff you would see in a college grad's room, just a bed and two dressers and that was basically it, his mind served as his way of escape. He found that there was no visual stimulant as powerful as his mind when he wanted to picture himself out of that room or outside of that town. Jonathan walked into the room and bent down to look under the bed, he kept his shoes as well as his suitcases under his bed. He grabbed the two suitcases and the rest of his shoes too. Next, he went through all of his drawers and cleared out his closet. It didn't take him long to completely transfer everything he had in his room into the suitcases. By the time he was finished he grabbed the suitcases and set them by the bed, so that way he could just grab them in the morning and head out. Although, it wasn't very late in the day Jonathan wanted to go to bed anyway because he figured the faster he went to sleep, the faster the next day would come. He closed his door turned off the light and hopped into bed. He didn't have a window in his room, so whenever he would cut the lights off it would get completely dark. It wouldn't matter if it was in the middle of the day or late at night because the room was so dark that you could never tell the difference. Jonathan laid there and closed his eyes as he allowed his mind to take him into a deep sleep and began to dream of the life that he would soon have when he finally left Winterville for good. When Jonathan opened his eyes again he couldn't see anything because the room was pitch-black, but he always kept a flashlight under his pillow so he would be able to see. He felt for the flashlight until he felt its rubber grip touch his hand. He grabbed it and pressed the button on the side and suddenly there was light in the room. He got out of bed and aimed the flashlight toward the door handle, and it lit up as he walked toward it. He kept the light on the handle so he could see it then opened the door, and pressed the button on the side of the flashlight again to turn it off. He walked into the living room almost bumping into the couch but he could see through the window that it was still dark outside. Jonathan figured that he hadn't been asleep very long and that it was just late into the night. He walked over to the kitchen to look at the clock to see if he was right. To his surprise the clock said **5:30 A.M.**, he rubbed his head and grinned as if he tasted his own excitement within the air. He knew that his time had finally come and he wasn't going to waste a moment of it. Even though it was early he didn't care, he went back to his room and took out one of his old pair of jeans with a grey V-neck shirt. Jonathan grabbed his suitcases and went into the garage. He lifted up the garage door and threw his bags onto the bed of the truck. He could feel freedom lightly touching his face as he held the car keys in his hand. He was ready to go but there was one last thing that he needed to do before he left…say goodbye. He turned around but was surprised to see his mother standing barefooted in the driveway. "You're up early" stated Jonathan. "That makes two of us" Ms. Cross replied, as she looked at Jonathan wondering where the time went. Jonathan wasn't much for long goodbyes so he walked over to his mother and gave her a hug, she held him tightly and whispered,

"I love you" in his ear.

"Love you too", he said.

Ms. Cross loosened her grip and took a step back,

"Call me when you get there."

"Will do" promised Jonathan.

"You sure you got everything?" asked Ms. Cross.

"Yea I'm sure" replied Jonathan.

As he made his way to the driver side door, he opened it and hopped in, turned the key in the ignition and felt the truck crank up. He looked at his mother as she stared at him and waved goodbye. Jonathan waved and slowly backed out of the driveway. He made sure his navigation system was placed on the dashboard, placed the truck in drive and pressed his foot on the gas. He turned one last time to see his house as he drove away. He knew that this was going to be *exactly* what he needed. He glanced down at the navigation system and headed toward the next highway. As he drove through some of Winterville to reach the highway, he thought to himself about how he was one of the lucky ones that was born with enough sense to know that there was much more to life than this small town. He looked up and saw the sign for the highway and turned off on the exit ramp, his journey was finally underway. Jonathan didn't mind the drive. He passed the time with mapping out his game plan of what he would do once he reached Silver Edge City. The hours seemed to pass by with decent speed. He kept driving using his excitement and determination as fuel. He drove and kept driving until he saw a sign that read "15 miles to Silver Edge City". Even without reading the sign, he knew that he was almost there. Jonathan looked around as he was driving and saw that the landscape was even different. He saw more cars on the road driving next to him, the type of cars that you would never see someone driving in Winterville, like a BMW or a Mercedes. Jonathan had seen these types of cars in magazines before but never actually saw them in person. As he continued to push Ole' Betty onward he noticed that he was approaching a large tunnel with bright lights on its ceiling and writing in big letters on the outside of the tunnel that read "The Silver Edge Connector". This was it! Jonathan had made it and now all he had to do was pass through the tunnel and he would be in a whole new world. As he drove into the tunnel he rolled down his windows and could hear the tires of all the cars rolling alongside the concrete road. It sounded like pure music to his ears. He kept driving and as he looked ahead to the end of the tunnel, he noticed a bright light. Surely he hadn't died while driving so he knew it must've been something else. As he approached the end of the tunnel, he began to see shapes forming inside the light. When he exited the tunnel he could now make out what the shapes were; they were skyscrapers as far as the eye could see. He was looking at the City unfold before him! With his window down he could hear the majestic roar of the city and behold its entire breathtaking splendor. Jonathan began to understand why he saw such an intense light in the tunnel. The buildings were so tall standing like formidable iron giants well equipped with crystal clear glass that they almost perfectly reflected the sun's light. Jonathan was definitely not disappointed. He could feel his heart beating in his chest as if it were dancing to its own music. His hands firmly gripped the steering wheel as he felt his palms starting to sweat. Jonathan shouted with a voice of triumph, "YES!" He was undeniably like a kid in a candy store except this store never closed and was bigger than he ever could have dreamed of. He knew that this place was his birthright, he was destined to be here and after all these years alas; Jonathan Cross was finally home.

CHAPTER FOUR
CONNECTIONS

The air was crisp and the sun continued to shine bright as Jonathan looked upward toward the skyscrapers that towered above the city. From his view, the buildings seemed to actually penetrate the sky. As he stood there in awe, he heard a sudden clicking sound. When he looked down, he saw that the meter on the gas pump had stopped running, right at $55 dollars. He pulled over to one of the gas stations that were a few miles outside of the tunnel. However, this wasn't one of the homely gas stations that one would see around and about Winterville; this gas station was completely state of the art. All of the pumps had digital touch screens; which was something that Jonathan had never seen before. Not to mention that the gas station itself looked like some sort of mini mall. After he paid at the pump he decided to head inside just to look around. It was a fairly large size, there was definitely nothing like this in Winterville. As Jonathan approached the station's double doors, he noticed that they were made of sharp clear glass with metal railings in the center so people could push or pull the door open. Jonathan entered the gas station and was greeted by the young store clerk who was seated behind the counter. He was wearing a red polo with the store's logo on the right side pocket. He looked like he had been there for a while but still managed to have a pretty chipper attitude. "Hello Sir, let me know if I can assist you in anyway" said the clerk. Jonathan silently nodded back at the young man in agreement, even though Jonathan doubted he would need the guy's help. He was perfectly capable of grabbing a bag of chips and soda without any ones assistance. Jonathan made his way down one of the aisles, he noticed that the floor was spotless and had some serious shine to it; like a car that had just been waxed on a Sunday afternoon. The place was definitely clean from top to bottom not to mention the fridge and freezer sections were completely stocked with everything from soda to caramel flavored ice cream sandwiches. Jonathan had only been in the city for about five minutes and he was already impressed with what he saw so far. Jonathan continued to browse the store as he could smell hot dogs being cooked. He suddenly remembered that he saw one of those slow cookers when he walked in and decided to grab one of the hot dogs, so he grabbed a bag of chips and a coke to go with it. As he took his food to the front, Jonathan thought about the fact that he was going to need a place to stay. Even though he had more than enough money for a hotel it would probably be best if he started looking for a place to live, that way he wouldn't be wasting his money on a temporary place. He had no clue where to start, so it looked like he was going to need the clerks' assistance after all. As he placed his items on the front counter he noticed that the young clerk had his back turned while stocking the cigarettes that were behind the counter on display. "Excuse me" said Jonathan. The young clerk turned his head to look over his shoulder to see who was calling him. He then turned around completely to give Jonathan his full attention, "Yes sir, ready to check out?" he asked. "Yeah" said Jonathan as he placed his items on the counter. As the store clerk rang up his small afternoon groceries, Jonathan began to ask the clerk where would be a good spot to start looking for a new place. "Hey, I just got into town and I'm trying to look for a place to stay, I was wondering if…" said Jonathan, as he was politely but ever so quickly cut off by the store clerk. "Say no more" said the clerk, as he reached beneath the counter and pulled out a short and thick red booklet, which had *Silver Edge Living* written on the front cover. Jonathan grabbed the booklet as the store clerk placed it on the counter. "That'll be five dollars and thirty five cents" said the clerk. Jonathan looked up with a touch of confusion in his eyes, thinking that the clerk was charging him five dollars for the book. It was when he saw the plastic bag lying on the counter with the hotdog still visible, that he remembered that he had yet to pay for his food. "Oh" said Jonathan as he pulled out a wrinkled ten dollar bill from his wallet and handed it to the clerk. Jonathan took his food and collected his change and put the booklet in his pocket as he left the store. While he was outside walking toward the truck he couldn't help but look up again into the skyline to see some of the towering buildings that seemed to be hogging up the sky. In fact, the buildings were so tall that Jonathan wasn't able to see the rest of the city, only the first line of metal giants that stood in his direct line of vision. Jonathan hopped back into the truck and pulled out of the gas station parking lot. Even though, he didn't know exactly where he was going he wasn't too concerned. After all, this was why he came to Silver Edge in the first place, for a new life and a little adventure. Besides, he had the booklet that the store clerk gave him and his navigation, so he wasn't completely left in the dark. Jonathan rolled down his window just like he did before on the highway so that he could get a clear and unhindered view of the city as he drove around and listened to its heartbeat and hear its voice speak through the people who inhabited its streets. It sounded like a symphony of life being lived to the fullest, to the point of overflowing. It seemed like the pace of life itself was different in this city, the people seemed to have a natural drive that you could see; even in the way they walked.

He saw the streets full of people who seemed to know what they wanted out of life, even some of the bums on the corner looked better than some of the people back in Winterville. He could see business men wearing designer suits with expensive haircuts texting on their blackberries and talking on their smart phones. He noticed pedestrians that were just as hungry for life as he was but he mostly saw himself. As he continued to people watch, suddenly Jonathan could see himself walking on the busy sidewalks alongside everyone else. He envisioned himself wearing one of the designer suits that the other businessmen were wearing and having a smart phone in his hand, no doubt e-mailing some top shot Corporate Exec. Oh yes, this was indeed a dream come true for Jonathan and much sweeter than he could have ever imagined. Jonathan continued to drive aimlessly through the city taking in the sights until he thought about the fact that gas wasn't exactly cheap and he should probably get started on looking for a place to stay. Although, he knew he probably wasn't going to find his new home that day, he figured it would be a good idea to at least get started. So he grabbed the red booklet that the store clerk had given him earlier and put it on the steering wheel so he could see it. As he continued to drive he tried to flip through the book while holding it with one hand and the other on the steering wheel. He managed to turn a few pages with his fingers, as he frequently glanced up to make sure that he was watching the road. He continued to flip through the pages as he saw local listings with pictures of some amazing condos. Jonathan was astounded that people actually lived in some of the places he saw in the booklet. His eyes continued to remain glued to the pages, when suddenly he looked up and saw that he was rapidly approaching the tail end of a grey SUV that was stopped at a red light. He saw its red tail lights growing bigger as he got closer; he immediately slammed his foot down on the brakes as hard as he could. He heard the tires let out a light squeal as they scrapped against the concrete. Luckily, Jonathan wasn't driving very fast so he was able to stop before he hit the car in front of him. For a moment, he sat there frozen in his seat thinking about how he almost just ruined his entire trip as he let out a sigh of relief that nothing actually happened.

He could see that the driver in front of him had his arm calmly draped out of the driver side window with a lit cigarette between his fingers. This let Jonathan know that the man was obviously oblivious to what just happened or what just *almost* happened. However, the drivers behind him weren't oblivious at all and in fact they were very much aware of what almost happened. Given the fact that they too had to slam on their brakes because Jonathan had made a sudden stop, they weren't very happy and made sure they voiced their opinion. "What the hell's going on up there!" shouted the driver behind Jonathan with his head stuck out of the window. Following this, the light at the intersection turned green, a few of the cars in Jonathan's lane immediately pulled out into the lane next to them shouting expletives as they drove by. Jonathan wasn't accustomed to the fast pace of the city. The way they drove in Winterville, there were more dirt roads than paved ones with a few people driving on them. Here in Silver Edge there were bigger streets packed with cars on all sides. Jonathan thought that it would be best to pull over so that he would avoid another close encounter. He drove through a few more lights until he saw a parking lot for a large Chinese restaurant. He pulled in the parking lot and parked the car. He whipped out the booklet again and began to circle the ads that would fit into his budget, although there weren't that many it was still better than nothing. As he continued to flip through the booklet it began to sink in his brain that his options were a bit limited at the moment and they would stay that way until he found a job. Although Jonathan thought about this before hand, it didn't register as hard or as clearly until now. Looking around Jonathan could see that the parking lot was rather full and he could smell a sweet aroma coming from the restaurant. The hot dog and chips that he had earlier had already worn off, and he always wanted to try Chinese food. He hopped out of the truck and headed toward the front door. The building was one level but very wide and it had an emerald green roof with fancy moldings at the corners, the building itself was made out of faded green brick. The front doors were wood that had been painted to match the rest of the building; the handles were made out of golden dragons that appeared to lunge toward the oncoming customers. The sign above the door read *The Emerald Palace*. Jonathan opened the door and entered the building it was dimly lit, no doubt to promote a more relaxed atmosphere. There were dark mahogany tables within the middle of the restaurant with leather booths placed alongside the side and back walls of the restaurant. The hostess seemed to be away from the front desk so Jonathan proceeded into the restaurant and decided to have a seat at the bar and eat from there. Jonathan took a seat on one of the leather bar stools; behind the counter was the bartender wiping the inside of a glass mug, he was a tall Asian man wearing a red vest with a white dress shirt underneath. He looked up and noticed Jonathan sitting down. "What are we having?" asked the bartender. "Actually, I'll have a look at the menu" said Jonathan. The bartender handed Jonathan a menu. The menu was emerald as well, keeping in touch with the unison theme of the building. Jonathan opened the menu it was filled with things he had never really heard of and could barely pronounce. However, there were a few things that Jonathan could make out, like Fried Rice and Kung Pao chicken. As Jonathan continued to look over the menu he saw out of the corner of his eye someone taking a seat a few chairs over from him.

Jonathan happened to glance over just out of pure human instinct to see who it was, and that's when he saw her. Her hair was long, dark, and flowed down to her shoulders. Jonathan stood frozen in her essence and it was if his mind would not allow his eyes to turn away. He noticed that her eyebrows were thin and stunningly sharp while exactly matching her hair color. Just by looking at her, he could tell that her skin was as soft as silk and her lips were full and ripe. She had lip gloss on and he liked the way they glistened. His eyes still locked on her as he continued to scan the rest of her extraordinary figure. Although his path of vision was slightly obscured by the counter he could still tell that her legs looked like they were carved out of marble and went on for days. To put it simply she was gorgeous, it seemed that once Jonathan's brain got its full, it allowed him to now look away, which was wonderful because if he stared at that woman any longer she would have undoubtedly noticed. Jonathan, now pretending to look over the menu overheard the bartender address the woman. "Hey Rachel, how's it going?" "You eating the usual today?" "Hey Tony!" "You know me too well and I'm going to have extra shrimp this time", answered the woman in a soft and pleasant tone of voice. Jonathan loved her voice even though he had only heard it for about five seconds. The beautiful mystery woman now had an identity. Her name was *Rachel* and he was determined to strike up some form of conversation with her. Jonathan gave the bartender his order while stealing glances of her. He could tell that she was young probably in her mid-twenties, which would put her close to Jonathan's age. Jonathan thought that this was good because this way he knew he had a better chance. Jonathan would never refer to himself as a ladies' man but he was never really shy and awkward around them either. He knew that if he was going to talk to this woman, the entry point of conversation was going to be random no matter what he said. So either way he looked at it, he would be coming out of left field so to speak. He glanced at her again; her sheer beauty was more than enough to motivate him to speak to her. "I hope the food's good" he said, while looking at her wondering if the two of them would have eye contact. She looked up, her eyes met his but not in a romantic way. She was purely trying to see who just spoke to her. "It is" she said, looking at Jonathan with a pleasant grin on her face; the same grin most people give someone when they just meet somebody yet they're trying to be polite. Jonathan stared at her but not too intently, he definitely didn't want to come across as some random creep. Rachel started to turn her attention to her hand bag that was propped up against her seat on the floor then suddenly turned her head back toward Jonathan. "You must be new in town" she said. Although you couldn't see it on his face, Jonathan was smiling hard on the inside, pleased at the fact that she was continuing the conversation. "Is it that obvious?" asked Jonathan. "Well it's just that there are not many people in this city who haven't eaten at *The Emerald*" Rachel attested. "Well I guess I'm in the right place then" he replied. Jonathan continued to secretly admire her beauty while thinking this was a good time to introduce himself. "I'm Jonathan" "Rachel" she said with a sultry tone. And there it was...his first connection in the big city.

The first real face he had the pleasure of getting to know and a pretty face at that! Things were going fairly well for his first day out "So where are you from?" asked Rachel. Jonathan hesitated for a moment before answering the question. He was thinking about whether or not he wanted to admit the fact that he was from such a place as nameless and minuscule as Winterville. However, he decided to go with the truth, it was just better that way. "I'm from Winterville" Jonathan answered. Rachel paused for a minute; her beautiful face draped with thought, "I'm not sure I've ever heard of it". She said with a wind of laughter under her breath. "Trust me, it's probably better that way", said Jonathan with a grin. "So what brings you in town? Rachel inquired. "I'm looking to make a fresh start and hopefully find a job" Jonathan replied. "Really, so what was your major in College?" asked Rachel. "Business Management" he said. Rachel nodded her head in agreement as she continued to listen, "You next." Jonathan said. "Well, I've been living here now for almost three years. I majored in Business Law and I'm currently working at Star Industries." Jonathan was impressed to say the least. This woman appeared to be the complete package; brains, beauty and ambition. Without a doubt, he never met a woman like her back home. "You know now that I think about it I overheard some people in Human Resources talking about job openings last week. You should check it out if you're interested" advised Rachel. She then whipped out a business card from inside her coat pocket. Jonathan took her card; it was a pale white business card with *Star Industries* written in blue, along with her contact information underneath. Jonathan made sure he withheld a wide smirk on his face, seeing how he just got her phone number without asking for it. He took the card and thanked her at the same time as the waiter came by and dropped her food off in a to-go box. "It was nice meeting you" said Jonathan. Rachel stood up and got her things together. "Same here", she replied. She then grabbed her belongings and headed out the door. As she walked by Jonathan could smell her sweet perfume beckoning him and felt it lightly tugging at his nostrils. He turned in his seat to watch her flawless frame as she exited the restaurant. He glanced down at the business card again, knowing full well that he was going to contact her regardless of whether he liked the job or not. "You know she comes in here every week" said the bartender as he watched Jonathan gawk at Rachel shortly after she left. He turned around and looked at the bar tender, "Good to know" said Jonathan. Shortly after, Jonathan ate his meal once it arrived and left the restaurant. The day brisk by as he continued to search for a new place to call home. However, like he expected he didn't find anything just yet and knew that it was a good chance he would be sleeping in the car tonight in order to avoid paying for a hotel. As night fall approached, Jonathan ended up pulling in the back of a grocery store parking lot for the night. He didn't have much of a problem sleeping in the truck, as far as he was concerned this was part of what it would take to make it in this new mega city he found himself in. He made sure to park away from the light poles so the light wouldn't wake him up. He sat there in the car with the seat pushed back, he dug down in his pocket and pulled out Rachel's card and noticed that her full name was at the bottom of the card; "*Rachel Monroe*". He thought to himself that it was a nice name as he held the card in his hand. As far as Jonathan was concerned this was a great ending to a great day, despite having to sleep in his car. He put the card on the dashboard, locked the doors and slipped his shoes off. He went to sleep with pride knowing that his life was now starting to come together and there was nothing that would be able to stand in his way.

CHAPTER FIVE
WANTING EVERYTHING

It had been a little over a week since Jonathan's brief rendezvous with Rachel, since then time seemed to only drip by like water from a faucet. However, he managed to call her from the number she gave him although it was her office line and not her cell phone. He hadn't thought about that when he originally got it but was only pleased at the fact that he got a number from her. Rachel was able to arrange an interview for Jonathan which led to him landing his first job in the city, at *Star Industries*. It was the largest business consulting firm in Edge City as well as one of the top firms in the country. In addition, Jonathan managed to find a cheap place in one of the more economically savvy parts of the city. It wasn't much; in fact it was just a bricked squared room with a sink and one window. Although it was small, it provided its purpose and was a lot better than sleeping on the cramped driver's seat in the truck. Things did indeed seem to be coming together for Jonathan but unfortunately things are not always what they appear to be.

Although Jonathan was where he wanted to be, he was still not quite where he *really* wanted to be. He now worked in a small cubicle with little contact with his other coworkers or "cubicle cell mates" as he liked to refer to them. He worked on the 10th floor of a 60 story building and the only view that he had on his floor, was a sea of cubicles that had a Prussian blue color to them. To make matters worse, Jonathan wasn't very fond of his new office manager   either; a Mr. Craig Spitz. For starters, his last name was Spitz, which immediately made him more unlikeable and led to a higher probability of him being a jerk…which he was. He was about 5'5 and weighed about 300 pounds. He was going bald in the middle of his head with hair just around the sides and his stomach seemed to be an entirely separate entity attached to his body. His gut oozed over his belt, often times covering it entirely. Whenever he walked around the office he seemed to move like a penguin, given the fact that he didn't actually walk per se it was more of an exaggerated waddle. To put it bluntly he was short and fat with a napoleon complex, not someone Jonathan enjoyed working under or working with at all for that matter. Although Jonathan understood that he was free from Winterville that still didn't keep him from occasionally visiting an unkind thought within the deep recesses of his mind and wondered if he had traded out one prison for another. However, he would quickly dismiss that thought because in his eyes he had already won. He managed to break free from the mundane clutches of his former life. So anything he had to do or experience from here on out was just part of the journey. As he sat in his small cubicle checking his e-mail he noticed one in particular toward the top of the screen that was from Rachel. However, before he could click on it he heard a raspy voice coming from behind him, "Jonathan" said the voice. He turned around to see who it was and to his utter dissatisfaction it was Mr. Spitz standing in the doorway of the cubicle. His hands on his hips with the look of disapproval lodged within his portly face, his black beady eyes staring at Jonathan. Jonathan swallowed and lightly clinched his teeth with his mouth closed in anticipation of an uncomfortable moment. "Yes Sir Mr. Spitz?" asked Jonathan trying to sound respectful, despite the fact that he had no respect for the man. "I didn't know we were paying you to check emails" responded Mr. Spitz. Jonathan couldn't stand to hear his voice half the time; he thought he sounded like a fat version of the crypt keeper. "I was checking to see if I had gotten a response to an e-mail I sent out earlier to one of the HR guys" said Jonathan, knowing good and well he never sent such an e-mail but it sounded good. Mr. Spitz continued to stare at Jonathan not really convinced of what he was saying. As he turned around to leave Jonathan's cubicle, Mr. Spitz warned, "Look, seeing as you just started working here I wouldn't get lazy, get back to work and try not to waste the company's time and money." Soon as he left, Jonathan slouched back in his chair with his hands behind his head and rolled his eyes. He spun the chair back toward the computer and saw that he had received an email from Rachel. He clicked on the email to open it. It turned out to be an invitation to the corporate party that was being held at the Fine Arts Museum in the upper east side of the city this Friday. The corporate party was held for the big wigs of the company such as shareholders, board members, and some of the upper level management. Rachel would be attending the party because she was the secretary of the chief financial officer of the company; Ronald Perkins. Jonathan smiled as he continued to read the rest of her e-mail, as he looked around to make sure no one was lurking around his cubicle. He managed to hold his outward composure as he read the e-mail but inside he was filled with optimism and excitement. Jonathan wasn't happy with where he was in the company or working under Mr. Spitz. He knew that this would be the perfect opportunity to meet someone of influence in the company and perhaps help in taking a step or two up the corporate ladder. This was the second time Jonathan had heard from Rachel since that afternoon at the restaurant. It seemed that Rachel had a knack for helping Jonathan out and he definitely began to take notice.

She sent him a copy of the virtual invitation, all he had to do was print it out and present it at the door on Friday and he would be good to go. Jonathan knew that there was a decent chance that Rachel felt the same way about him as he did about her. After all, she was the one who landed him the job and now he was going to be rubbing elbows with the top dogs of the company. Jonathan replied to the e-mail with a big "thank you" attached to show his gratitude and thought about asking her to meet for coffee. However, he quickly changed his mind and figured that it would be better to ask her out in person instead of hiding behind a keyboard. So he sent the e-mail and printed out the invitation at the copier, he folded the invitation once it finished printing so no one would see it and headed back to his desk. Then he unfolded it again so he could get a good look at it and he noticed toward the bottom of the invitation that it stated the key note speaker would be a gentleman named *Mr. K. Edwards* who is the founder and CEO of Star Industries. Jonathan heard mentions and whispers of this man before but hadn't really gotten many details; after all he had just started working at the company and just moved to the city. However, Jonathan didn't need to know everything about the keynote speaker or all the other guests to know that this would be a great opportunity from him. The rest of the afternoon turned into a blur; speaking to potential clients and helping with low level office projects were the things that filled Jonathan's day. By the time five o' clock came around he was ready to leave and his apartment was about 25 minutes away from the office. He wasn't used to that kind of commute which was one of the reasons he liked it so much because it was unfamiliar. It also gave him a chance to view the city as he drove through its busy streets. Once he arrived at his apartment he would make his trek up several flights of stairs and into his room. He would lie on the cheap bed that he had nested in the corner of the room and stared at the ceiling while thoughts lingered towards the possibilities that everything he wanted in life could be found within this massive city. Now, all he had to do was go get it and that is exactly what he planned on doing.

Jonathan glided through the rest of the week with the anticipation of Friday night; he was ready to get a peek at the upper echelon of Star Industries. Although he wasn't Rachel's date this would at least give him another opportunity for her to see him in a different light. He bought a black suit for the occasion, some new dress shoes and a nice tie to match. He was dressed to impress and looking for an opportunity from both Rachel and life. As he navigated his way through the city, he noticed that the city seemed to transform into a whole different animal at night. It would undergo a metamorphosis and not the one that caterpillars go through when they turn into butterflies. As the city came alive at night, it seemed to be more of a menacing transformation like Dr. Jekyll and Mr. Hyde. The lofty skyscrapers that were bright reflecting beacons of light during the day became ominous giants that had piercing beams shining through their windows. The blanket of stars that covered the city at night reflected beautifully on its concrete streets. While taking it all in, Jonathan made sure he was paying attention to the navigation system as it was directing his path. He eagerly drove with the windows down on his way to the museum. Jonathan enjoyed hearing the sounds of the city. On the navigation screen and due to the sudden increase in traffic, he could see that he was getting closer to the museum. From what Jonathan could tell the entire city was something to stand in awe of; however this particular part of the city was even nicer. The shops had clear glass walls and some of the streets were paved with old stone, not regular concrete. It gave it a sort of old money appeal to it, despite the fact that this was a relatively new part of the city. As Jonathan continued to drive down the street, the navigation system spoke in that annoying monotone electric voice, "Destination on the left." Jonathan could now visibly see the museum. It was a colossal structure that was firmly laid on the left side on the street. By the looks of it, it took up a vast majority of the entire street and by its architectural design; it looked like something the Romans would have built. Huge in stature, dramatic in presentation and fit for Caesar, it had long giant steps and large pillars at the top of the stairs. The building itself was a work of art and fittingly so. Jonathan continued to drive by the front while catching fading glimpses of fancy people getting out of even fancier cars. He definitely felt out of place driving by in ole' Beatty but it was dark so he was counting on no one noticing. He pulled further down the street and parked in a metered parking space by the curb. It was a nice little walk; still Jonathan didn't care, he would have walked a mile if he had to. As he walked across the stone street he pulled out the folded invitation from his pocket. When he arrived to the base of the steps there was still a decent crowd of people moseying along into the entrance while enjoying one another's company. Jonathan walked up the steps and passed the giant columns at the top of the stairs. He could see through the doors at the front entrance where there were more people standing and talking. Jonathan walked in through the front doors that were being held open by two doormen dressed in black suites. Inside, it was surely a sight to see, the lobby floor was coated in a beautiful layer of marble. At the front desk they were checking tickets, something Jonathan was slightly concerned about even though he had an invitation. Nevertheless, he approached the front desk and presented the invitation to one of the receptionist. The receptionist looked at the invitation for a moment, as Jonathan stood there worrying that he might get embarrassed and be asked to leave. Instead, the receptionist looked up and politely smiled "The Fine Arts Museum welcomes you Mr. Cross, enjoy your night." Jonathan smiled back at her and made his way down the hall to the art gallery.

Within the hallway both sides of the walls had expensive paintings of artwork from local to international artists. At the end of the hallway was another set of glass doors that lead to the art gallery. Jonathan walked down the hall and into the art gallery; it was full of tuxedos and stilettos and the place was absolutely overflowing with dignitaries and corporate figure heads. Jonathan felt that he definitely looked the part and now it was time to act it out. As he looked around the gallery, it was utterly breathtaking. The room was decorated to suit the occasion and there were waiters dressed in white suits, serving high-end Hors d'oeuvres. A side bar was setup to serve champagne and wine as well as a continuance of the fine art Jonathan encountered in the hallway. Jonathan noticed toward the front of the room that there was a very nice stage with a podium that had been set up for the event. Behind the podium, there was a large banner which had the Star Industries logo embedded on it. Jonathan started to walk around the gallery unable to avoid looking out of place; although he managed to compensate for his uneasiness by keeping silent as he studied people's conversations. A lot of the conversations were full of the stereotypical things people think the rich talk about. Such as how they did last quarter in the stock market and how their net worth is looking this year, or whether or not their kids got into that new private school. "This didn't come as a surprise to Jonathan in the least; he was actually expecting to hear some of the things that came from the lips of the affluent. As he continued to walk around, he heard the sound of a microphone being cut on through the speakers in the front. A woman dressed in an all-white gown walked up to the podium and grabbed the mic. "Good evening everyone, thank you for coming out to the corporate mixer." Once that announcement was made, it was everyone's cue to begin their applause and they followed suit. The woman continued to speak but was lost in Jonathan's ears as he scanned the room to see if there were any signs of Rachel. He noticed a woman who was standing toward the front of the podium with her back turned to the rest of the room. Her hair was long and swathed on her neck and her bare back showed through the ruby dress that she was wearing; it was Rachel. He didn't need to see her face to know it was her, he just knew. While he was caressing her body with his eyes the woman's voice in the background appeared to cease and a loud applause erupted in the gallery with some dignified cheers. Jonathan looked toward the podium to see what was going on, he noticed an older gentleman stepping toward the podium. His walk was calm but with a powerful stride, it seemed that with each step he took toward the podium the cheers and applause got louder. Surely this couldn't be the same room full of the stately rich individuals who were talking about caviar and portfolios only moments ago. More importantly, who was this man who all of a sudden had everyone's undivided attention including Jonathan's? When he finally reached the podium he stood there for a moment while the crowd continued to cheer. He was an average height and build but beyond that there was nothing average about this man. His suit was tailored; it was deep blue almost to the point of being black. He had a pink dress shirt underneath with a matching tie, same color as the suit. His hair was jet black with a few sprinkles of gray hairs showing themselves proudly, with his goatee displaying the same color pattern. He looked upon the crowd for a moment like a general overlooking his army; this man commanded attention but he did it without even opening his mouth.

The people calmed down enough for him to finally get a word out. "Good evening ladies and gentleman," he said pausing for a second to let the crowd settle. "I wanted to come before you all tonight to personally thank you for your dedication in helping make Star Industries a frontrunner in Corporate America" the gentleman continued. As he spoke, Jonathan watched as this man controlled the room. Then it crossed his mind that this must be the CEO of the company just like the invitation stated. No other man could embody this kind of power and business swag and <u>not</u> be the CEO this *had* to be Mr. Edwards. He finished addressing the crowd and retracted from the podium while the applause echoed throughout the gallery to honor his presence. Jonathan watched him as he exited the stage while the people exuberantly surrounded him, hoping to grab a mere particle of his time. Jonathan thought to himself this was the type of man that he wanted to be. Someone who was important, who had complete control over his life and wasn't subject to the situations nor the people around him. This man was the embodiment of everything Jonathan had hoped of becoming; he had never seen anything like this up close before. In all the confusion Jonathan lost sight of Rachel, she had disappeared somewhere. However, it wasn't a big deal because for the time being his focus was on Mr. Edwards. He grabbed one of the complimentary glasses of champagne even though he had only been exposed to alcohol less than four times in his entire life... but when in Rome. As he took a sip he felt a light tap on his shoulder, "I didn't peg you for a champagne kind of guy", said the soft voice. Jonathan turned around and saw Rachel who was looking absolutely stunning in her dress. Jonathan was excited but didn't want to come off as overly eager. "Well, I figured I'd roll with the punches for a change" "I wanted to say thank you once again for the invite; this is truly amazing" said Jonathan as he looked around the room while admiring the moment. Rachel looked back with a slight smile on her face but before she could reply, a man interjected. "There you are Rachel, I've been looking for you" "There are some investors I want you to meet" said the gentleman. Rachel looked back at the gentleman and introduced him to Jonathan. "This is Ron..." said Rachel but before she could finish the man shoved his hand almost directly into Jonathan's chest, "Ronald Perkins." he said. Jonathan shook his hand, "Jonathan, pleasure to meet you sir." "Likewise" replied Mr. Perkins. Jonathan stood there as he watched the two walk away while Ron placed his hand on Rachel's back. Jonathan felt a rush of jealousy ball up in the back of his neck. He wondered if she was dating this Perkins guy or if he was just infatuated with Rachel just like Jonathan was. Either way it felt like Rachel was being stolen from him. Even though he had no basis for being upset other than the fact that he was beginning to develop intense feelings for this woman. Jonathan gulped down the rest of his glass of champagne and began to walk the room. He walked around and pretended to mingle for about another half hour before deciding to head home. So he left the gallery and headed toward the lobby and noticed there weren't many people still hanging around. Jonathan exited the main lobby doors and headed outside where he felt the cool air brush against his face with the back-drop of the city howling back at him. He walked down the huge steps while noticing a big body sedan parked at the bottom of the steps. The closer he got to the car he noticed that it was no ordinary sedan, but a Rolls-Royce. There were three men standing toward the front of the car, one of them was tall and built, like a bodybuilder, he looked like some sort of titan gladiator from the days of old. The other man had his back to Jonathan and he too was tall except bald and skinny. As Jonathan got closer he was able to get a better view of the third man, to his astonishment it was none other than Mr. Edwards. Jonathan almost stopped dead in his tracks but his mind refused to let his legs hold him back. He finally reached the bottom of the stairs and stood over to the side as not to disturb the three gentlemen. It seemed that Mr. Edwards was talking to the tall slim man while the other, whom Jonathan assumed was a body guard, remained silent. Oddly enough there was no one else outside besides the four of them. Jonathan stood there somewhat frozen in the moment because only a few feet away from him was a clear model of the type of man Jonathan wanted to be. Although he didn't know him, he had seen everything he needed to see inside the art gallery. Without over thinking the moment Jonathan seized the opportunity and walked toward Mr. Edwards. "Excuse me sir." said Jonathan, as he nervously walked over almost stuttering in his steps. The body guard took a step toward Jonathan extending his arm in order to stop Jonathan from getting any closer. However, before the man could touch Jonathan, Mr. Edwards spoke up, "It's all right Percy I believe the young man just wishes to speak." His voice was calm yet prevailing all at the same time. "How may I help you Mr...." inquired Mr. Edwards, while waiting for Jonathan to finish his sentence. "Cross, I mean Jonathan Cross sir, it's a pleasure to meet you." "The pleasure is mine, how can I help you?" Jonathan didn't know what to say but he knew he couldn't drop the ball now so he had to think of something. "I just wanted to say that as an employee I feel very confident about the direction Star Industries is going" stated Jonathan. "Is that right? Well I'm glad you feel that way young man." said Mr. Edwards. "Yes, sir" affirmed Jonathan. Jonathan began to feel nervous as he looked into Mr. Edward's eyes as if he could see into Jonathan's mind and read his every thought. Jonathan thought about breaking eye contact but he couldn't because he was locked in. "You know I rarely have an employee who has the courage to speak to me let alone someone who just started working for the company" noted Mr. Edwards. Jonathan wondered how he knew that he had just started working there but before he could ask, Mr. Edwards answered the question for him, "Don't be offended, I just know green when I see it" "Let me ask you something Jonathan, what do you want out of life?" continued Mr. Edwards. Jonathan didn't realize it then but how he answered this question would ultimately change everything in his life, perhaps if he did he would've answered the question differently. He paused for a second to think and then blurted out the first thing that came to mind, "Everything" he said. Mr. Edwards looked at him for a moment but in that second his look changed, it became an intense look similar to that of a lion before it pounces for the kill. Mr. Edwards nodded his head thinking about Jonathan's response. "Tell you what, come by my office Monday morning and we'll further discuss your future" said Mr. Edwards. Jonathan was in complete shock! He didn't understand what had just happened but answered back anyway, "Yes sir!" Even though he had no idea how he was going to be able to get in contact with him. While the bodyguard held the door open, Mr. Edwards climbed in the back of his car while the bald man sat in the driver's seat. Jonathan stood there in disbelief at what just happened as he intensely watched the Rolls-Royce pull off from the curb and followed its red tail lights with his eyes, until it disappeared into the distance of the night. Whether or not he understood what just took place, had yet to be seen. However, come Monday morning, things were *definitely* about to change for Jonathan Cross.

CHAPTER SIX
PERFECTION

The music was soothing but not soothing enough. Jonathan's palms were getting moist so he rubbed them alongside his dress pants. He was traveling in the elevator alone nothing but his thoughts to keep him company and they were doing a pretty good job of it too. In fact they were running the show as the elevator continued to climb to the top floor. He imagined what Mr. Edwards might ask him or if he would be able to hold a steady conversation with him. He thought about how he had been given the shot of a life time but might let this amazing chance slip through his fingers if he didn't impress this man. The pressure was definitely building within Jonathan but he couldn't let it win, he refused. After all, Mr. Edwards mentioned something about discussing Jonathan's future so this had to be an indication of something good. That is, unless Jonathan's immediate future involved him getting fired from Star Industries. Either way in about another 10 seconds he was about to get off that elevator and enter the office of arguably one of the most powerful men in the city. Suddenly the elevator stopped and a chime through the speakers sounded off as the doors opened. There was a large reception desk with the star Industries logo propped on the wall behind it. There was a petite woman behind the desk wearing a white blouse with her hair pulled in a bun that was highlighted even more by her bright red lip gloss. She looked at Jonathan with a cheerful expression, "You must be Mr. Cross" asked the woman. Jonathan took a step forward and answered, "Yes, I'm here to see…" but before Jonathan could finish his sentence the receptionist interjected, "He's been expecting you, right this way." Jonathan followed the woman to a set of mahogany doors. When they approached the doors the woman hesitantly stopped at the door, "Just wait here a moment and someone should be right with you" she instructed. Jonathan had to admit that this was a tad strange that the receptionist would only lead him right to the door and not through it. So Jonathan was once again left to himself with only his thoughts to keep him company, except this time around he decided to put them on mute. Seeing how those thoughts didn't add any value to the moment at hand and they only seemed to make him more anxious than he already was. It was odd because Jonathan had always wanted the opportunity to take himself to lofty heights. However, now that the opportunity was real it also came with the realization that real failure could come with it, but Jonathan wasn't going to let that keep him from going forward. He would rather take the shot and miss then be too afraid to take one at all. So he stood at the door checking to make sure that he had himself together. By the time Jonathan looked around to see if he saw the receptionist still walking down the hall, she was already gone. While he looked down the hall he felt a touch of cool air brush up against his back, he turned around to see what it was. The door was open with a man standing out halfway with most of his body in the doorway. It was the thin bald man that was with Mr. Edwards the other night at the museum but this time Jonathan was able to get a closer look at him. His eyes were dark and piercing as if they could look into the soul of anyone that they encountered. His face was barren and there was no facial hair beside his eyebrows; and even those were barely there. He looked directly at Jonathan with a semi intense gaze, "He'll see you now" said the *bald eagle* in a voice that was minutely scratchy. When Jonathan walked through the doorway his shoes clicked and echoed on the wooden floor.

The office was enormous with large glass windows that went from floor to ceiling, revealing a truly breathtaking view of the city. In the middle of the room there was a long conference table which undoubtedly was the meeting ground for many high end deals that

Mr. Edwards was involved in. The table itself was a deep burnt oak with black leather chairs surrounding it and at the right side of the room Jonathan could see another doorway. The bald man continued to escort Jonathan through the other doorway until he stopped to let Jonathan walk in front of him. Jonathan walked into what appeared to be a personal condo that was an extension of the office. There was no room for doubt that Jonathan was about to be in the company of a very wealthy man. The condo was complete with everything you would expect a condo has; full kitchen, spacious living room with a master bedroom that was around the corner from the kitchen. Although Jonathan couldn't see for a fact that there was a bedroom he decided to just take an educated guess. For the lack of a better word, the entire place was RICH and it was clear that this man indulged himself in the finer things of life. There was a bottle of what was undoubtedly expensive champagne placed on the counter top in the kitchen, along with what appeared to be a Rolex watch resting gently against the bottle.

The place was spotless, undoubtedly maintained by the building's cleaning crew. It was immaculate yet empty. Jonathan began to wonder if the bald man made a mistake and maybe he wasn't supposed to be in the condo. Jonathan hesitantly walked toward the living room trying to see if anyone was there but there was no one except a fireplace and a view. "Dreams of Grandeur" said a voice coming from behind Jonathan who slightly startled him, he quickly turned around. It was Mr. Edwards standing in the doorway dressed in a grey pin stripped suit, with his hands resting in his pockets. The look on Jonathan's face suggested that he didn't catch what Mr. Edwards had said. "I said, Dreams of Grandeur boy, that's how it all started" Mr. Edwards repeated. "If any man wants to succeed in life he has to have a vision, otherwise he won't know where he's going." "Would you agree?" asked Mr. Edwards. "Yes sir" responded Jonathan. Mr. Edwards entered the room walking toward Jonathan's direction; Jonathan felt anxious as Mr. Edwards advanced toward him. The sunlight passed through the window illuminating Mr. Edwards' face so that Jonathan could see his eyes; he remembered those eyes from the other night. They were proud and fierce. Those eyes looked like they could read the hearts of men with a simple glance, and now they were focused directly onto Jonathan. Mr. Edwards stopped about a foot away from Jonathan, "Did you mean it?" he asked. "I'm sorry?" asked Jonathan with a confused look written on his face. "I asked you a question on Friday about what you wanted out of life and you said *everything*." "Did you mean what you said?" asked Mr. Edwards. Jonathan thought back to that conversation and remembered what he had said and thought nothing of it. "Yes sir" Jonathan responded. Mr. Edwards nodded his head and turned toward the large glass window that doubled as a wall overlooking the city. He stood there staring at the skyline looking down into the streets below and watching the people going through the hustle and bustle of their everyday lives. He stood there like a king looking over his kingdom and to Jonathan this man was just that; a King. "So tell me about yourself," Mr. Edwards bluntly asked, still looking out of the window. Jonathan stood there in the foyer thinking of what to say but only the obnoxious truth came floating out into the surface of his brain. "I graduated from Winterville Community College with a 3.5 GPA. I also majored in Business Management…" while Jonathan was still speaking Mr. Edwards interjected, "Ahhh, so you like to lead…good…continue" said Mr. Edwards.

"I moved here about a month ago, although my mother didn't seem to think it was the best idea" said Jonathan continued. "What about your father?" Mr. Edwards once again interrupted Jonathan paused for a moment while a vivid memory of his father teaching him how to throw a baseball out in Denny's Field on the outskirts of town flashed across his mind. He blinked and looked at the floor for a brief moment then looked up at Mr. Edwards. He tightened his jaw muscles then answered the question, "He's dead". Jonathan was now burning a hole in the back of Mr. Edwards' suit. "He died in prison eight years ago" Jonathan continued in a monotone voice. Mr. Edwards turned his head halfway to the side but not all the way around. "May I ask what was he in prison for?" Jonathan rubbed his face knowing that he never really spoke of his father much, as he found himself giving away secrets. "Armed Robbery" Jonathan replied. "He held up a bank with a shotgun a few towns over. The police caught him as he was making a run for it just outside Winterville city limits." He felt different after saying all of that out loud. At this point Mr. Edwards had finally graced Jonathan with his full attention and turned around to face him. He paused for a moment looking Jonathan up and down, "Would you like a drink?" Mr. Edwards asked as he walked toward the kitchen grabbing the bottle of champagne. "Jonathan nervously cleared his throat, "I'm not much of a drinker." Mr. Edwards still proceeded to pour two glasses of champagne anyway, "Never insult prestige, son." said Mr. Edwards while holding a glass out for Jonathan to grab. Jonathan took a slight sip, it was room temperature but it tingled going down his throat. "I'm sorry about your father, I can tell he was a good man, never let anyone including yourself tell you any different" said Mr. Edwards. Jonathan didn't verbally respond but only nodded his head as he held on to his half a glass of champagne. "Thank you Jonathan, this little meeting has been most informative, Adrian will see you out." Jonathan turned around and the bald skinny man was standing just inside the doorway. "Adrian, so *that* was his name!" Jonathan had been wondering what the guy's name was but he had to admit this was an abrupt ending to a pretty short meeting. Jonathan exited the room with Adrian thinking about what just transpired and how to make sense of it all. Adrian escorted him back to the original hallway where the receptionist dropped him off and pointed down the hall. "The Elevator's right down the hall", Adrian said as his voice now seemed to be a bit heavier this time around making the scratchiness amplified. With Adrian's hand still extended Jonathan noticed that it had been badly burned, possibly third degree. Jonathan pulled his eyes off Adrian's hand so that he wouldn't get caught staring. Jonathan thanked him, and headed on his way out while he thought about everything walking through the lobby, riding the elevator and even when he climbed into his truck. He was curious about what would happen next, though he thought it best not to get too excited because there was no telling what could happen.

Back at his apartment, Jonathan lied on his mattress during the middle of the day not being able to shake off his meeting with Mr. Edwards. He started to nick pick over every detail about the meeting including what he could have said, what he shouldn't have said, and all the usual things people get antsy about when they look back on an event that was important to them. Lately, it seemed like Jonathan's mind was a busy place with a lot of traffic going through it. Like a series of events with everything ranging from Rachel to the tainted memory of his father. All he had to do was take his pick of what he wanted to think about, but then his phone rang loudly and obnoxiously with one of the preprogrammed ringtones that came with the phone. Jonathan looked at the phone, it was a number that he didn't recognize but he decided to answer it anyway. "Mr. Cross" said the voice on the other end of the phone. Jonathan immediately knew who it was; it was Adrian from Mr. Edwards' office. Although he had only heard him speak earlier this afternoon, Jonathan could now recognize Adrian's voice anywhere. Jonathan was unsure of how he could have gotten his number but he didn't give it too much thought for there was no time for that. "Yes sir, how can I help you?" Jonathan asked with disgust at himself for sounding like some cheap store clerk. Adrian continued, "Your employer would like to extend an invitation for you to join him at his estate, he's having a private party and he would like you to be there", Jonathan rose to his feet doubtful of what he just heard. "*Really*???" "I mean Wonderful!" Jonathan exclaimed. All the while, still not fully understanding what was going on. "I'll send you the address and promptness isn't an option." confirmed Adrian. "Sounds good sir…..Uhh-Hello?" replied Jonathan but then he realized that Adrian had abruptly hung up. He stood in his wrinkled boxer briefs and a dress shirt wondering what to make of it all. He ran his hand through his hair, making sure all of what he was experiencing was real. His phone then sounded off again signaling that he had just received a text message, it was from Adrian sending the location and time of the party. The text read, "Hillcrest Estates, 8351 Ravenside Drive at 7:30 p.m. It appeared that Jonathan was about to get a sneak peek behind the curtain of wealth. Apparently, Jonathan made a better impression on Mr. Edwards than he previously thought and that things were looking up. It was only a Monday but this week was already off to a great start, with the party being slated for Wednesday.

On Tuesday Jonathan was back at the office going through the daily ritual but this time, with a bit more pep in his step and a smirk that wanted to tear through his face. Regardless, he managed to keep his composure, nothing was written in stone. For all he knew this whole thing could be built on a house of cards that could come tumbling down. Nevertheless, against his better judgment he believed that there was more to it than that and that something bigger and greater was on the horizon of his life. There was no going back for him so he could only move forward; wherever that may take him. Things were strange because he went about his normal day with no one the wiser to the fact that in this cubicle, its dweller had a private meeting with the CEO of the company. Not only that but the CEO liked him enough to invite him to his house, this of course had to mean something because men like that just don't invite people to be around them for the fun of it. Progress had arrived and Jonathan intended to meet it head on. As he worked at his desk, he went through the bombardment of emails and telephone calls that came his way. There was one e-mail that caught his attention and it was from the CFO Ronald Perkins describing some department restructures for meeting budget cuts.

It made him think of Rachel, he wondered if there was anything going on between her and Ronald. He thought about how Ronald touched her back at the party, maybe they were an item. Maybe she was using him to get ahead or maybe she wasn't. Jonathan didn't know and the only thing that he really knew about Rachel was that he liked her but perhaps she was unobtainable. Either way, he couldn't help but feel that he wanted more from her. For now, he would have to put his feelings on hold and concentrate on more important things, such as his second meeting with Mr. Edwards.

He packed up his things and headed toward the lower parking decks. On his way there he would have to pass through the lobby were there was always an abundance of human traffic. It was just understood that you would have people you didn't know bumping up against you to get to where they were going anytime you stepped foot into the lobby after five. Jonathan thought of it like walking on campus just with smarter and sometimes prettier individuals bumping into you. Today was no exception it was packed as usual with people moving like worker ants and if you were to ask the right person they would agree. Jonathan was making his way to the elevator leading down to the parking deck when he ran smack dab into Rachel. "Oh excuse me" They both said it at the same time almost entirely in sync. It took about half a millisecond for Jonathan to realize who was standing before him. "Heeeeyyy..." he said while holding his hand up to her shoulder to make sure she was alright. "I'm fine" she assured him. Right when it was about ten seconds from becoming awkward, Jonathan realized he was still touching her shoulder. "So how's the country boy adjusting to the big city?" asked Rachel. Jonathan responded, "It's been the highlight of my life" accompanied with a clever smirk making its debut on his face. Rachel, clearly entertained with his previous comment, smiled back but not wanting to divulge whether or not it was a flirtatious smile or just a polite one. There was a brief silence that hung between them; Jonathan felt his brain going slightly numb not knowing what to say next. So he said the only thing that was in his mind "Would you like to have dinner with me?" he asked. The words just flew out of his mouth with a mind of their own. He felt nervous almost instantly but stood firm to avoid looking like a wuss. Rachel brushed her hair back over her left ear with her hand, all while staring Jonathan directly in his face. "Sure" she replied it took a few seconds for the words to hit Jonathan's ears and process it. He continued to look at her until he realized that he needed to respond, "How does Saturday work for you?" he asked, "That should work." Rachel answered; in the midst of a busy crowd the two of them seemed to be the only people not moving. Which, in all actuality they were the only two not moving in the lobby. Rachel slipped Jonathan another one of her business cards, this time her real number was written on the back. He held it in his hand and looked at it for a second; he thought that even her handwriting was beautiful. When he looked back up she was already gone but he didn't care as long as he saw her over the weekend. Jonathan made his way out of the lobby and into his truck; he was on cloud nine and this had turned out to be the best week of his entire life. He couldn't believe his luck he didn't know what to make of everything that had been coming his way lately so Jonathan decided to embrace it all! Things were far past just okay and slowly creeping alongside great with the possibility of getting even….better.

Back at his apartment he crawled into the bed and turned off all the lights as he laid in the still darkness resting peacefully on the thoughts of his upcoming future. It didn't take long for him to fall asleep because his brain and body needed a well-deserved rest from all the excitement. The next morning came quickly and Jonathan was awakened by the sound of his alarm clock. The repetitive task of being ripped out of a peaceful sleep by an alarm clock was beginning to wear down on his patience as he slammed his hand on the clock that was sounding off near the mattress. Regardless of the fact that today was the big day of Mr. Edwards's party, as Jonathan got up, he sensed something was different about the morning, he could just feel it. He then looked around the room and it seemed as if it had gotten smaller overnight, like the walls magically shifted closer together. He pulled himself up and headed down the hall towards the showers. The beating of the water helped open his eyes and the rest of his body. Once he was done he headed back to his room, got dressed, and headed to work. Most of the workday was a blur; he was there physically but mentally far, far away. The only thing he really remembered was Mr. Spitz and the odor of onions on his breath. When the day ended Jonathan rushed down to the lobby in hopes that he might run into Rachel again but no such luck. However, all was not lost because the highlight of his day had yet to take place. By the time he left the building, headed home, and got back to the apartment, he had no time to unwind but to simply freshen up again and change his clothes. Jonathan briefly felt embarrassed that it was the same suit he had worn to the art museum but quickly dismissed the thought because he was a college grad on a budget so, it would have to do. By the time he had finished getting ready it was about time for him to leave. He headed out the door just in time to see the sun making its departure to the other side of the world. He realized that he still had the directions to Mr. Edwards' house saved on his phone as he walked through the building's parking deck and hopped inside ole' Beatty. He plugged the address in the navigation and headed out to his destination. He drove through the city for about half an hour, by this time the sun had already disappeared and the city was making its nightly transformation. Jonathan continued to drive crossing over a bridge that overlooked a large river that he had no idea existed. He was surprised that there even were any rivers in Silver Edge. As he crossed the bridge the water lit up reflecting the dancing moon above it. He saw that the tall skyscrapers had disappeared and the loud hustle and bustle of the city had been silenced. Buildings had been replaced with homes with normal size lawns and street lamps. There were trees there now when before there were none. Jonathan continued to drive through this unfamiliar part of the city, not knowing if it even was a part of the city. This area truly was beautiful; Jonathan could see the appeal for someone who was always in the city wanting to live out here. As he continued to drive he noticed that he was getting closer to the house as he saw a well-lit, gated subdivision in the distance. He drove up to the gate. It was black with giant initials "H" and "C" in the middle. Stationed next to the gate was a security post like someone would see crossing a toll bridge and there was a well-built middle aged man with a cheap army hair cut at the post, "Can I help you?" he asked. "I'm looking for the Edwards Estate" asked Jonathan. The gentleman then looked down at a clipboard with a white sheet on it. "Name" asked, the gentleman not bothering to look back up. "Jonathan Cross" replied Jonathan, as he sat in his truck wondering whether or not *Sergeant Peabody* over here was going to send him back over the bridge. He then saw the man press a button and the gate began to open. Jonathan looked back at the man "Welcome to Hill Crest, sir." said the guard. Jonathan nodded and waved his hand. Truthfully, Jonathan meant neither but he just felt that it was something that he should do when he pulled forward as the gate parted like the red sea. Although it was night time, you could see the homes because they were extremely well-lit. Perfectly handcrafted with fine detail, anyone could tell that the lighting had been professionally done. The name definitely suited this community because these homes weren't just mere homes at all but mansions sitting on what had to be at least 15 acres a piece. Each one looked like a complete work of art something to behold and gawk at. You could see each one in all its glory even during the night but the land between them mimicked that of a black sea, blades of grass made black by the shade of night swaying back and forth from the night's cool breeze. Jonathan kept driving admiring the lifestyles of the rich and powerful, until he finally turned in on Ravenside Drive. There were only two homes on the street, one on each side. The one on the right had to be

Mr. Edwards' given the ensemble of cars parked outside. Jonathan drove up slowly to the house which was elegant and regal. It had a large circular driveway made out of cobblestone with a fountain in the front. There were two large men standing at the front entrance and a shorter gentleman dressed in all black with a clipboard in his hand. Jonathan parked ole' Betty a few cars length behind the last car on the curb, to distance himself from the rest of the group. As he got out and headed toward the house, he fixed his suit jacket. The gentleman at the door gave a polite smile and asked for Jonathan's name. The two big men behind him had tight muscle shirts on and were standing over six feet each; and they were **not** smiling. Jonathan gave the man his name; the gentleman flipped a few pages and scanned them up and down. He paused for a moment and then looked at Jonathan and said, "Welcome Mr. Cross, please enjoy your evening", Jonathan told the gentleman thank you and walked up the stairs. The two bouncers at the door stood firm, stared straight ahead, and didn't bother to look at Jonathan as he walked past them. He entered the front door and couldn't believe his eyes of how amazing this place was. The floor was dark marble with two winding staircases leading upstairs. There were people scattered about all dressed to impress. Honestly, it looked like a rerun of the museum except the setting was by far even nicer. Jonathan suddenly thought to himself, what the heck was he was doing there and awkwardly felt out of place. He was grateful to be there but didn't really feel like he belonged. This made sense seeing how he was probably the youngest and poorest person within a twenty mile radius. He then wondered how he was going to find Mr. Edwards in this crowd which looked like something fresh out of a Forbes magazine and he obviously wasn't going to go looking around the man's mansion calling out his name. Suddenly he felt a hand firmly grab his shoulder; as he quickly thought it might have been one of the bouncers not totally convinced that he was invited to the party. To his surprise it wasn't one of the bouncers revoking his invite but instead it was Mr.

Adrian from Mr. Edward's office. Jonathan couldn't help but notice Adrian's hand; it was the one that had been badly burned which was now resting on Jonathan's shoulder. Suddenly feeling embarrassed, Jonathan quickly changed his focus so that he wouldn't appear rude. "He would like to see you in his study" instructed Adrian.

Jonathan followed Adrian through the rather large living room filled with guests and down the hall where no one was present. There was a room at the end of the hallway on the right, Jonathan walked in and saw Mr. Edwards sitting on a leather couch smoking a cigar. Even at his home he was well dressed, white shirt with the sleeves rolled up, dress slacks with a belt and some suede loafers. "Jonathan, glad you could make it" said Mr. Edwards. Jonathan heard the sound of the door closing behind him, "Thank you for having me" he responded as he thought about why exactly he was invited there in the first place. Mr. Edwards still remained on the couch steadily staring Jonathan in the eyes as if his inner most thoughts were an open book waiting for its pages to be read. There was a silence that rested in the air and it was fairly quiet for there to be a party taking place in the same house. Maybe the room was sound proof which would make this meeting of theirs even more awkward. Mr. Edwards finally stood up and asked, "Are you hungry Jonathan?", "No sir, I had something earlier I'm fine." He answered. Mr. Edwards took another puff of his Cuban cigar and blew the potent smoke in the air. "No….I mean are you hungry?" "Are you hungry for life, are you hungry for passion, are you hungry for more, are you hungry for your true potential…Are-you-hungry?" asked Mr. Edwards. Jonathan without any hesitation answered, "Well in that case sir, I'm starving." After those words flew out his mouth, he felt a sense of pride and courage swell up inside him. It was as if he knew those words were to be spoken for this moment. Mr. Edwards stepped forward pulling the cigar out of his mouth, "Good" "You've got an animal in you, boy!" Mr. Edwards continued, "That's good, treat it right and it'll serve you well; you defend it and it will defend you." "Those who stand against you and *it*, will be ripped to shreds and left for dead behind you" he continued. Jonathan stood there listening to what Mr. Edwards was saying but he was merely listening, not fully understanding. "I want you to come work for Me," Mr. Edwards requested. Jonathan paused with confusion at the request and replied, "I already do, Sir." "No, I mean I want you to work DIRECTLY with me, you'll have no one to report to but ME" said Mr. Edwards. Jonathan lost his breath for a second as he felt his chest begin to tightened; he couldn't believe what he just heard. He scratched the back of his head glancing at the couch trying to make sure that the moment was real. He responded quickly, not wanting to give the impression that he wasn't going to take Mr. Edwards up on his offer. "That sounds like an amazing opportunity" said Jonathan; his head still in a fog how all of this was just an inch or two past reality. Mr. Edwards took another puff from his cigar and then extinguished it out in a crystal clear ashtray that was resting on a nearby book shelf. "Outstanding" he said. "I see something in you that I like and that's a rare thing" said Mr. Edwards this was all a bit shocking and overwhelming. However, Jonathan managed to keep himself together by glancing around the room every few seconds whenever Mr. Edwards wasn't looking at him. Jonathan stood there soaking in the moment allowing himself to feel the plethora of emotions that was going on all at the same time as he stood there with feelings of shock and awe quickly turning into gratification. Although, he never thought something like this would ever happen, he always envisioned himself here. For the rest of the conversation, Jonathan walked on egg shells making sure he did nothing to jeopardize this wonderful gift that he had just been given. The two continued to talk until Adrian abruptly opened the door to the study.

Adrian stared at Jonathan for a moment not saying anything as he stood in the doorway. Mr. Edwards must have known why he opened the door because he cut the conversation short; "It was a pleasure Mr. Cross, we'll be seeing each other again, Adrian will escort you out". "You must excuse me I have some business that beckons my attention" said Mr. Edwards as he excused himself. "Yes Sir" Jonathan replied, as he leaned forward and extended his hand for a handshake. Mr. Edwards grabbed his hand. His grip was rock solid, like a cobra squeezing the life out of its prey. Jonathan tried to tighten up his grip but he was overpowered and could do nothing but leave his hand there. Mr. Edwards continued to maintain his unyielding grip until he decided to let Jonathan's hand go, allowing him to leave the room. Jonathan walked out with Adrian wiping his hand on the side by his waist so that Adrian wouldn't see. Adrian walked him back through the house again, people still laughing and socializing enjoying the ambiance of their elite lives while the two of them headed toward the front entrance. Adrian stopped once they got to the door allowing Jonathan to take the rest of the journey on his own. Jonathan walked briskly back to the truck and drove off, once again with the windows down so he could hear the sounds of the night. It served as a backdrop for his thoughts, it was all so surreal. The entire way back he thought about how a door had just been opened and what was on the other side of it. However, he already had a pretty good idea of what was on the other side of that door; everything that he had always wanted. This made the rest of the ride home a blur. He still couldn't believe how great a week it had been and such a perfect day to go along with it. By the time he made it back to his side of town he was pretty exhausted. He pulled into the parking deck and parked the truck. It was dark as usual so he pulled out his tucked in shirt and unbuttoned the top few buttons. He headed toward the elevator to go up to his apartment, when he suddenly felt a sharp pain in his back right below his shoulder blades. The pain was so excruciating that it made him fall to his knees. He reached to touch the spot where the pain was coming from but before he could do that he felt another sharp blow. This time it caused him to fall completely down and roll over on his back. As he laid there he looked up and saw a man in a black ski mask standing over him holding a wooden bat. He then realized those blows he felt weren't from natural causes but from a hit caused by that bat. It was then, when fear quickly crept in overpowering Jonathan. As he stared at the man in the mask he could see the man's cold steel blue eyes staring angrily back at him and felt the hatred seeping through the mask. He tried to move but felt a heavy kick from a boot on the side of his face. At that point, his brain registered that there were in fact two men and that Jonathan was being attacked more than likely from a common city mugging. He couldn't move he felt the force of the man's boots dig into his back already bruised from being hit with the bat. He heard one of the men shout "Grab Him!!" to the other and then felt his hands being pulled over his head as he began to receive heavy blows to his face. He felt the knuckles of an iron fist grind heavily into his face the first one caused his nose to split open at the bottom sending blood gushing out. The ones that followed were worse, each blow intensifying; the punches had such force behind them that each one felt like it was bringing him closer to death. Surely he would not survive this, each hit caused him to slowly lose consciousness and he could almost hear the skin on his lip tear as he laid there taking an onslaught of punches. His mind tried to take him elsewhere, anywhere but there but unfortunately all he could do was focus on the pain and pray that each hit would be the last one until suddenly it stopped. Jonathan couldn't move, he couldn't speak and could barely hear, all he could do was feel. He felt pain throughout his whole body and some warm liquid touching his face. His left eye was almost swollen shut be he managed to catch a fading glimpse of the warm liquid; it was his blood. He lay there alone on the cold pavement, in the dark with nothing but pain and agony to comfort him; it now seemed that his once perfect day wasn't so perfect after all.

CHAPTER SEVEN
WORKING FOR MR. EDWARDS

"I already told you I couldn't see his face he had a mask on!" said Jonathan. This was probably the tenth time the police had taken his statement. He'd been in the hospital for about four days now and was growing weary of all the questions including the salty Jell-O. His wounds were taking their time to heal but the swelling on his lip was finally starting to go down. His left eye still had bruising around it and his back was still sore with a few bumps and bruises on it as well. As he was talking to the police officer, Jonathan just laid there in one of those typical hospital gowns under the covers with the bed propped up so he could sit up straight. The officer's uniform was all black and his badge was silver, looking like it had been polished every morning. Engraved across the bottom of the badge were the letters S.E.P.D. Yes, indeed one of the Silver Edge Police Department's finest was at Jonathan's bedside proving to be more trouble than he was worth. "And you're sure you don't want me to notify your next of kin?" asked the Officer. Jonathan couldn't allow his mother to find out about what had happened. It would only amplify her fear of him moving into the city, besides he didn't want her to worry herself to death. "No, there's no need to do that" "Let's just file the report and see if you guys can catch the two idiots that did this" affirmed Jonathan, as he tried his best to keep from brushing his tongue alongside the inside of his lip. There was a cut both on the outside and inside of his lip. He could still taste some of the blood from the cuts; it had a copper tinge to it, almost as if he had a roll of pennies in his mouth. "Well, the report's already been filed but I just needed to get a few details on some things." The officer continued. "If anything else comes to mind or if you have any further questions you can call our office downtown" he said. As he reached into his front pocket to hand Jonathan the Police Department's telephone number. "I've already got one." said Jonathan, glancing over to the nightstand where two of the same cards were laying. The officer nodded and headed out the room.

With the bed still propped up, Jonathan stared at the wall catching glimpses in his mind about what happened. He wondered how the hell that day went from amazing to ending with him being beaten in the parking deck of his building. He looked around and saw some of the get well cards from his co-workers at Star Industries. There was even a card from Mr. Spitz. The one that he read the most was the one from Rachel. It was a personally hand written card telling him to get well soon and she was there if he needed someone to talk to. News seemed to travel fast within Star Industries because Mr. Edwards sent Adrian to check on him when they found out. Jonathan thought about how he just needed to make sure that the news didn't make its way back to Winterville and hit Marianne Cross' doorstep.

He then heard footsteps clanking outside the door coming closer. The door opened and one of the doctors walked in the room. He looked like a typical doctor with a white lab coat, clipboard in hand, a stethoscope around his neck and with white hair to match the coat. From the look on the doctor's face, Jonathan could tell that he was going to be released today which would be good news because lying in that bed made him feel as if he were on his deathbed. "Mr. Cross, how are you feeling?" the doctor asked. Jonathan directly looked at the doctor thinking how that wasn't the brightest question in the world, "Like someone beat me with a bat" he responded. The doctor smirked back "Fair enough" He then flipped a few pages on his clipboard as he walked closer to Jonathan's bed. "Well, you seem to be healing nicely and everything looks to be in order, I'd say you're free to go" the doctor instructed. "That's exactly what I wanted to hear doc, thanks" said Jonathan. "If you should experience any light headedness, nausea, or unexpected bleeding please give my office a call." the doctor further instructed. "Will do" Jonathan replied, as he began to make his way out of the bed. The doctor headed toward the door, "Your clothes are hanging up in the closet." "I took the liberty of telling the nurses to have your clothes washed" the doctor said as he exited the room closing the door gently behind him. Jonathan gathered his things and began to change his clothes. He managed to put his pants and shoes on without thinking about what happened. However, by the time he got to putting on his shirt he began to think back to that parking garage and he could still feel the bat hammering against his back. He paused for a minute trying to shake the thoughts but another thought lunged forward into his mind and he now saw a tightly clinched hand hurling toward his face. He dropped his shirt with slight nervousness. Jonathan always tried to keep a level head in tough situations. But he had to admit that he found himself a bit rattled about what happened but he continued to change his clothes. He was fully dressed when he heard the door open again. He turned around expecting to see the doctor, however to his surprise it was Adrian standing in the doorway. Adrian stared at Jonathan for a moment looking him up and down, "He wanted me to make sure that you made it home safely this time" assured Adrian. Jonathan wasn't sure if he was trying to be funny or was displaying some kind of genuine concern. Either way it didn't matter to him because truthfully, he was still a bit anxious and didn't feel like driving home anyway. Jonathan followed Adrian out of the hospital without saying much; more of the same continued once they got into the car. They rode the entire way without speaking. Jonathan stared out the window once again looking out into the city. It still had its beauty even though it was now the place where he had been robbed and beaten up for the first time in his life. However, Jonathan wasn't going to allow this event to darken his entire experience in Edge City. He stared at the buildings thinking that he wasn't going to let this hinder him and he wasn't going to give anyone or anything the satisfaction of him giving up. It wasn't long before they arrived back at the apartment. Adrian pulled in to the parking deck on the ground level and drove up to the second level and dropped Jonathan off. "He'll be in touch" said Adrian, while looking out the front window examining the parking lot. He looked as if he was about to ask if this was where Jonathan was attacked; which it was. "Thanks" mumbled Jonathan as he got out of the car. He then heard the sound of tires peeling off but he didn't bother to turn around. He walked quickly to the elevator door, not stopping to look around to see anything; he preferred to go straight ahead up to his room.

That night was different than any other night he had spent in the city. He actually felt alone. The room was quiet and brought no comfort, no words of wisdom from his mother, and he hadn't spoken to his friend David since he left home. For once he felt like the small town kid lost in the big city. It all sort of hit him at once. Thoughts of the whole incident were a bit overwhelming for a moment as if water had rushed into the room and he was struggling to keep his head above it. Jonathan's attitude and determination would have to act as his life jacket because he refused to let this get the best of him. He couldn't and wouldn't turn around now as he began to pace back and forth in the room thinking to himself about what he would do from here. He had almost completely forgotten about Mr. Edwards' offer and wondered if this would affect his position with him in any way. Jonathan's line of thinking didn't make much sense but at this particular time in his life a lot of things weren't making sense. He stopped for a second to think about what his father would do if he were there. However, Jonathan already knew the answer to that question because he knew his father was not a man to give up so easily if at all. No, there would be no going back or rethinking about where he was going to live. He already knew the path he was going to take, it was becoming crystal clear; he was going to work for Mr. Edwards.

Early Monday morning Jonathan headed back to Star Industries, riding in ole' Betty with the windows down. He still enjoyed the voice of the city even though it had recently dealt him a tough blow. The feeling he had as he headed into the building was similar to that of a walk of shame. Although, he realized that he did nothing wrong by getting blindsided in a parking lot and being beaten to a pulp, there was still an underline of embarrassment that came with it. Nevertheless, Jonathan still held his head up high not trying to hide the still noticeable bruises on his face. The building was full of people going through the normal Monday rituals. Jonathan felt the presence of someone anxiously walking with him almost touching his hand as he moved through the hordes of people in the lobby. He made his way through and headed straight for Mr. Edwards' office. However, that feat was slightly easier said than done for two reasons. The first being the last time he made his way up was through an invite. Second, Jonathan would have to get off on the 35th floor and go to its front desk just to get security clearance to reach the executive floor. None of the other elevators went all the way to the top, so anyone going to the top floor would have to take two elevators, and vice versa. However, none of this really mattered to Jonathan at the moment; for he was being fueled by a I'll-deal-with-it-when-I-get-there mentality. He boarded the elevator, and there were three other people that rode up with him to the 35th floor. Neither of them spoke to one another, they were all occupied with their own lives and agendas; there was no room for idle talk. Jonathan just watched the numbers light up as the elevator passed each floor. When it stopped everyone looked up in unison and walked out the door, heading their separate ways. The floor had its own lobby, which was nowhere nearly as crowded as the main lobby downstairs. The reception desk was located toward the center of the room, there was a dark haired man probably within his early thirties seated behind the desk. Jonathan began to make his way over to the desk and realized how loud his dress shoes clicked & clacked against the floor with every step. The man must have heard it too because he looked directly up at Jonathan as he was walking over. "May I help you?" asked the man, as if he was already annoyed this morning. "Yes" Jonathan replied. "I was trying to see Mr. Edwards this morning" The man gave Jonathan a cross eyed stare and began to look him up and down. Not that anyone could blame him because after all, here was a twenty something year old kid with a black eye wanting to see the CEO of probably the most powerful company in the city. Now the man looked as if he was beginning to get angry, "And you would be who?" the man inquired. "My name is Jonathan…" but before Jonathan could finish he heard a rough scratchy voice projected from behind his shoulder, "He's with me, Jerry" said the voice. Jonathan already knew who it was without even turning around. "Oh no, problem Mr. Adrian, you two have a wonderful day" said the man. Adrian began to make his way over to one of the other elevators, with Jonathan following suit. "Thank you, sir." said Jonathan, Adrian remained quiet and pulled out a green security card and swiped it across a panel next to the elevator. The two of them entered the elevator and rode up in silence. Jonathan couldn't quite read Adrian's personality yet besides the obvious; that he was a man of few words. He decided not to say anything else and figure he too would remain silent. They arrived at the executive floor and headed toward Mr. Edward's office. This time when Jonathan entered the office Mr. Edwards was already standing by the conference table talking on the phone. They had walked in on the tail end of his conversation; no doubt talking about something that would make himself and his company richer. "That sounds like something of interest, have a proposal sent to my office and I'll give it a glance." said Mr. Edwards then abruptly hung up the phone before the conversation was over. However, whoever was on the other end of the phone assumingly got the point when the next sound they heard was that of a dial tone. Then there was a moment of silence. Jonathan looked to his left and saw that Adrian was no longer there and only he and Mr. Edwards remained. "I never call a man, a man until I've seen him get knocked down and rise to his feet." "So today I call you a man" said Mr. Edwards, as he gazed at Jonathan. There was something in his eye that let Jonathan know that he was impressed, as if he just received another stamp of approval. "Well I would have preferred if I wasn't literally knocked down" said Jonathan. "Oh of course you would but we rarely if ever get to choose how we're going to be hit." "But one thing's for certain, the hits do come" stated Mr. Edwards. Jonathan then said, "I came to see you today because I wanted to get started, sir." "I mean I want to take you up on your offer to work under you." he clarified. Jonathan didn't know what to expect from this man but he knew it had to be better than what he was doing and definitely better than where he came from. He knew there were things he could learn and places he could go. Jonathan knew that his future was going to be tied to this man but for how long he had no idea but for now, he didn't care. "I'm glad to hear that" said Mr. Edwards, as he walked over to Jonathan he extended his hand in order to seal the deal. It's amazing how a simple gesture such as two individuals touching one another's hand can have such a profound meaning to one person but not the other. It meant the world to Jonathan to be in this moment, he would have widely smiled to show it but he feared his lip would split back open so he opted not to. Mr. Edwards' face was calm but a subtle hint of satisfaction was hidden in his face almost to the point where it was unrecognizable to the common eye and Jonathan was no exception. Yes, there is power in a simple handshake, immense power that Jonathan knew nothing about, but would soon find out.

As the weeks passed by, so did the rest of Jonathan's bruises while things had begun to change. He had been given a raise and was now receiving extra money from Mr. Edwards for miscellaneous activities from arranging his dry cleaning to be picked up, to assisting him during executive meetings. At this point some people had definitely begun to take notice that there was a new face on the roster of Mr.

Edwards. Jonathan took notice of the changes as well, he was no longer working on the 10th floor under the fat thumb of Mr. Spitz and people around the office started to look at him differently. He was finally able to furnish his small one bedroom and was actually starting to make plans to move out. He had only been having vague conversations with his mom as to how things were going back home. She was oblivious to the fact that her son had almost been beaten to death and that he was now working under probably the most influential man in the city. There was a certain demeanor that Mr. Edwards carried and that was subtly transferring over to Jonathan. He was even beginning to dress better. Mr. Edwards insisted that he buy him some nicer suits, if he was going to be working closely with him. Adrian still kept Jonathan at arm's length and watched him with a close and suspecting eye; so nothing seemed to change in that area. Things were undoubtedly on the rise and Jonathan was stepping into the faster lane of life and enjoying the cross over. He paid close attention to how Mr. Edwards would conduct business, and how he would respond to certain situations always managing to stay calm and in control of the moment. Although on this particular afternoon, Jonathan perhaps saw more than he wanted to.

All three of them took a trip down to the city docks to see an old meat packing plant that had been closed down some time ago. It was right next to the Huntington River named after the first mayor of the city. The place was run down and dirty almost completely over run by rust and some of the ground close to the building had a red hue to it. Undoubtedly, from the blood of the entire meat carcass' that had been processed there years ago. Maybe the lack of cleanliness was why it was shut down before; no one really knew. They arrived in a black town car with Adrian behind the wheel. When they arrived, there was a short man wearing a dress shirt and slacks talking on the phone. They all got out of the car and the man was still talking but paused for a moment when he saw Mr. Edwards step out of the car. "Yea, I hear ya but hey look, they're here so I'll talk to ya later on." said the man as he hung up the phone shortly after. "How are you Mr. Edwards, sir?" asked the man with his hand extended. Mr. Edwards shook his hand and with a straight face replied, "Well, depending on how this conversation goes I could be having a good day and I would like it to stay that way." Mr. Edwards then looked over at the building for a moment and inquired, "So do you have any news for me?" The man took a deep breath before he nervously spoke looking at both Adrian and Mr. Edwards. "Well I'm not sure if we'll be able to get the zoning permit for you to expand on the building; those guys down at corporate get pretty particular about this crap!" You could tell the man was nervous by the shallowness of his voice. "I see" replied Mr. Edwards while continuing to look at the building not bothering to look at the man, he then looked at Adrian and nodded. Adrian turned to the man and reached for the inside pocket of his jacket while the man stared at Adrian with a nervous look watching to see what he was gonna pull out. Jonathan also found himself focused on Adrian's hand but all he pulled out was a white envelope. The man's face still held an anxious expression as he grabbed the envelope but that look quickly transformed into a wide grin when he looked inside. The envelope was full of money and the man looked up again and said, "What the boys at corporate don't know won't hurt 'em, I'll make sure you get those permits." He then tried to shake Mr. Edwards' hand but Mr. Edwards turned his back and headed toward the building. The man dug in his pockets and gave Adrian a key to the building. "Well I see no harm in you guys having a key until we finalize things" reassured the man. Adrian took the key and remained silent. Jonathan stood there trying to get a grasp of what just took place. He never witnessed someone bribe a man before or a man accept one either. Jonathan then nervously looked around to see if anyone else was watching but there was no one in sight. He too stayed silent and just stared at the river and watched how water moved at a swift pace building up a current. He felt as if he had just committed a crime; perhaps because he just witnessed something illegal take place. But still he said nothing; he kept quiet and watched Mr. Edwards and Adrian head toward the building. "That man knows how to get things down" the man commented while staring at Jonathan with a wide eyed grin. Jonathan nodded his head but didn't verbally respond as he gave the man a dirty glance, looked back at the building, and then started to walk toward it. There was nothing that he could, should, or would say. He chose to remain silent because that was the way things were and the way things were going to be now that he was working for Mr. Edwards.

CHAPTER EIGHT
THE ART OF DISILLUSION

For some reason, the sun always seemed to shine extra bright in the city and today it was a testament to that notion because it was hotter than ever. It looked and felt as if GOD had taken a flashlight and placed it right above Edge City. Soon, Jonathan would be able to see the city more clearly from the view of his new loft that he just recently put a down payment on. He was all grins at the signing; it was a great come up from the single room unit he had just left. He took pictures of the place and sent them to his mother, which made her absolutely ecstatic. She planned on coming up sometime in the next few months; it was better this way because this allowed Jonathan to get some things in order. He hadn't seen his mother since he left Winterville and was eager to show her that he was indeed making it in the big city. He was outside of the building looking up at the sign that said Parlor Lofts… it was beautiful. Life was becoming more and more stimulating now that he was working for Mr. Edwards. As he looked at the sign he couldn't help but think about what he saw over a week ago down by the docks. He didn't know what to think of it really, here was a man that he had grown to admire bribing someone just so he could get a zoning permit. Jonathan had to admit, it wasn't the most flattering thing that Mr. Edwards could have done in front of him. Nevertheless, he convinced himself that it was really no big deal. After all, this is the majors and everyone knows that they play differently. So he let it go or at least for now since there was no need to cry over spilt milk. He entered the building and headed up for another look before he brought all his furniture over; which at this point was the one mattress he had bought for the other place. His new unit number was 303. It was a lot bigger than his previous digs and he felt like he could actually breathe in this place. The wooden floors had a nice gloss almost as if they were smiling back at him. It had three bedrooms and the master had an amazing view. It was this new loft that made Jonathan realize that his dreams were coming true. He was now moving up in the world and enjoying the ascension; life had finally begun to be exciting. He smiled to himself knowing that this was only the beginning and things were going to get even better!

He did a brief walk through of the place again before heading out; he had made it to the elevator when his phone began to ring. He decided not to look at it because he knew he was getting ready to get on the elevator and the signal would be lost, so there was no need to answer it. He got on the elevator accompanied by an elderly woman holding a Chihuahua and a man dressed in cycling gear. The elderly woman smiled at Jonathan. "Hello Dear" she said. Jonathan smiled back, "Hi, how are you?" he asked. The woman smiled and stared at Jonathan for a moment but did not answer back. Jonathan turned and faced the front of the elevator as the doors closed; wondering whether or not the woman heard him. The doors closed and he rode the elevator down to the first floor. Upon exiting, he took his phone out to see who had called him. The phone displayed a missed call from Adrian; he quickly redialed the number as he was leaving the building. He heard the phone ringing, as he wondered what Adrian had called him about. Jonathan never really enjoyed talking to Adrian very much but at this point it proved to be a necessary evil that he would just have to endure. The phone stopped ringing when he heard it click over. "Hello" said Adrian in his infamous scratchy tone. Jonathan thought how it was actually amazing because even his greetings didn't sound friendly. Most people's voices sound inviting when they say "hello" but when Adrian responds it sounds more like he's really agitated than anything else. "I missed your call." said Jonathan. For a moment, the phone was silent on the other end when he heard   Adrian mumble something but he couldn't quite make it out. Jonathan thought it wise to not even bother asking him what he said, he figured if Adrian wanted him to know what he said then he would have said it louder. " He wants you to be at his office within an hour." Adrian instructed. He then paused again and continued, "His downtown office" he further instructed. Jonathan wasn't very sure on how to get downtown and had no idea where the downtown office was. "I'll send you the address" said Adrian, right before Jonathan could even ask for it. "Ok sounds good" Jonathan affirmed but heard no response after that except the dial tone from Adrian abruptly hanging up the phone. Jonathan looked at the phone shaking his head while thinking to himself that this guy was a bit of a jerk; although he would cut him some slack because after all Adrian did drive him home from the hospital. Nevertheless, he shook it off and waited for the message to come through, once he got it he figured he'd go ahead and start heading over there now. That way if he got turned around he'd have some time to correct himself. Furthermore, with the traffic in this city it could sometimes take an hour to make a 20 minute trip. He headed around the corner to the guest parking lot where his truck was. He hopped in and put the address in his navigation system and rode off, as he rode through the city he thought of Adrian again. Jonathan had questions about him that he wanted answers to but didn't know how to get them without having to ask. Which was something that was completely out of the question but he still wondered who was he really besides being Mr. Edwards' go-to-man? Why did his voice sound like that? And how did he get those burns on his hand? One of the few things that his father taught him was to always be aware of your surroundings, and right now Jonathan was trying to get his bearings together.

He had to admit that he didn't really know everything that was going on and how could he? Silver Edge was a whole new world and Mr. Edwards and his often silent associate Adrian were two men that seemed to be incased in mystery and opulence. So, at this point he only knew what he had seen, and there was probably more to see which he was sure that there was. Jonathan was just going to have to wait for the opportunity to reveal itself but until then, he was along for the ride. He drove ole' Betty through the streets of this iron city he found himself emerged in; the traffic was fairly light it was about 1:15 in the afternoon and most people were already back at the office from their lunch break. Jonathan was enjoying the new found freedom of his new schedule. Although it was weird in a sense because now that he was on call for Mr. Edwards he no longer had to suffer the mundane 9 to 5. But that also meant that he could get a call late in the night and he would be expected to respond. So it sort of balanced out but Jonathan didn't mind it, he was now able to get out of the office and learn hands on from a man who knows business like the back of his hand. As a matter of fact, Jonathan heard that there were those from the business world that referred to Mr. Edwards as "The Right Hand of Business" He seemed to always be ahead of everyone else even at times when it didn't appear that Star Industries was doing well; he would miraculously find a way to pull ahead. He was a walking legend in Edge City, a breathing myth that was capable of anything. Jonathan looked at it as a privilege to have the opportunity to be in this man's presence which made it easier to overlook any of his faults, like the harbor incident. The drive was fairly easy it didn't take as long as he expected to get to downtown. Jonathan glanced over at the navigation and saw that he was approaching the address that Adrian had given him. It was yet another nice building but less than half the size of the Star Industries Tower. This one looked high end but had more of a modern look to it. Jonathan got lucky there was a spot on the curb right in front of the building, a few cars down from the street meter. He got out and hesitantly did his civic duty and put coins in the meter as he headed inside the building lobby and pulled out his cell phone to call Adrian and let him know that he had arrived. Yet, right as he was about to dial the number, he saw one of the elevator doors open, and out walked Adrian. Dressed in his usual get up black suit and tie, he motioned for Jonathan to come over to the elevator. Jonathan walked over and got on, once again he found himself caught in a game of hush mouth with Adrian, neither one of them said a word. Jonathan was standing to Adrian's right side but slightly behind him and thought it best not to say anything. However, he couldn't quite help the fact that he was tired of being on pins and needles around this guy. So he decided to say something, anything to get this lifeless man to speak. "Do you know why he wanted to see me?" asked Jonathan. Adrian continued looking straight ahead at the elevator doors, "No" he said. Jonathan standing behind him shook his head thinking to himself that this guy was impossible to talk to. Thankfully, the elevator stopped and the doors opened up with Adrian silently leading the way. Jonathan managed to get a glimpse of the place as he was walking, it was a completely different feel and look in this building and the modern styled theme continued on the inside just as it showed on the outside. There was no one around either, which seemed odd but Jonathan paid it no mind. They soon arrived at a big corner office, the doors were glass so anyone could see in but seeing how there was no one around to see anything, it wasn't really an issue. Adrian opened the door, it was a fully furnished office but no one was there besides the two of them. Now looking back on it Jonathan didn't notice anyone else in the entire building as he came up. He wondered was this a fully furnished building void of any people to inhabit it. He then heard the door open behind them before he turned around he felt something different in the room. The atmosphere felt like it shifted, nothing over the top but still it just somehow felt different. As he turned around he saw Mr. Edwards, dressed sharply as usual, Mr. Edwards then nodded to Adrian giving him the signal to leave. Adrian then exited the room shortly after that. Jonathan watched Adrian as he walked out of the room; and then turned his attention over to Mr. Edwards. He watched him as he moved across the room, unbuttoning his suit jacket and placing it on the leather couch that was against the wall. "In life there are those who wish to challenge your destiny" said Mr. Edwards. "Their presence is inevitable and their existence is essential" He continued. "It is essential to your growth, to your will, your strength, and your mind" "An adversary should never be avoided or ignored Mr. Cross" said Mr. Edwards. Jonathan stared and listened wondering where he was going with this speech. "Do you understand what I'm saying Jonathan?" asked Mr. Edwards. For a spilt second he felt nervous, knowing that he would have to give an account to what he had just heard. It was funny that even though he had spoken to Mr. Edwards on several occasions he would still find himself being a bit uneasy from time to time. "I believe so sir" said Jonathan. At this point, Mr. Edwards walked over to Jonathan so that the two of them were standing face to face. "Good." said Mr. Edwards, "Because everything I am today is the result of an advisory I conquered yesterday" "Which brings me to my next point," he continued, while placing his hand on Jonathan's shoulder. "I now face a new opponent, a new advisory who wishes to put a halt to my progress" he said. Jonathan stood there trying not to look as confused as he really was. "Does the name Julian Caesar mean anything to you?" asked Mr. Edwards. Jonathan thought about whether or not the name rang a bell but he couldn't think of anything. "No sir" Jonathan replied and at this point Mr. Edwards had dropped his hand from Jonathan's shoulder. "Well I digress; I wanted to talk to you about enlisting your services" Mr. Edwards said. "I have a special project that I'm working on that's going to require a bit more of a hands on approach" "And I'm afraid that I simply don't have that kind of time to devote my attention to such matters" he said. Jonathan still a bit clueless as to what this conversation pertained to then asked, "What is it that you want me to do sir?" "I'll have Adrian fill you in on the details but I'm thinking that you're the right man for the job" instructed Mr. Edwards. Jonathan still clueless as to what he was talking about further extended his services "I'm sure I'll at least be able to lend a hand" assured Jonathan; Mr. Edwards looked at him for a moment and nodded. "I'm sure" Mr. Edwards concurred. "You know you remind me of someone Jonathan" said Mr. Edwards. "A young man that I knew a long time ago" "Well, I'll take that as a good thing" stated Jonathan. "It is" replied Mr. Edwards. "He was a good man" he said, as he gazed out of the office window. "Do you still talk to him much?" asked Jonathan. "I'm afraid not, he died quite some time ago" said Mr. Edwards. "I'm sorry to hear that, sir." Jonathan replied. Mr. Edwards turned from looking out of the window and looked at Jonathan, "Don't be" "It was for the best" Jonathan looked confused at what he said however, he quickly changed his face in order not to give any clue what he was thinking. Before he could say anything else, Adrian entered the room again....right on cue. "As I said Adrian will fill you in on all the details" said Mr. Edwards. Adrian stood in the middle of the doorway silent and grim as usual giving Jonathan a look that suggested he should leave. Jonathan took the hint and headed toward the door. "I thank you for your time Jonathan" said Mr. Edwards as Jonathan made his way toward the door. Jonathan stopped just before he walked out, "Not a problem, sir." he said as he proceeded to leave. On the way out Jonathan began to replay what had just taken place in his mind. He wondered why he needed to come all the way down here for a five minute meeting and also wondered why there appeared to be no one else in that building. He wanted to know who was the young guy Mr. Edwards was talking about? He also wanted to know what the hell was going on? As he left the building the sun was still in its place shining bright in the sky illuminating Edge City while its inhabitants were moving about as usual. Jonathan tried to get a grip on what was going on but he still had to admit that the bribe was swimming around in the back of his head trying to scratch to the surface of his conscious. However, the allure of standing beside the most powerful man in the city outweighed any guilt or doubts that his mind could conjure up. He then thought of who he could unload his concerns and excitement on, there was one name that stood out; Rachel. He thought that maybe she could serve as his sound board for a few minutes, and he could bounce some of his thoughts off of her.

He made it back to his old place, now sitting on his bed, the floor was a bit messy, some of his clothes were on the floor hanging out of the few moving boxes that he had. He scrolled through the names on his phone and paused when he got to Rachel's. He gave it a second thought before he started dialing and decided it wouldn't hurt. The phone began to ring. He thought about what he would say or what he should say. The next sound he heard was her answering the phone with that soft angelic voice of hers resonating over the phone. "Hello" Rachel said but Jonathan remained silent "Hello?" she repeated. There was a pause for a moment then she spoke again "Jonathan?" she asked. Jonathan felt a nervousness and sense of embarrassment come over him. Without thinking he quickly hung up the phone and rubbed his head thinking to himself that was possibly the dumbest thing he had ever done. He dropped the phone on the bed and looked at it for a moment, when suddenly it began to ring. He stared at the screen as it glared Rachel's name on the caller ID. Jonathan quickly grabbed the phone and switched it to vibrate. The phone stopped ringing and displayed one missed call. He breathed a sigh of relief, now thinking about why he couldn't talk to Rachel. He knew good and well he needed to keep his mouth shut and that's what he planned to do. He then felt a tingle on the bed and looked over and saw that the phone was vibrating yet again. He could hear it vibrating, while shaking around on the bed but did nothing but stare at the phone hoping that Rachel wouldn't press the issue and let it go. After all, Jonathan didn't fully understand what was going on and there was no way he was going to drag her into to this or at least that's what he'd hoped.

CHAPTER NINE
SPECIAL DELIVERY

"So what's it look like Johnny!?" she asked, "You'd love it mom, it's got a great view." said Jonathan; as he stood by the window looking out as the sun was making its departure from the sky. It gave off a funny color as it was going down, making the sky appear to be a beautiful combination of pink leading into purple while turning into blue. "Yeah, it's a nice change of pace." said Jonathan glancing back at the living room. "I'm proud of you Johnny" said Ms. Cross. "But you haven't seen it yet" said Jonathan, "I don't need to see your new place to know that your dreams are coming true Johnny" "I can hear it in your voice" said Ms. Cross. "I'll have to come up soon." "If I can ever get some time off", she said. "Well let me know when and I'll get the ticket" said Jonathan. "Oh I'll get my own ticket, you save up that money, you hear?" said Ms. Cross. "I wish I had done some things differently when I was your age." she reminisced. "Well the piggy bank's getting fed more on a regular basis now", said Jonathan; which was true because he was making about three thousand dollars a week. Jonathan had never seen this kind of money before in his life. Although he only had about $25,000 in his bank account, it felt as if he were a millionaire; it was just beyond real to him. "Well, look at you on your own for a few months and already measuring your wallet", teased Ms. Cross. Jonathan smiled and sat down on the couch propping his feet up on his newly purchased coffee table. Something he knew he could never do at home for fear of getting his feet cut off, "Things are definitely looking up I'll say that much" said Jonathan, "Well, like I said I'm proud of you, I love you and I'll see you soon kiddo" said Ms. Cross. "Love you too", Jonathan replied. He held the phone to his ear as he heard the phone click. He sat there look-ing at his dark reflection through the Plasma TV that he also recently purchased. Jonathan knew things were great and he wanted them to not only stay this way but get even better. Although he admitted to himself that things with Mr. Edwards were less than clear, he still couldn't shake the fact that things were the best they had ever been in his life. He couldn't just throw all of this away because he had a few unanswered questions and faint inhibitions.

Besides, anytime Jonathan found himself around Mr. Edwards, it seemed to feel right; as if the missing piece to his life was put in place. In Jonathan's chain of evolution Mr. Edwards was his missing link so to speak. He thought, without Mr. Edwards, he wouldn't have the necessary pieces to survive, he knew that he needed him for more reasons than one. However, he wasn't the only one aware of this fact and he could tell that Mr. Edwards knew this too. There was no doubt the presence of a bond that had been formed between the two of them. One appeared to need one more than the other but the truth of the matter was that they both needed each other. One thing was clear; Mr. Edwards had found something in Jonathan that he had not seen in a long time. However, what it was exactly that Mr. Edwards saw in him was still a mystery to Jonathan. Maybe he would never know but if he didn't that was fine because he tried his best not to get caught up in things like that. Why is the sky blue? Why do people fall in love? All he knew was that there was a good thing forming here and if his time with Mr. Edwards had taught him anything thus far, it was that things were already complicated with this man. Therefore, adding questions to the equation was like adding salt to the wound, something that would only make things worse. This is why he'd been dodging Rachel for the past few days. She already left a voice message on his phone. He had been contemplating the idea that he should fill her in on what was happening but just thought perhaps doing it in an indirect way. He still didn't exactly have it all figured out but he knew that he had to talk to someone just to get it off his chest. There was definitely a dichotomy taking place in this situation. On one hand, Jonathan wanted to keep his mouth shut but on the other he wanted to get some outside perspective on this just in case he wasn't doing the right thing. The only thing that he knew for sure was that he was going to have to pull himself together and get a grip.

He once again found himself at beck and call; Adrian had left him a message on his phone earlier in the day. Actually, he left it around midnight to be exact; it was now 2:15 in the afternoon. The message told him to meet Adrian later on tonight around eight, so he still had some time to kill. He sat still on the couch while occasionally glancing over at the phone wrestling with the idea to return Rachel's call. He rationalized how he could make up some excuse as to why he was now giving her a call and the reason for his delayed response in returning her call. Deep down he knew that if he gave her a call that the conversation would inevitably take a detour to talk about his life and what being on the fast track with Mr. Edwards was like. Obviously it was a topic that Jonathan wanted to avoid. However, he no longer wanted to avoid Rachel, so he dialed her number wondering what to expect next. Was she mad that he had ignored her? Was she going to bring up the weird phone call when he hung up on her? He had no idea what to expect from her all he knew was that he was throwing a dart in the dark by dialing her number. The phone rang for a moment; still having no idea as to what he was going to say if she actually answered the phone. The next thing he heard was a soft voice, "Hey Stranger, glad to see that your hands work and you can dial somebody's number" she said. "Yea I just been rippin' and runnin' non-stop these days" Jonathan replied. "So I hear that you've become someone's new golden boy" Rachel said. But before Jonathan could say anything else; Rachel interjected, "News travels fast, slick" she continued. Jonathan couldn't argue with her at this point because it was definitely no secret that he had been spending a lot of time with Mr. Edwards and knew that people were already taking notice. It would have been hard to miss the fact that Jonathan was promoted from a ground level position at the company to now being the new preferred shadow of the CEO. "Yeah", said Jonathan in a way that really didn't leave any room for him to say anything else. "So why did you call me a few days ago?" asked Rachel. Jonathan knew this would happen. He almost wanted to throw the phone down when she asked that question; he slightly grinded his teeth for a second before he tried to come up with an answer. "I wanted to get your opinion on something." he said, taking a second to realize that he came up with a pretty good answer which was actually truthful. He really did want to get her advice on what to do without throwing Mr. Edwards name out there. "My opinion?" said Rachel; her voice suggesting that she was unconvinced to Jonathan's response. "Yea, I just wanted to run a few things by you, maybe we can talk about it over dinner; my place" said Jonathan. There was a loud silence that lasted a few seconds too long before Rachel said anything. "Wow, so you pretty much did this all wrong" said Rachel. "You called me several days ago, didn't leave a message, wouldn't return my calls and now you're asking me out over the phone?" Rachel asked. Jonathan rubbed his hand over his head thinking to himself that he sounded like a real idiot when she put it like that! As he tried to come up with a rebuttal or something clever to say, she once again beat him to the punch. "Luckily for you, I tend to have a soft spot for guys who screw up", quipped Rachel. "Well, I aim to please", Jonathan sarcastically responded; fully aware that Rachel was right about his approach. Nevertheless, he was just thankful that his opportunity with Rachel wasn't completely out the window. "Send me your address, Romeo", she asked. "Yeah, I'll get it to you", replied Jonathan. "Can we make it a late dinner?" he asked. "Well you really know how to push the envelope", Rachel said sarcastically. Jonathan was getting frustrated with his inability to keep his foot out of his mouth. He figured he should quickly hang up the phone while he was still somewhat on Rachel's good side. "I'm sorry, it's just that I have a couple of things that I need to take care of." Jonathan said. All the while he'd hoped that he wasn't digging himself into a deeper hole. "I'm sure" said Rachel. Well, I'll let you get back to whatever it is that you do these days and I'll see you later on", she said. "Sounds good" said Jonathan with a somewhat nervous smirk beginning to show all over his face. He wasn't sure if Rachel was completely happy in his sincerity about joining him for dinner or still annoyed with the fact that he took so long to call her back. Either way he was having dinner with her, which gave him a chance to redeem himself. However, the dinner plans were going to have to wait because he knew he had other business to tend to with Adrian. He was going to have to deal with whatever new task Mr. Edwards had presented him.

The rest of the day carried itself along with Jonathan making sure he had things in place for tonight. He wanted the place to be spotless, nowhere near resemblance to the one bedroom junk pile he just left. This was a new start within a new place and he wasn't going to blow it. By this time it was a little bit before seven and Jonathan wanted to make sure he gave himself enough time to meet Adrian by 8'oclock. So he headed out the door taking a final glance making sure things looked up to par before leaving the apartment. He wanted everything to be perfect for tonight to make up for his behavior lately. He perused over the room for another few seconds before closing the door. He glanced down at his watch, it was now 7:05; he knew he had time but he still moved as if he had somewhere to be.

By the time he got into the car he found himself already yearning for the night to fast forward itself so he could be back at the loft with Rachel. Lord knows he definitely didn't feel like entertaining another one of Mr. Edwards' late night mystery sessions. Adrian had already sent him the address and Jonathan had it plugged into his GPS. Jonathan had to admit that it was starting to get a little strenuous constantly driving to different parts of the city. Nevertheless, he knew that on the bright side, he was learning the lay of the land. The night sky had settled in and stars were beginning to come forth from their solar slumber; when Jonathan arrived at the address he saw that it was a restaurant only a few miles from the city bridge. It was an old mom & pop diner, complete with its own set of old timers reminiscing about their glory days. Adrian was already in the parking lot standing by a blacked out town car, like the grim reaper waiting for the next unlucky soul. Jonathan pulled into the parking space beside him; Adrian had his back up against the car silently staring off into the distance. He barely acknowledged Jonathan when he pulled up, which was nothing new however there was something different about Adrian. He seemed a bit more agitated than normal, his amorphous demeanor normally made it hard to get a read on him. However, tonight was different, he seemed more like an open book or at least a half cracked one showing the reader he definitely didn't want to be there. Jonathan stepped out of the truck; by now he figured he wouldn't bother with saying hello because he knew that generally ended in Jonathan feeling like an idiot. So instead he stood there for a moment letting the awkward silence run its course. Adrian continued to stare out in the night for a moment before turning his head looking Jonathan over from head to toe with a semi quick glance. "Get in the car" Adrian instructed.   Jonathan did as he was told and got in. As Jonathan slid in the front passenger seat he undoubtedly felt that Adrian's mood was on edge. This made Jonathan feel even more uncomfortable but at this point, there wasn't much he could do about it. Adrian drove off, pulling out of the diner parking lot like a bat straight out of hell. There was no mistaking the fact that Adrian clearly didn't want to be there, or do whatever it was they were going to do. Adrian drove through the city streets driving way over the speed limit. Jonathan didn't want to give the impression that he was nervous even though he was, so he quietly grabbed the inside of the door handle. At this time, things made no sense which only caused Jonathan to doubt the whole situation even more. He wondered where in the world they were going and why Adrian was driving so fast? Were they running from some unknown assailant? Was Adrian scared of something? Or was he trying to get pulled over on purpose? Although strangely it seemed like there were no cops in sight, giving Adrian free range to sprint freely throughout the city streets.

Jonathan looked outside of the window seeing shades of the night pass by his window in an almost artistic sequence. He could tell that they were crossing the bridge that was close to the diner, for a second Jonathan thought that they were heading to Mr. Edwards's estate. However, he remembered that the bridge he was thinking of was located on the other side of the city. Like the other bridge, this one seemed to be a connector between two different worlds. Adrian continued to speed until they got to the other side of the bridge, it was a miracle that they didn't get pulled over but then again maybe it wasn't. Jonathan almost hoped that they would have because maybe the police could save him from what looked like another night of the whole cloak and dagger routine. That kind of luck seemed to have evaded him tonight; there was no one coming to his rescue. Once again, the scenery was different it looked like another round of the suburban life outside of the city. Although the area was nice it wasn't as nice as Mr. Edwards's neighborhood. If Mr. Edwards' neighborhood was reserved for the rich, then this area must have been for the upper-middle class. Although, like last time it was dark so Jonathan couldn't get the best view these streets had to offer. At this point he figured he'd open up his mouth " Where are we going?" Jonathan asked. Adrian looked over at him for a second then looked back at the road. As Adrian continued driving, the car's headlights were lighting up the pavement in front of it as it drove onward then suddenly he cut the lights off. The road was now black with only a few sporadic street lights to illuminate the way. Adrian turned to Jonathan with his face still halfway visible; "To tie up some loose ends"Adrian replied. Jonathan had to admit to himself that at this point he was completely uneasy about the whole situation. He was wondering what the hell "tying up loose ends" meant; because it almost sounded as if Adrian was talking about killing someone. Had this been anyone else, Jonathan would've not worried about what they said but he was quickly discovering that he had to take everything this man said seriously and not take any of his actions lightly. Jonathan noticed that Adrian was slowing down, so he looked out of the window to see where they were exactly. It looked like Adrian was getting ready to pull into a subdivision on the right side of the street. Jonathan managed to make out the name because the sign had light shining on it from the bottom; the name on the sign was Pine Ridge. Adrian turned into the community as Jonathan slowly leaned forward in his seat to get a closer look at the street. Jonathan wasn't stupid he knew that if they were riding through a nice neighborhood at night in a black car with the lights off, then chances are they didn't have an open invitation to whosever house they were going to. The homes were nice with spacious lots. Adrian parked the car on the curb. He silently sat in the seat for a moment staring out of the window at the sole brick house across from where they were parked. Adrian continued to look out the window for what seemed like an hour but it was actually only about two minutes. "Listen when we get in here you keep sharp" Adrian sternly instructed. He then reached for a white envelope sitting in the back seat. Adrian looked over at Jonathan once again as he slightly looked him up and down, "We'll see if he's right" said Adrian; as he opened up the car door. Jonathan took this as his key to follow suit and got out of the car as well; his heart started racing. He had no idea what was going on but he began to get the feeling that from Adrian's comment, this might be something of a final test. It was late but surprisingly Adrian wasn't cloaking his way through the bushes, he walked boldly down the street as if he lived in one of the homes. Jonathan followed Adrian while keeping his head slightly tilted to the ground just in case some nosey old lady was looking outside of her window. Adrian continued on until he got close to the brick house; it was the third house down from where he parked the car. The house was beautifully designed and looked spacious, if Jonathan had to guess it was probably around 5000 sq ft. Adrian began to head around the side of the house between the house next to it. He quickly maneuvered from around the side to the back of the house. There was a wooden fence in the back with one of those metal locks for a door handle. Adrian stopped at the door and reached in his pocket, Jonathan turned around to see if anyone was watching. Although, it wasn't like he would have gotten a good look at anybody in the dark unless they were very close. Adrian pulled out a key and unlocked the gate it was obvious that he was prepared and undoubtedly cased the place out beforehand because he knew exactly where he was going. Once inside the gate Adrian told Jonathan to close it, the two of them then proceeded to the back door entrance of the basement. Adrian then pulled out another key and unlocked the basement door. He apparently must have somehow gotten some copies made of the owner's keys because this definitely wasn't Adrian's house. By now, Jonathan knew what they were doing was illegal but his better judgment was apparently on vacation. Adrian twisted the key and turned the knob slowly as he entered the house. He walked in motioning Jonathan to follow him inside. "Close the door" whispered Adrian. Naturally, the house was dark, so Jonathan tried not to look around somehow thinking that if he didn't look, this wouldn't be real. However, he knew it was and he was going to accept the situation for what it was. As he tip toed behind Adrian he managed to get a look at the basement, it was finished with plush carpet and there was also a custom made pool table next to a custom built wet bar. As Jonathan kept inching along he wondered if everyone in Silver Edge was rich besides him. Adrian led the way with a flashlight that didn't seem to add much light, but knowing Adrian that was something that was done on purpose. The two made their way to a stairway that looked like it led to the main floor of the house. As they walked up, Jonathan began to think about all the scenarios of what could possibly occur. He wondered if someone actually saw the two of them sneak into this house; perhaps someone called the police and they were already on their way. Or what if someone was home and waiting for the two of them on the other side of the door at the top of the stairs, waiting to blow their chest out with a sawed off shotgun? Maybe, some of that fear was evoked from when Jonathan got a sneak peek of the gun holstered under Adrian's jacket. When they reached the top of the stairs Adrian opened the door without hesitating, it was almost as if he knew for a fact that no one was home. This level of the house actually had some dim lighting so the flashlight was no longer necessary. Adrian stood still for a minute as he looked around. "Stay here" he said. "Sure", mumbled Jonathan. Once Adrian left his sight, Jonathan could no longer hear him. Jonathan thought about how if this was his house and Adrian was sneaking around he would have no idea he was there. It was almost frightening how stealthy Adrian could be when he wanted to. Jonathan thought about what he would do if all of a sudden a brigade of police officers came smashing through the front door. That thought was suddenly interrupted when Adrian appeared from around the corner still carrying the white envelope from the car in his hand. He walked over to Jonathan and handed it to him, "Here take this" he said. "I want you to go upstairs and put this in the master bedroom." "It's the one at the end of the hall, place it on the bed and get out!" Adrian further instructed. While looking at Jonathan with a piercing stare; Jonathan looked at the envelope then back at Adrian. "What's in…" Jonathan started to ask the question but he knew better. He took the envelope and headed upstairs but he wasn't as stealthy as Adrian. He could hear his shoes press against the wooden stairs. Jonathan wanted to look back to see if Adrian was still at the bottom of the steps but he didn't want to look like a kid on his first day of school looking back for his mother. So he pushed on looking down the hall. He could tell it was the master bedroom because it had double doors; Jonathan wondered just what exactly was going on. Whose house was he in? What in the world was in the envelope and why did they do all of this just so he could put an envelope on somebody's bed? Nevertheless, Jonathan was more concerned with getting out of there so he moved quickly towards the bedroom. He opened the door on the right side and gently pushed it over with his hand. He eased his body into the room from a sideways angle, just in case he needed to make a dash toward the stairs. The room was almost pitch black. So much that Jonathan could barely see but he could make out the big bed in the middle of the room. He took a few steps forward and tossed the envelope onto the bed. Then he turned around to head out the door. Jonathan quickly walked back downstairs but when he got there, Adrian was gone. Jonathan felt a weird filling swirl through his stomach, wild thoughts began to seep in his mind. Maybe it was a setup. Maybe Adrian left him here so he could get caught. He looked around and didn't see him anywhere and given the situation, it wouldn't have been appropriate for Jonathan to start shouting out Adrian's name. Right then, Jonathan saw flashes of light coming from the front of the house. Jonathan bent down as he looked out the front window wondering what that was until his brain registered that those flashes of light were actually headlights! Apparently the owner of the home was back and pulling into the driveway. Jonathan's almost got weak in the knees and a moment of sheer panic came rushing down from his heart into his body. Jonathan immediately bolted down the stairs and headed for the back door. He pushed the door wide open. He then saw that the outside gate was still open, he immediately ducked down and headed outside the gate. Since he was coming from the back side of the house he tried to look to the front to see if he could see anything but no luck. He stayed low and headed towards the back of the house next door and then came up to the street from the other side. He looked to see if Adrian's car was still there, he felt a bit of relief when he saw that it was. The car was sitting idle with the lights off. Jonathan kept his head down and headed for the car. Once he opened the door and got in, Adrian immediately whipped the car around and headed out of the neighborhood. At this point Jonathan was breathing heavily, he heaved in and out like a vacuum of air as it filled and released from his lungs. He looked at Adrian as he tried to collect himself for a moment. At this point Jonathan wasn't concerned about being intimidated by Adrian, he was pissed and planned on expressing himself. "You mind telling me what the hell was that about?!" shouted Jonathan. Adrian remained silent as he looked over at Jonathan and looked back at the road. Jonathan began to get angry and rubbed his hands on his pants and looked out at the window. He closed his eyes and took a deep breath, "Look man I want…" but before Jonathan could say anything, Adrian interrupted, "He'll be pleased to know that you followed through", he said. Jonathan stared at Adrian for a second and then looked outside the window. Still angry he sat in silence, as was the norm for the two of them. He then slouched back in his seat and turned his head toward the window and looked out. He knew it would be a long ride back so he settled in his seat and tried to focus on ending the night on a good note. He prayed that his dinner with Rachel would go well because at this point, Jonathan realized he was going to need someone to help take his mind off of his new life.

CHAPTER TEN
REFORMATORY

"Be careful" she told him. This was how Rachel ended their two and a half hour conversation. He could still see the look on her face, that look of anxiety dancing around the corners of her eyes. He all but spilt everything but managed to leave out some of the more disagreeable details of some parts. However, she pretty much got the gist of the fact that Jonathan was becoming a bit anxious about the things that had been going on lately. Everything from the brutal beating he took in the parking garage to the uncomfortable midnight rendezvous with Adrian that he so painfully enjoyed. Yet, it wasn't all bleak there was a bit of spark that came alive in the conversation when it wasn't on the path of melancholy. Once again that underlying connection between the two of them reared its head. There was no question that Jonathan had fallen for Rachel; he didn't classify it as love yet because he had no point of reference to describe what he felt for her. He had never met a woman like Rachel before, all the girls from his past were unmatched and out classed when it came to her. He could think of no one that could even begin to compare to her. This brought up the question as to whether or not Rachel should know about everything that was going on. Jonathan wasn't fearful of anything drastic happening to Rachel like her untimely death or anything like that but there was an uneasiness of the thought that she could possibly lose her job. That she could suddenly find her beautiful name on the top of some corporate black list never gaining employment again.

Jonathan didn't want that for her nor did he want that for himself. Although, once he was able to lay everything out on the table of his mind he managed to take a step back as to what he really saw. So far he witnessed a bribe, met up with Adrian at awkward times for some semi-sketchy meetings, and he now recently broke into some-one's home to drop off a mystery envelope. Besides the last one, there wasn't anything too incriminating, it wasn't like he was the head of some Mafia crime family. Although Adrian did have the look of a man who was familiar with violence; Jonathan would never come right out and say it but anyone with half a brain could see that Adrian just wasn't a very nice person to be around. It had only been a few days since Rachel and Jonathan had their semi heart to heart. Since that short window of time, the two of them had exchanged their fair share of text messages and late night conversations over the phone. More importantly, Jonathan had not heard from Adrian since that night at the house, nor had he heard anything from Mr. Edwards. He didn't mind it too much because it gave him a chance to clear his head. Or at least that's what he tried to tell himself. Truthfully, deep down he knew that he was still just as nervous as he was when he was running out of that house. He didn't know what the silent treatment meant, he just didn't know what to expect. Hopefully, he hadn't been cut off; which was an ironic feeling that he had been facing. Lately, it seemed like he was on both sides of the coin at the same time; part of him didn't want to know if he wanted to go any further with whatever this was. The other side of him was compelled to stay because he couldn't and wouldn't go back to the dungeon of a life from whence he came. He had finally made it over the hill and he could see his rainbow with a pot of gold at the end.

All he needed to do was just relax because he knew that he came too far and that there was too much potential for his life to be-come everything that he had always dreamed of for him to turn back now. Jonathan found himself lying on his plush bed, a far cry from that worn torn mattress he had back when he was at the one room apartment. His bedroom had a glass wall that served up a nice view of the surrounding area. He laid there in an undershirt and black bas-ketball shorts; from the way his bed was positioned all he had to do was look to the right and he could see out of the glass wall from his bedroom. As he watched the view he figured that he would have to end this run of silence and make the first move of contact. Surprisingly, he thought of calling Adrian first simply because Mr. Edwards was a bit hard to get a hold of at times; which was probably the way he liked it. Besides, Jonathan didn't have his direct line anyway. He only had the line to his office which was screened by the receptionist. He climbed out of bed and headed to the shower which was now conveniently located in his condo and not outside and down the hall this time. As he made his walk toward the bathroom he heard a loud knock at the door, the immediate surprise of the sound in the air caused Jonathan to stop and turn around. It wasn't even 11 o'clock yet on a Wednesday. Who could it have possibly been? He turned around only to hear another loud knock at the door. This time it was three knocks and a voice from the other side of the door shouting, "Police open up!"

Jonathan felt a cold chill enter his veins and travel to his back then violently wrapped itself around his spine. He was paralyzed for a moment as he thought back to that night when he and Adrian went traipsing through that house. He wondered if he had been caught, perhaps one of the neighbors did see him after all. Jonathan tried to take a moment to collect himself but he wasn't given one; the banging forcefully continued and increasingly intensified by the second. "S.E.P.D, open up!!" shouted a man from behind the door. No doubt he was probably some trigger happy cop looking for an excuse to make an arrest or worse quick to put a bullet into someone. Jonathan had no choice but to walk toward the door, his mind being clouded with fear he had no time to create a story to get out of this. He had no idea what was waiting for him on the other side of that door. Obviously he knew that cops were on the other side but what else? Was it cops with an eye witness who got a good look at Jonathan's face, waiting for him to open the door so they could say, "That's him officer, arrest him!" Also, Jonathan didn't know what the going rate was for prison sentencing for breaking and entering. Whatever the case, it was Jonathan who was completely unprepared, his mind in an all blank state of panic. He got closer to the door and reached for the door knob, this time he could see the door shake as it was being pounded on. He grabbed the knob and quickly unlocked it to open up the door. There were two cops in black uniforms just like the one from the hospital. One looked like he had been on the job for too long and had a look of discontentment plastered over his face. By the looks of it, he had to be in his early 60's it was almost surprising that he was still working the streets at that age. The other one was staring Jonathan right in the face going to work on a piece of gum that he was chewing. He had a thick mustache and thick aviator glasses on. "Goodness kid, you deaf?!" asked the officer. "Uh No...No sir" Jonathan replied; Jonathan, trying hard not to sound and look nervous even though he was doing a lousy job of both. He felt his palms beginning to get moist, he tried to wipe his hands on his shorts but that didn't help much. Since the shorts were made of nylon his damp hands felt like they just glided across the top of the fabric. "How can I help you?" asked Jonathan. The officer continued to chew his gum before answering. At this point Jonathan's mind was racing a mile a minute, he was already on the verge of throwing up because he was so nervous. This added to fact that the officer seemed to be amplifying the situation by taking his time in answering Jonathan's question. The one with the glasses looked back at his partner and then looked back at Jonathan. "Yea, we're here because there was an attempted break in that occurred last night on this floor and we're trying to track down any leads", the officer finally replied. After the officer said this Jonathan immediately felt like someone had removed a hundred pound weight from his chest. That feeling of fear that had wrapped around his spine like some sort of deadly Anaconda had suddenly loosened its grip and gone limp.

Jonathan wanted to let out a huge sigh of relief, but saner thoughts prevailed. "The break in was down the hall but we're going door to door on this floor to see if anyone saw or heard anything suspicious last night" said the Officer, as he continued to chew his gum. From the way he was chewing it; it had probably lost its flavor hours ago. "So how 'bout it?" asked the officer. "How 'bout what?" Jonathan asked. The older officer shook his head as if to suggest that Jonathan just asked a stupid question. The officer in the front took off his glasses and swallowed his gum. "I'm asking you if you heard or saw anything last night that might help us out" asserted the officer. As he looked at Jonathan there was something familiar about his face. Jonathan slightly squinted as if he was trying to get a clearer view of some small detail. But then again he knew that he had never met the officer before so it was nothing for him to pay too much attention to. Jonathan then realized that they were still awaiting an answer, spoke up quickly, "No sir I didn't" Jonathan replied. The officer looked at Jonathan for a brief moment without saying anything and then looked back at his partner. "Let's go", said the officer as he put his glasses back on. Jonathan waited for them to walk off before he closed the door. He didn't want to seem like he was being overly eager to get away from them.

He closed the door and turned around, putting his back up against the door. Then he slowly slid down to the floor. He placed his hands on his head for a moment pondering on what could have happened if the police were knocking on his door for a different reason. It was a scary thought to think about what the alternative could have been. He rubbed his hands back and forth for a moment on his head then got back up to his feet. He needed to try and clear his head so he hopped in the shower and stayed in there for about half an hour. By the time he was finished he felt a bit better but still found himself replaying what had just happened in his mind. Maybe it was all from the excitement but he heard his stomach groaning for his attention. He got dressed and realized that it was lunch time anyway so he figured he would go out for a drive and grab something to eat. As he left the loft he looked around as if he was a fugitive being careful to make sure that the coast was clear. He walked down the hall looking to see if he saw where the break in occurred and sure enough he saw one of the rooms around the corner had a door that had been kicked in with the classic yellow police tape covering the doorway. It looked like a scene straight out of a movie except there was no dead body being zipped up in a black bag.

After viewing the so called crime scene he headed down to the parking garage. As he headed down he once again thought about Mr. Edwards and what was going to happen from here. Although he had to admit that he was definitely getting some of the adventure that he had always craved for, he just didn't foresee his adventure involving breaking in to people's homes and being paranoid while talking to the police. He got off the elevator and headed to his truck. He reached inside his pocket for his keys, as he pulled them out he noticed that someone had parked in his spot. Jonathan paused for a moment and turned around to make sure that he was in the right spot. He looked up at the one of the signs on one of the concrete pillars and it said that he was in section "F", which was where he was supposed to be because the building had assigned parking. Jonathan dropped his keys and stared at the number where his car was supposed to be and sure enough it was the right number. He looked with disbelief because this meant that someone had stolen his car! "Oh you can't be serious!" shouted Jonathan, spewing a passionate mix of both panic and anger from his vocal cords. He took a few steps and looked back at the sign on the pillar again as well as the parking space number to double check that he was in the right spot. Although he knew that he didn't need to do that because he already knew that he was in the right place. He refused to believe that this happened; he stared at the car that was in his spot intensely. It must have belonged to some corporate exec, or high paid lawyer that probably lived in one of the bigger units. It was a dark gray Porsche, a two-seater that the owner undoubtedly drove fiercely through the city streets. As Jonathan looked at the car he noticed that there was a white note propped up in the corner of the front window. Jonathan took a step closer to see what the note said, on the note it read, "He sends his regards". Jonathan looked at the car and then looked around again to see if anyone was around. However, he saw no one and now his once boiling anger was now beginning to subside into a mild curiosity. What was this? Was it some sort of joke or was there more going on here that he didn't understand. He looked at the note as he moved closer and made his way to the driver side of the door. Resting in the driver's seat was a black box; Jonathan once again turned to see if there was someone watching; but still he saw no one. He paused for one last time before reaching for the door handle. He wondered was this car really for him? Was this some sort of grandiose gesture from Mr. Edwards? His hand wrapped around the door handle as he pulled it to see if it was open and sure enough, it was. He got in, moved a black box that was nestled in the driver's seat and closed the door. That classic new car smell rushed into his nostrils as he looked around the car in disbelief. This couldn't be real. Jonathan knew enough about cars to know that this thing probably ran north of $90,000. Not in his wildest dreams would he have thought of something like this happening. He continued to look around the car, now allowing his hands to look as well, as he ran them across the dashboard and onto the pitch black leather seats. He turned around and looked at the small back seats still trying to grab ahold of the reality that this exotic piece of machinery now belonged to him. Suddenly, he then remembered the black box that he moved out of the driver's seat. He frantically looked for it for about two seconds as he realized that it was right next to him in the passenger seat. He picked it up and opened it and inside was a set of keys. He took them out of the box and looked at the steering wheel; he then put the keys into the ignition and closed his eyes. He turned the key in anticipation of hearing the car start up. Indeed it did, his call was answered by the car's engine as he heard it awake from it slumber sending the sounds of over 400 horsepower vibrating through the hood.

"You gotta be kidding" said Jonathan aloud, this time with a wide eyed smile coming across his face. It looked like the transmission had a paddle shift as well as having a standard automatic mode. Jonathan decided to leave the paddle shift to the professionals and put the car in automatic and pulled out of the parking spot. It rode smoothly across the cold pavement of the parking deck and then onto the busy streets of Edge City. By now, Jonathan had the windows down; surprisingly there wasn't much traffic, which gave him free reign to see what this piece of automotive art could really do. Jonathan pressed down on the accelerator before even giving himself a chance to reconsider what he was doing. Although he wasn't quite prepared for the force of the car as it shot out, dashing forward like a launched missile. "Yes!!" he screamed, almost at the top of his lungs as he saw a blurred version of a green light pass through his eyes. After he got a taste of its power he decided it was best to slow down, after all he wasn't trying to have two run-ins with law in one day. When he reached the next red light he noticed that some of the other drivers around him took notice of him in the car, they probably thought that he was some hot shot attorney or some power hungry stock broker kid who just got his first bonus. Either way, Jonathan now found himself on the other side of the glass, realizing that he was no longer on the outside looking in at the life he always wanted. NOW he was on the inside looking out and thought to himself how things were coming together. Suddenly, he now found himself not being concerned about all of the drama he was worrying about before, he just wanted to enjoy the moment.

However, his moment was cut short as he heard his phone ringing, the caller ID displayed that the call was coming from Star Industries. He answered the call and placed it on speaker. "Hello" he said. "I trust everything is to your liking", it was Mr. Edwards; speaking with usual confidence knowing good and well what the answer was.

Jonathan really didn't know what to say but he did the best he could. "I'm…I'm…a bit speechless, Sir." "Is this really mine?" asked Jonathan; unable to contain himself. "Anything you have you've earned, remember that" said Mr. Edwards. Jonathan took that as his round-about way of saying, yes. "Where are you now?" asked Mr. Edwards, "I'm actually out now not too far from my building" he said. "Good, I want you to come by the manor later I have some things that I would like to discuss" instructed Mr. Edwards. "Yes Sir, of course" Jonathan replied. At this point his mind was far removed from the thoughts of yesterday on how he had broken into someone's house for this man. It seemed like Jonathan's present state of euphoria had taken care of the problem for him. "We have much to discuss and if you're willing to listen, you'll have much to learn" said Mr. Edwards. "I'm willing" said Jonathan. "I know" Mr. Edwards replied. It was odd the way Mr. Edwards always managed to ask a question to make someone feel as if they had some sort of choice in the matter. Only for that person to later realize that he already knew what they were going to do to begin with. "I'll see you around 6 o'clock", Mr. Edwards asserted. "Sounds good, Sir" said Jonathan.

The two of them hung up the phone simultaneously as Jonathan glanced down at the dashboard again still in disbelief that he owned a Porsche. Although, it didn't take long for him to remember that his truck was gone and he didn't know what they had done with it. Although Jonathan at times considered that truck to be a piece of junk, it was still his dad's old piece of junk. This wasn't enough to bring him down from his high though, but he did wonder about Ole' Betty and figured he would ask about it when he saw Mr. Edwards later on tonight. However, before he could give that scenario too much thought his phone started ringing yet again. Except this time it was Rachel calling; he answered quickly. "Hello" he said. "Hey" replied Rachel, in her soft tone of voice. She could make Jonathan's ears melt over the phone just by the sound of her voice. "Hey what are you doing right now?" she asked, "I'm just driving around" trying to disguise his excitement. Jonathan didn't think he should mention that he just got a new car just yet. Seeing how they had such an in-depth conversation about some of the things that he was concerned about in regards to his new found role in the life of Mr. Edwards', he wasn't ready to share the news of his latest automotive upgrade just yet. "Well, I wanted to talk to you some more about your new found friend" said Rachel

Both a nervous and guilty feeling sunk its way into Jonathan's heart when Rachel said this. He really didn't want to keep talking to her about all of this crazy stuff. Also, he didn't want their conversations to somehow make it back to the ears of Mr. Edwards. The guilt began to seep in because he felt like a bit of a hypocrite driving around in a new car paid for by the same man that he was beginning to have second thoughts about. Jonathan also wondered what it said about his own character; as if he could be bought. If he could be bought then he had to admit that he must be pretty expensive to be given such a lavish gift. "What's going on?" asked Jonathan. "I was trying to look up some info on your boy, I didn't manage to find much of what everyone in Silver Edge already knows" affirmed Rachel. "What do you mean?" asked Jonathan. "I mean there's no real info out there on the guy, nothing telling you who he really is" she said. "Besides the rags to riches tale of him being a foster child who later grew up to become the greatest business mind this city has ever seen" she said. "No foster care parent info, biological parent info, and nothing prior to his life before he hit Edge City" she said. "Well that makes since because aren't foster records supposed to be sealed and stuff like that?" Jonathan inquired, "No cowboy, in this day and age nothing's really sealed unless you work for the pentagon", Rachel said. "And even some of that stuff is easy to hack" Rachel continued. "Besides when you're somebody like Kane Edwards, you don't have a personal life, everything is played out in public" "Heck, the only thing men like him can keep private is their preferred brand of toilet paper and that's if their careful." said Rachel, "Kane?" asked Jonathan abruptly, "His first name is Kane?" Jonathan paused for a minute to think about the fact that he didn't even know the man's first name. "Are you serious?" asked Rachel. The phone got quiet for a minute before Rachel said anything else. "You mean to tell me you've been working with this man for months now and you didn't even know his first name", quipped Rachel; Jonathan could almost hear her shake her head over the phone. Now that he thought about it, he had to admit it was a bit odd that he didn't know that. He also took note that the opportunity never really presented itself. Jonathan was too nervous and awe struck to ask these questions when they first met and he recently spent so much time trying to figure out what was going on, he never even stop to think about it. "So I guess they really do grow them slow out there in the country" Rachel teased. "Well, what can I say, it takes time to produce such a sweet crop" Jonathan replied, "Wow, even your jokes are slow" said Rachel. Jonathan let out a slight sigh as he was getting a bit annoyed at the whole country bumpkin skit. "Relax lover boy I'm sure where you come from you're the talk of the town" said Rachel. "Man, a guy can't catch a break" said Jonathan; grinning at the irony of that statement as he looked around the car's interior while holding the steering wheel. Anyway look, I wanted to see if you were free later so we could talk more about this?" inquired Rachel.

"Yea sure" Jonathan said, "What time?" he asked. "Probably sometime tonight I'll call you and let you know for sure." said Rachel, "Ok" replied Jonathan. Once he hung up the phone he remembered that he was supposed to be meeting with Mr. Edwards or should he say Kane later on. What kind of name was that anyway? In all honesty it sounded like the name of some sort of psychopathic serial killer or at best a villainous mastermind, somehow plotting world domination. Either way you looked at it, it was definitely a unique moniker to say the least. Jonathan drove around for a while, by now he was a lot more familiar with the city and his confidence had risen to the point where he didn't really need to use the navigation anymore. Besides he wasn't going to look a gift horse in the mouth or at least for now he wasn't. Jonathan had placed a call to destiny earlier in his life but it seemed that she was always busy with someone else or just simply chose to ignore his call. Though she took her time it seemed like destiny finally returned Jonathan's call and the phone was ringing loud and clear. Hours went by as Jonathan spent his time out and about in the city streets, the day appeared to have a grander spread of beauty to it. This was undoubtedly due to his now seeing the glass half full approach that was surely brought upon by receiving an expensive gift. He later stopped for gas and a cheap hot dog on the way to Mr. Edwards's part of town. For some reason he didn't want to go over there with an empty stomach. Once again he made that scenic drive across the bridge into the world of affluence and privilege, a world that now seemed to recognize the once unassuming young man. Once Jonathan made it to the front of the neighborhood, he stopped at the security post where the middle aged man with the bad haircut he met last time was. However, this time the man didn't leave the booth he simply looked out from the glass and nodded signifying that he recognized Jonathan and opened the gate.

Honestly, it was a weird feeling. Is this what power felt like? The power someone gets from having a certain last name or stacking up zero's in their bank account. No questions asked just the respecter of person that people secretly hope for. The mere act of access granted just by facial recognition or a lofty title. It might have been shallow but Jonathan would have been lying to himself if he said that he didn't like it. The whole feel of the situation was different. When he made it to the estate, there wasn't a stuffy crowd of old hedge fund babies like there were the last time he was there. Also there was no auto show of vintage cars and rare exotics owned by the super-rich. By the looks of it, it looked like a mansion with no one inside; although the place was so huge that it would be foolish to come to that conclusion without someone actually looking inside, but perhaps that was part of the point of owning a piece of real estate of this caliber. Jonathan pulled up to the curb in front of the house, as he reached for the gear to put the car in park he looked over at the driveway. Something about tonight was making him feel bold, so he decided to park in the driveway this time. As he cut the car off it was like someone putting a mussel on a lion as the purr of the engine faded to silence in the presence of the cool night. He got out of the car and walked over to the front door, which was a reasonable distance since the place was so big. Once he got to the door he saw an intercom system that he didn't notice before. He pressed the button. "Hello, its Jonathan"; he stood there for a moment waiting to hear a response back but he heard nothing. He pressed the button again and said, "Hello" but he still received no response. He stood there for a moment before turning around to see Mr. Edwards standing behind him at the bottom of the front steps with a drink in his hand. "Hello Mr. Edwards Sir, I didn't see you standing there" said Jonathan. A bit startled at how he seemingly just appeared out of nowhere Jonathan paused in a state of mild confusion, Mr. Edwards stayed silent while he gazed back at Jonathan as he took a sip of what was probably a glass of $2,000 wine. He then glanced at the car then back at Jonathan. "Come with me, we have some things to discuss" Mr. Edwards instructed. Jonathan wasn't quite sure of what to make of that since he couldn't tell what exactly was going on which at this point was the norm. Jonathan followed Mr. Edwards as he walked around the side of the estate, even at night the place was well lite and a sight to see. "You've proven to be useful Jonathan and I think it's time to start bringing you into the fold" stated Mr. Edwards. Jonathan had to admit that he was a bit taken aback by that comment because he thought that he was well into the fold at this point. The next couple of words that came out of Mr. Edwards' mouth, Jonathan didn't fully hear as he was still a bit puzzled as to what Mr. Edwards meant. The next thing Jonathan knew he was walking in the back door of the lower level of the mansion. It was the lower level because homes like these didn't have basements but levels. As he walked in; the place looked like a separate and very spacious home probably around 6,000 sq. ft. It came equipped with the classic wet bar and expensive pool table that you would find in most super estates like these. The floor was a mixture of hard wood and some spot marble, it seemed like this man might have had something against carpet. Besides that, the place was completely decked out pretty much what you'd expect from an older wealthy man. There was a flat screen plasma TV that was in the upper right hand corner behind the bar. It looked like the news was on but Jonathan didn't pay too much attention to what was on the screen. He was more focused on the moment he found himself in. "I told Adrian that you have what it takes", said Mr. Edwards. "I told you before that you have an animal in you", he continued. "I've got news for you kid, whether you realize it or not it's in your very nature to win" said Mr. Edwards; as he said this he slowly started to move toward Jonathan almost in a stalking manner. As he inched his way toward Jonathan, there was a thud that came from behind one of the doors that was on the other side of the room. It was across a large seating area in the middle of the room. Jonathan looked over in to the direction of where he heard the noise come from. By the time he looked back Mr. Edwards was right in front of him; almost directly in his face. It startled Jonathan as he took half a step back, "You're a natural born killer, you just don't know it yet", Mr. Edwards commented. Jonathan felt that nervous feeling he had earlier that morning with the police. He didn't enjoy feeling that way, "Excuse me?" asked Jonathan; again he heard a thud come from one of the rooms but this time he didn't look away. Something else grabbed his attention from the corner of his eyes. It was the TV behind the bar, the news channel was still on but on the screen there was a helicopter view of a house that looked very familiar. Jonathan began to focus on the house more intensely as they zoomed in; he did recognize the house. It was the very home that he and Adrian so elegantly invaded a few nights ago. Alongside the house was a still shot of a man who was dressed in a suit waving his hand, while standing behind a podium. At the bottom the caption read "Mayor Caesar's home vandalized more details at 11." Jonathan's face all but dropped to the floor, his heart began to race as if it was being chased. He thought about how he had no idea that the house he was instructed to break into belonged to the mayor of the city. Once again there was a distant thud in the background. Jonathan said nothing and looked at Mr. Edwards, as he stood there in his face and took another sip of wine. "Come with me" instructed Mr. Edwards. Jonathan couldn't believe it, he had too many emotions flooding him at once, he hated and admired this man all at the same time. He was getting tired of this emotional rollercoaster that he had been riding lately and it was becoming a burden on his conscience as well as his sanity. His body shifted completely into zombie mode because his mind was gone but his body seemed to be following Mr. Edwards toward one of the doors where the noise was coming from. His mind was back at that night when they broke into the house, all the while hanging on to the caption where it stated that the house had been vandalized. However, that was impossible because all Jonathan did was place an envelope on the bed before high tailing it out of there with Adrian. What was going on? And what was in that envelope? Unfortunately these were a set of questions that would have to wait because it seemed that another situation was waiting behind this door that Mr. Edwards was walking over to. The next thing Jonathan knew, he was in the room and heard the sound of someone groaning followed by another thud. Suddenly, his mind and focus came to as if he where awakening from a deep sleep. He first noticed that the room was completely white and that there was a bright light, he then noticed a well-built man in a muscle shirt with his back to Jonathan. There were two other men, one on each side of the mystery bodybuilder in the center of the room. The one to the right looked at

Jonathan as he walked in, their eyes ineptly locked. As Jonathan snapped out of; his zombie like state he noticed that there was something familiar about the man, but he didn't stare for too long. These weren't the kind of men who took kindly to the eyes of another man sizing them up. Jonathan decided to focus his attention on the man in the middle of the room. This time the man had his right hand drawn back; from the looks of it he had some red stuff on the side of it. He then swung his right arm forward with such force that all Jonathan heard was the sound of bone hitting bone. He stood in shock as the scene before him began to unfold. "That's enough Percy", Mr. Edwards commanded. "I still want to be able to hear him talk" "So don't break his entire face or at least not yet…" said Mr. Edwards.

Once the man stepped to the side, Jonathan then saw another man tied down in the chair; his face was pretty bruised up his left eye was swollen shut while blood flowed from his nose. That explained the red stuff Jonathan saw on the big guy's hand. All of the sudden, Jonathan felt sick as if he was about to throw up. It was like the air in the room hit his gut then wrapped its hand around his throat, he almost couldn't breathe, he was speechless. Jonathan now recognized the man after Mr. Edwards said his name; it was his bodyguard from that night at the museum. He was a big guy that looked capable of snapping a man in half with ease. That wasn't too hard to believe seeing how the man tied to the chair was wearing a sample of Percy's strength on his face for everyone to see. Jonathan couldn't move; he listened to his heart beat as it continued to climb while vibrating in his chest sending blood rushing through his veins at break neck speed. He didn't recognize the man that was standing before him, this couldn't be the same Mr. Edwards; perhaps in a way he was right. Maybe this was Kane. Maybe this was sort of an ulterior version of himself that enjoyed having men tied and beaten in his basement, like some sort of schizophrenic psychopath. But then again was this really such a stretch from the actions Jonathan had seen from this man thus far? Either way his eyes were wide open and there was no room for misinterpretation or confusion anymore; this man was dangerous.

Mr. Edwards with his drink still intact, walked towards the man in the chair, "You have to understand that you chose to be in this predicament that you find yourself in tonight" All the while, the man looked like he was slipping in and out of consciousness, as if his body was trying to find a way to escape the harsh reality of what was going on but there was no escape. Mr. Edwards poured the rest of his drink on the man's head as the stinging alcohol ran over the open cuts on the man's face. The man clinched his teeth in pain, "Pleeeee-ase", the man mumbled, but before he could finish, Mr. Edwards interjected. "No need to give the full fledge plea for your life", he unsympathetically said. "I'm not going to kill you, but I do want you to deliver a message for me", Mr. Edwards said. "I want you to tell your boss that the next time he tries to steal a shipment from me he should remember this, any moves he tries to make, I've already thought of" I'll always be at least five steps ahead of him!" Mr. Edwards said with confidence. As Mr. Edwards said this, he looked directly at Jonathan as if he were indirectly giving him some sort of forewarning. Mr. Edwards's cold gaze alone dismissed any thoughts of Jonathan telling someone of what he had just witnessed. Although he didn't have to try hard because at this point Jonathan was officially afraid of Mr. Edwards and what he could do. Yet, that seemed to be the worst part because he knew that this man was capable of doing anything and was extremely unpredictable. After a few moments, the man's body refused to stay awake any longer to suffer further torture as he quickly passed out. Mr. Edwards dropped the wine glass in the man's lap. "Percy, clean this up!" commanded Mr. Edwards. Jonathan watched as the hulk-like henchman began to untie the man and hoisted him over his left shoulder. Jonathan glanced to his right and the man who looked familiar to him was staring intensely. There was something about his eyes that had a cold look of death to them. They were eyes that had probably seen their fair share of violence and bloodshed. Jonathan looked away trying not to give these lions the scent of fear, if it wasn't already too late.

Mr. Edwards walked over to Jonathan and placed his hand on his shoulder, although he said nothing, the silence was deafening. He patted Jonathan on the shoulder and looked at him for a moment. Jonathan lifted his head slowly and looked at Mr. Edwards; still there was silence but only for a moment. "Adrian is going to call you later but for now I want you to go home", said Mr. Edwards. "You know you all make a good team." he said. "What?" asked Jonathan. His voice trembled from the immense fear that held him hostage in his own body. "You, Adrian, and Percy" "Quite the trio I might add." said Mr. Edwards. Jonathan was still confused as he stood there with no sign of comprehension making itself available to him. "Percy?" asked Jonathan, his voice still shaky. "Yes he was the one who…shall I say redecorated the mayor's house after you and Adrian left." said Mr. Edwards. It then dawned on Jonathan that the car he saw that night as he made a mad dash out of the house wasn't the mayor; it was Percy coming to commence part two of the criminal act that was committed that night. "Oh and if you were wondering what was in that envelope, it was some evidence of the mayors extra-curricular activities with his secretary and her sister." said Mr. Edwards. "I'm sure his wife wouldn't approve and neither would the citizens of this fine city." He said. "So now that he knows that I know he's not the innocent white knight that the people of Edge City think he is, he'll get out of my way." Mr. Edwards explained. "You see Jonathan I plan on running this city in more ways than one, and my next step is to be mayor." "And I had to put the so-called competition on notice." "Now go get some rest kid, you look tired", he said in a very nonchalant tone; as he walked out. Percy and his gang followed suit with the beaten man slung over Percy's shoulder. The man with the cold eyes walked out last as he continued to stare at Jonathan, he stared but said nothing.

His eyes did all the talking and they told Jonathan that he'd be next if he didn't keep his mouth shut. After everyone left the room, Jonathan stood there dazed and confused. He felt like a weight was closing in on his body. He knew that feeling and it wasn't a weight but a set of bars, like a jail cell. Actually, he knew the feeling well because he woke up to it every day in Winterville. He stood there as a tear welded up in his left eye, until it spilled over to his cheek and slowly danced down his face. The unreal but existent thought came into his mind that Jonathan had gotten a clear view of the truth tonight. Not just about Mr. Edwards but about himself because he now realized an inconvenient truth. That he hadn't escaped anything by leaving Winterville; he simply traded one prison for the other.

CHAPTER ELEVEN
THE BURDEN OF PROGRESS

It's always odd how the perception of something can change when it's looked at with the right lighting. It's like watching a movie for the second time; you tend to notice things that you didn't see before. The minute details that were once indiscernible to the naked eye now seem to blare out while daring you not to notice. There was no denying or turning away from the horrific deeds that had taken place right in front of Jonathan's eyes the night before. He found himself now walking through the streets as the sun danced its power on the top of the buildings towering above him. The sky played as a beautiful backdrop with clouds white enough to catch anyone's eye that looked up. However, the beauty of the city wasn't enough to take Jonathan's mind off of what was going on around him. It was official; that the man he worked for wasn't just some hardworking man who made his fortune on gumption and pulling up his life by the boot straps. To the ill-fated contrary he proved himself to be some sort of corrupt Kingpin willing to do whatever it took to get what he wanted. Not only that but this madman wanted to run the city, literally; he wanted to be mayor. This was a far cry from the shadow of his supposed former self that Jonathan had seen that night at the museum. Perhaps Jonathan was the one who felt betrayed the most because he was the one who believed the most; he bought into the dream. The dream that everybody has lying in wait at the end of their mouth but sits idly by on their unspoken lips; the dream that rests in their hearts but gets disturbed by their cynical minds. Some call it the American dream but surely thoughts of a better life complete with life pleasures is a universal aspiration and not tied down to one specific region of the world. Although now it didn't matter what region it was indigenous to because the allure of its beauty had fallen. The violent reality of what Jonathan witnessed last night was enough to snuff out the pleasant thoughts of the dream he had once envisioned. The truth pulled his head into the game so he could get a clear view of what was really going on.

He was making his way down Ladd Street which was only a few blocks over from his place. He preferred the walk today; he wasn't really in the mood to drive a car that was purchased with blood money. The enticement of the new car smell faded with the image of that pummeled man tied down to a raggedy chair. So instead he used his own legs, he figured he could use the air anyway. As he walked through the busy streets of the city that operated as its veins; constantly flowing with people. He wondered if any of these people knew the kinds of things that were going on. Jonathan would hate to admit it but this just wasn't something he could relate to coming from a small town. Back home, he never witnessed that level of vice, he had already knew that he would be a fish out of water in Edge City. Though he never imagined that it would be like this; he was in over his head. But oddly enough this was also somewhat of a familiar scene to him just on a grander scale because just as he felt like an outsider in Winterville he now felt like an outsider in the big city. It's ironic how he traveled so far and worked so hard, only to find himself in a different version of the same situation. Maybe he wanted too much from life. Or maybe this was some derisive form of karma spitting back in his face for thinking he could have it all. He gnawed on this obnoxious notion as he roved through the streets, blending in with the very people he wanted so desperately to fit in with. He got his wish but in a demented way, he had also gotten status like he wanted but it was equipped with the dread of infamy. He felt like he got the girl he always wanted but he couldn't enjoy her company without worrying about her safety. He left home like he wanted but only to join a sea full of sharks; this was not what he wanted. The disappointment and confusion was enough to make anyone hungry, so Jonathan figured he would try and get something in his system so he could maybe formulate some sort of plan to unearth himself from the unforgiving and unforeseeable turn of events.

By the time he had gotten to the end of Ladd Street he was at the corner of 75th which was a pretty good stretch of buildings that offered everything from the postal office to brick oven pizza. Seeing how he had always been a sucker for pepperoni, Jonathan figured he would grab some pizza. That seemed to be a pretty normal thing to eat and right now he was in desperate need of normalcy in his life. He headed into one of the pizzerias called "The 75th Slice" an obvious nod to the street that it was on. It was definitely an old school spot; it had the look of history to it as if the owner of the place had his array of three hour stories to tell. As the hostess approached Jonathan, it made him think of checking his account balance; although he knew there was money in his account he was still in his old mind set of making sure he had enough money to pay for his food. The whole idea that he now had excess cash and a steady sizeable income was a new thing to him. It was one of the few new things in his life that didn't seem to cause problems. He looked up his statement as the hostess was directing him to his seat, the screen was taking a minute to load so he placed the phone down on the table as he waited. He picked the phone back up as he saw the waitress making her way to the table. He looked at the phone, and his eyes went toward the bottom where his savings account information was; he knew he had a good $15,000 in the account. However, that was a far cry of what was actually in there. The number that was next to the word savings account was $750,000 and right above that was his checking account which stated that he had exactly $250,000. He felt the phone began to slide through his hand as he loosened his grip; the phone fell on the table. He sat frozen in his seat, speechless and motionless staring at the phone almost in terror but with a faint blend of doubt. Could he have read that right? Did he just see that he had a total of a million dollars in his accounts? "Can I get you anything to drink sir?" asked the waitress. Jonathan had barely noticed that she had even walked over to the table let alone heard what she just said. He looked up at her a bit dazed, the room felt like it was spinning and everything else was in slow motion. He looked at the waitress' face; she had a blank stare on it that looked as if she was awaiting a response. Again she asked, "Sir, can I get you anything to drink?" Jonathan still didn't really hear what she said but this time he managed to read her lips. "Uh no…..no……excuse me" he said; as he hopped out of his seat and rushed past the waitress. He headed out the restaurant door while staring at his phone he didn't have the opportunity to notice the middle aged married couple that he suddenly ran right into. "Watch it kid!" said the man; while looking Jonathan up and down as if he were some escaped lunatic. "Excuse me, I'm sorry" Jonathan replied in a very preoccupied tone of voice. Did he look at the phone wrong? Was there some sort of mistake made? Or maybe the phone had a glitch and showed the wrong information. After he thought about this he stopped and figured that was a sensible explanation, so he decided to reload the screen. He exited out of his account page then reentered his password; he stood in the middle of the street anxiously waiting for the account screen to come back up. His attempt to deny what his eyes told him was to no avail, the accounts still read the same. Jonathan began to breathe heavily; under normal circumstances anyone who received a sudden windfall of money like this would be beyond elated. However these weren't normal circumstances and considering the source of where the money came from; elated was the last thing Jonathan was. After what Jonathan had seen last night and now having his account being stuffed with money he knew he was in over his head. At this point he ewas considering maybe skipping town but he didn't want to run from something like this because for all he knew he could very well find himself being the next one who was tied to a chair and being beaten like a rag doll. That wasn't something that sounded too appealing and then to add to the fact that the woman he loved would be left behind within arm's reach of Kane Edwards wasn't exactly the most comforting of thoughts either.

Jonathan tried to breathe deep and continued to walk slowly down the street with his hands on top of his head. He was trying to step outside of the situation and get a grip but he couldn't, he needed to talk to somebody. He tried to call Rachel but the phone went straight to her voicemail. The fact that the call went straight to voicemail was a bit odd, she normally kept her phone on. For a second he wondered if something might have happened to her but he didn't want to jump to conclusions. Besides, that really wouldn't make any sense for Mr. Edwards to harm Rachel because for all he knew Jonathan was cooperating. Then Jonathan's mind took a step further down the road of thought and realized that he wasn't even sure if Mr. Edwards knew anything about Rachel or the fact that they had feelings for one another. She was safe or at least that's what he had to tell himself for now just to keep it together.

It was a lot to take in; it was a good thing that he was already outside because he definitely found himself needing the comfort of good old fashion oxygen. Jonathan knew that things were beyond him at this point, he had no point of reference as to what he could relate this to. He walked for about another 15 minutes down the street feeling numb to everything that was around him; yet alive to everything that was inside of him. All of his emotions good or bad were having a rather large get together and the party didn't look like it was going to stop anytime soon. He continued on until he heard his phone ring, "Finally" mumbled Jonathan, he grabbed the phone from his pocket and put it up to his ear. "Hey, where are you?" asked Jonathan. However, to his surprise a man's voice answered back, "Well, I'm actually taking a joy ride if you really must know. Jonathan frowned as he tried to figure out who he was talking to. He quickly pulled the phone away from his ear to see if the number showed up on the caller

ID. Surprisingly, the number did in fact show up; it was his friend David from Winterville. Jonathan hadn't spoken to David in months not since their mini throw down in the cafeteria that day. In fact he wasn't even sure if David considered him a friend anymore. "Oh…. hey Dave", said Jonathan. "Well goodness Cross I know we had our little pow-wow back at school but you could sound a bit more excited than that!" quipped David. Jonathan still shaken up wasn't very engaged in the conversation. "Uh…yea…hey man what's …what's… what's going on?" asked Jonathan. "I'm doing great man!" "Dad just made me store manager last week and I decided to give myself the day off today." said David. Jonathan could tell David was pretty pleased with himself; he didn't really care but he did find himself envying David for a moment. Although, it was a brief moment Jonathan thought about all the drama and corruption David was innocently missing out on and had he been in David's shoes he would be too. Instead he found himself hundreds of miles away from home working for a man who was definitely dangerous and quite possibly psychotic. "Come on now Cross tell me something" said David, "I know by now you must have some crazy story to tell, living all the way in Edge City." Jonathan stood silent for a second and just looked off in the distant staring into space. "crazy story" said Jonathan; as a halfway smirk emerged from his lips but once truly formed turned into more of a nervous smile. "Yea, a few." said Jonathan "Yea, you better because I hope you're not up there sulking around and crap looking like a zombie like you were back here" said David. Although it was a random call, Jonathan could to some extent appreciate the fact that he was talking to someone he considered a close friend. He hadn't spoken to him in months; it's just that the timing wasn't the best. He had other things that were fighting for his attention and were winning the fight by a long shot. As he stayed on the phone he heard a beep signaling that someone was trying to get through on the other line. He hoped it was Rachel because it was getting close to being about half an hour since he first called her which felt more like three hours. He was desperate to talk to her whether Jonathan realized it or not Rachel had become his unofficial sounding board. She was his release and right now he definitely needed to get some things off of his chest. "Hey Dave, look man glad to catch up but let me call you back." said Jonathan and without waiting for a response Jonathan abruptly hung up and clicked over to the other line. "Hey, where are you?" asked Jonathan; his tone of voice almost entirely blanketed with anxiety. "Easy tiger, stalking isn't your forte" said Rachel. "No, I'm serious." He continued. "So am I" said Rachel. "Rachel…." said Jonathan, this time in a sterner tone, "Look, I'm just making sure everything's….normal on your end" said Jonathan. "Yea, I'm fine, what's going on with you?" asked Rachel, as she was beginning to get slightly annoyed. "I..uh..I don't want to talk over the phone" Jonathan replied. "Just meet me at my place in an hour" he said. "Sure thing boss" Rachel said in a sarcastic voice. After they hung up Jonathan began to start making the trek back to his loft, it was about a half hour away. That gave him enough time to get back, try to refresh his thoughts, and get a grip before he saw Rachel. The city could be kind when it wanted to be. Jonathan for the first time took a second to notice that it was absolutely gorgeous outside. It wasn't surprising to see how easily beauty could be eclipsed by negative situations. He didn't have the time or will to engage in what now seemed like child's play; being the bright eyed college kid from the small town that wanted to explore a brave new world. Besides this new world that he had discovered seemed to be having its way with him; and its way was not an easy one.

By the time Jonathan had made it back to his place it was safe to say that Rachel would be there at any moment. He walked through the door and tried to unwind but it was a bit hard to do with a million dollars' worth of dirty money staining his bank account. He sat down for a moment on the couch with his hands pressed firmly over his face, almost as if he wanted to suffocate himself. No doubt a form of punishment he subconsciously wanted to inflict upon himself for letting himself fall in a situation like this. He felt his warm breath bounce off his hands and over his face as he breathed semi-heavily. His innocent suicide was interrupted when he heard a faint but existing knock at the door. He got up slowly, not too anxious to unfold the next subchapter of his already morally challenging day. He walked over to the door knowing that Rachel would be on the other side. He was just a few inches away from the door as if he was about to engage it in conversation; that's when the thought came in his head that it could be someone else on the other side of the door. He looked at the door and heard another knock, then followed by a swift ring of the doorbell. Jonathan placed his hand on the door "Who is it?" he asked, "It's me Mr. Paranoia open up." Jonathan recognized Rachel's voice. Even though it was slightly muffled from the sound traveling through the door he could identify the tenderness of her soothing voice. He opened the door and saw her standing there; for once she was dressed down. She was wearing a pair of jeans that hugged her legs perfectly with a light gray tank top, with her hair pulled into a ponytail. They embraced as she walked in the door Jonathan held her tightly the smell of her perfume was somewhat calming to him "What's going on with you?" asked Rachel, Jonathan said nothing as he loosened his grip and looked straight into her eyes. He pulled her even closer and kissed her, he felt her soft lips message against his own; he was tired of thinking and over analyzing, his mind needed a break from all of that; right now he was operating on instinct.

They held that position for what felt like an hour but in actuality was only a minute. He continued to kiss her then slowly pulled back; she gazed back at him her hands now wrapped around the back of his head while running her fingers through his hair. "Well… that was pleasant" said Rachel. "I would apologize but I'm not sorry that I did that" Jonathan replied. The romantic chemistry between the two of them was enough to calm the seas of his emotions; which at this point

were in full blown hurricane season. "You know I swear trying to figure you out can be a full time job" said Rachel. Jonathan smiled for a
quick second to allow himself the pleasure of the moment. "I needed
to see you" said Jonathan. He was passed wondering whether or not
he should continue to involve Rachel in what was going on. His own
selfish reasons proved to be more than enough to coax him into telling
Rachel what was going on. The pressure and weight of keeping his
sanity intact seemed to thoughtlessly outweigh his guilt. Reluctantly
letting Rachel go, he took a step back and rubbed his right hand back
and forth over his head as if to scratch some unsatisfied itch. Rachel
had her eyes fixed on Jonathan patiently waiting on what he had to
say; while still recovering from his show of affection. "I'm not
sure…" uttered, Jonathan not fully getting out what he wanted to say.
"I can show you", he continued but, at this point the lack of complete
sentences had Rachel a bit puzzled. "You're not going to start acting
weird are you?" She asked. "Just wait there for a second" he   said.
He quickly went into the other room and brought out his laptop. He
walked past Rachel and set it down on the kitchen counter. He typed
quickly, his eyes fastened to the screen; he didn't bother to look up at
Rachel to see that her confusion was turning into annoyance. "Jonathan what's going on?" asked Rachel. Jonathan not answering her
question spun the laptop around so that it faced her direction. Rachel
walked toward the screen, not fully seeing at first what it was that she
was looking at. As she got closer she slightly bent down, "What, this
looks like you're…." She failed to finish her sentence as she looked
up at Jonathan. The expression on her face said everything that she
might have been thinking within that moment. Jonathan stared back at
her. "Yeah" said Jonathan, responding to Rachel's unspoken question
as to whether or not what she was looking at was in fact real. "This
is your account?" asked Rachel, she still needed clarity by asking the
question out loud. "Yes" Jonathan said, as he leaned up against the
kitchen sink. "That was in there this morning, or at least I'm assuming

it was." "I haven't checked my account in a few days." He said.

Once again Jonathan found himself in that all too familiar place; the awkward silence that seemed to follow him ever since he stepped foot in the city. By this point he had begun to learn how to navigate around the silence and deal with its presence. "This is what I wanted to talk to you about", he said; trying to pause so he could somehow think of how he was going to convey this information to her. "I don't understand. Where did this come from?" she asked; still staring at the computer screen. Before Jonathan could answer Rachel looked up and asked, "Did he give this to you?" Jonathan looked directly back at her and simply nodded his head. "For what?!?" hollered Rachel. Jonathan stepped away from the wall putting his hand up, kindly signaling for her to keep her voice down. "Well, what the hell have you been doing for him to give you that kind of money?!" she asked. Although it seemed that her question was mingled with a command; almost demanding that Jonathan give her an answer. All things considered, Rachel had been more than a good sport about the things that had been going on lately; in all honesty she was entitled to have a bit of an outburst. "Jonathan this doesn't make any sense" said Rachel. She had taken a few half steps back from the laptop with her attention directly focused on Jonathan. "I know" said Jonathan "That's why I called you, I wanted to…" "You know?" asked Rachel. "Well that's good to know that you know cause none of this makes sense" snapped Rachel. "Look, try to relax for a minute." Jonathan said; realizing that the conversation wasn't going the way he thought it would.

Nevertheless, he had to be honest with himself and admit that he didn't really know what to expect. At this point, him not knowing what to expect was pretty much standard operating procedure. Jonathan rubbed his hand over his head and held them there as he stared off into space. "Look…I…I…don't know what to do" he said. Rachel looked back at him, "Goodness Jonathan" as she shook her head. It wasn't the shake of disgust but of concern and perhaps a sense of disappointment. "Look, I know you're new here from that littleville town you call home but there's no such thing as a free lunch, especially in this city" Rachel explained. By this time, the atmosphere of the room had shifted from the ballads of love that seemed to be ever so present only minutes ago from when they shared a passionate kiss to a thick cloud filled with stress and anxiety.

"There's more" Jonathan hesitantly continued. "The other night I was over his house, and there was this guy in a chair" Jonathan struggling trying very hard to pull his thoughts together and still not knowing how to go about saying what he was trying to say. "What guy?" interjected Rachel. "I don't know" Jonathan replied. "I don't know who he was." "All I know is that he was tied up and the man looked like he had been beaten within an inch of his life." "What?!?" screamed Rachel, with her face distorted as if she were looking at some other worldly creature as opposed to the man she now had feelings for. "I know how this sounds", Jonathan pleaded; making his way over to Rachel with his arm extended in an attempt to provide some sort of comfort. "I don't think you do Jonathan" snapped Rachel; her eyes were starting to get full, Jonathan could see that water had glazed over them from the emergence of tears starting to form. "No, I don't think you have any idea how this sounds." Rachel replied. "But let me help you out", she continued. "It looks like you have embedded yourself in deep with the wrong people and I don't know what road you're going down and I'm not sure I want to go down that road with you"; her voice slightly cracking between words showing her discomfort. By now a tear ran down the side of her face as evidence from the dramatic moment seeming all too real for Jonathan. "Just let me explain", Jonathan desperately pleaded with Rachel as she lifted her head and looked off into to space. "*Maaan,* I know how to pick 'em; every single time without fail." Rachel said to herself. "GET out of my way" she said. Jonathan moved aside for fear of making it worse, he did nothing but watch her back as she left. His mind almost didn't register the fact that she was leaving and the next thing he knew the door closed and he was alone. Once again he found himself with nothing but his thoughts for company and they were too vile and negative for him to entertain, so at that point he didn't even have that as an outlet. He looked at the door in silence and stood there until he could muster up the strength to try and come up with something to get himself out of this. He wanted to go the police but he knew that he already had dirt under his own fingernails from the break-in of the mayor's house. Maybe he could run but he didn't know where to go, there was no way he was going to go back to Winterville after all he had been through to get out of there. Perhaps, that didn't mean that he couldn't go somewhere else but for all he knew these people could follow him. He didn't know what to think and after last night he wasn't about to go to Mr. Edwards and tell him he was leaving. He wasn't trying to have a run in with Percy like the man in the chair. So there he sat, head in his hands trying to forcefully pull some miracle solution out of the ether. However, there was nothing for him to grab, he couldn't think straight, not now and not with so much on his mind. He could feel his head getting heavy from the weight of the stress. When all seemed to be lost he heard his phone ring, he moved quickly to answer it, hoping that it was Rachel.

He looked at the phone but he didn't recognize the number, he thought about letting it ring but deep down he had a pretty good idea of who it might be. Adrian was always the go between for him and the now dark world that Jonathan was an unwilling participant of, yet becoming acclimated to it. He wanted to yell and cuss at the phone but he didn't, instead he looked at it in anger; his eyes wishing they alone had the strength to destroy it. Jonathan was beginning to feel defiant; his anger had given him some sort of wrathful courage while he continued to stare at the phone as it rang. It stopped after a few seconds, the phone then flashed a missed call message across the screen. It wasn't two seconds before the phone began to ring again and as quickly as his wrathful courage entered his body it just as easily left as he watched the phone ring again. What was he going to do, just simply ignore the entire situation? He knew he couldn't ignore them forever, besides they would find him long before he had a chance to ever leave town. So, he picked up the phone, his mind wanting to resist but his body prevailed as he picked it up. He answered the phone and put it to his ear as he said nothing for a few seconds not really wanting to go through with the whole thing. "Hello?" answered Jonathan. "Mr. Cross, so good of you to answer the phone", said the man. Immediately Jonathan felt chills travel from his ears into the depths of his soul. He knew that voice, and it wasn't the scratchy one he was expecting.

This time he didn't have his right hand make the call, however it was; Mr. Edwards himself. Jonathan was a bit afraid to speak but he knew that he had to, "Hello, Sir." said Jonathan, almost stuttering to get it out. "I was calling to see how you were doing?" Mr. Edwards inquired. "How was I doing?" Jonathan wondered what kind of question was that. Considering the events that Jonathan witnessed the other night and the fact that he had become a millionaire overnight. The only thing Jonathan could do in that moment was lie, "I'm fine" he replied while trying to filter the traces of annoyance in his voice. "Really?" asked Mr. Edwards. "You know Jonathan over the course of my life I have seen and encountered great men." "I've seen men come from nothing and then acquire everything" "I've seen men come from greatness only to die in the shadows." Mr. Edwards continued. "Do you know what I've found that has been a common denominator in the ones who failed?" asked Mr. Edwards. Jonathan said nothing he only listened; he could tell that he wasn't really expecting him to answer. "Distractions" said Mr. Edwards. "Distractions, Jonathan they always come in one form or another", said Mr. Edwards. "For some men its drugs, for some it's laziness, and for others it could be some consuming addiction to distasteful behavior that runs contradictory to the lifestyle they enjoy" said Mr. Edwards. "But don't be lead to believe that those are the only types of distractions." Mr. Edwards continued. "Like I said they come in a wide variety of forms, it could even be as simple as a woman", he said. After those last words, there was a brief pause on the phone as neither one of them said a word.

Jonathan wondered for a moment what Mr. Edwards was getting at but he couldn't quite put his finger on it. Then Mr. Edwards spoke again "So I ask you Jonathan, are there any distractions in your life?" By the tone of his voice, it suggested that he already knew the answer to his own question. It was becoming clear to Jonathan what Mr. Edwards was getting at; he knew that he was talking about Rachel. Although the real question at hand was how? How did he know to ask Jonathan that question? How did he even know about Rachel in the first place? Jonathan looked around the room for a minute, his eyes scanning the room for something out of place. For all he knew, the place could have been bugged, there could be some high tech camera recording his every move at this very second. Although he didn't see any clues to confirm his suspicion, that didn't stop his mind from going a mile a minute on the seemingly infinite scenarios that could have led up to Mr. Edwards finding out about Rachel. "Don't we all have some sort of distraction sir?" asked Jonathan, as he made his way over to the window. He looked out of the window frantically trying to see if there was some black unmarked car with men holding binoculars looking inside his place. Although he saw nothing he still drew the curtains, as to block any unseen prying eyes.

"I mean I don't think it would be possible for anybody to not have any kind of distractions whatsoever," Jonathan rebutted. "Don't be fooled by mediocrity Jonathan, that's always the downfall of any potential that a man might possess on the inside." Mr. Edwards insisted; his voice was sharp like a razor; quick to cut down the ideology of languid men. "You don't have to allow your focus to wane, it's a choice." suggested Mr. Edwards. "Choices that I hope you are making the right decisions about." He continued, "It would be beyond tragic and a gross disservice to yourself to let something or someone get you off track." Mr. Edwards advised. As Jonathan was still listening, he continued to make his rounds around the place, checking to see if he found some hidden camera stored in a corner somewhere. Though Jonathan was a bit spent, between the emotional heavyweight bout with Rachel and now this, he was running out of gas so he dropped down by his bed when he entered his room; his phone still clinging to his ear listening to Mr. Edwards. Jonathan didn't say anything and he could hear his heart beating faster as the sound seemed to start drowning out what Mr. Edwards was saying. "You can be so much more if you chose to be; that is a truth few men tend to acknowledge and a choice that even fewer men make", said Mr. Edwards.

"Now, I would love to continue our conversation but I have some business matters that require my attention", said Mr. Edwards. "Why don't you come by Star Industries later on this evening and we'll discuss this further?" Mr. Edwards suggested. Jonathan cringed at the thought of having another meeting with this man, now that he knew he was dangerous. Jonathan wanted to chuck the phone at the wall and maybe make a mad dash out of town and that's assuming that he wouldn't be followed by anyone. Though Jonathan now believed that to be the case. He couldn't muster up a reply, nor did Mr. Edwards require one at the time; they both simply hung up the phone almost simultaneously. Jonathan sat there by his bed, his anger starting to take the place of his fear; he had a slight suspicion before that Mr. Edwards might have been keeping tabs on him but nothing ever to really confirm it. That is until now, Jonathan knew that Mr. Edwards was talking about Rachel, the question was how? Jonathan never noticed anything out of the ordinary. He never saw anybody following him on the street or some suspicious car tailing him on the road. Then again Jonathan had to be honest with himself and take into account that he was never really paying attention as to whether someone was follow-ing him. He was so caught up in everything that was going on in front of him that he had no time to give thought to what might have been going on behind him.

As he got up, he continued to think and it hit him hard like a lightning bolt of revelation. If Mr. Edwards knew about Rachel it was also possible that he could have her followed! Jonathan grabbed his phone again and dialed Rachel's number. The phone rang but no one answered. This was probably due to the fact that Rachel wasn't in the mood to talk to Jonathan. Once her voicemail came on Jonathan left her a message,, "Hey it's me, look I know your upset but I was just calling to make sure you're ok…look…just pay attention and be care-ful", he then hung up. He tried not to let his mind run wild with all the possibilities that might take place. He thought about how he could try to follow Rachel but then he remembered that he has never been over to her place before and he had no clue as to where she was. He knew the probability of her calling him back at this point was low. He was starting to feel heavy again he didn't know what to do or even if Mr. Edwards was having Rachel followed or not. Maybe he was blow-ing this whole thing out of proportion. As he was halfway through entertaining that thought an image of the man tied down to that chair flashed in his mind again. That image alone suggested that Jonathan wasn't crazy to think that the possibility of something happening to Rachel wasn't so farfetched.

With no way to contact her, Jonathan felt a bit hopeless and frus-trated and knew that if he continued to just stay there he would drive himself insane. So he got himself together or at least to the best of his ability and headed out. He wasn't going to wait, there was no way he could survive the uncertainty as to whether or not Rachel was okay and the answers to what now seemed like an insurmountable array of concerns and questions that were now taking up permanent residence in his young conscience. He made up his mind that he was going to head straight to Star Industries, although he had no idea as to what he was going to say or do once he got there but all he knew was that he was going over there. He also knew that going over there was only really half the battle or maybe even less than that and he also knew that once he got there he was going to have to have to do something. Something more than the usual; in fact he was going to have to do the inevitable. He was going to have to confront Mr. Edwards.

CHAPTER TWELVE
THE ARRIVAL

The drive over was different than any other time before, for some reason even the simplest of things seemed to leave an impression. A random face on the street as he drove by had more clarity than usual, a vivid image not some blur caused by the speeding by of objects. It was as if time slowed down enough for his eyes to catch the little things. Although it wasn't so much that time was slowing down but more of his body dealing with the anxiety it was going through. Too far to walk; the office was located toward center of the city. So Jonathan made his way to Star Industries with much hesitation pacing back and forth in the depths of his stomach. What on earth was he going to say, or would he even say anything at all for that matter? He really had to ask himself what exactly it was that he was going to do; if anything. He wondered if he was really going to go through with it but it seemed the thought of Rachel being in danger or the thought of her fate being tied to the hands of an unforgiving man was enough to keep Jonathan moving forward.

It wasn't long before he arrived at his daunting destination; he was still numb to the whole possibility of him coming face to face with the man who had the potential to cause lasting bodily harm to both himself and the woman he loved. But he mustered through pulling the strength from some unintended form of nervousness. He pulled into a parking lot across the street from Star industries, at this point Jonathan felt that being over cautious was probably the safest bet. So he took no chances assuming that Mr. Edwards had cameras probably all over the building and would be notified the moment that Jonathan's car drove on the lot. So Jonathan made his way across the street not thinking about the fact that if there were cameras watching. Those same cameras he feared seeing him drive up would now be the same cameras watching his physical body as he approached the building. He also thought about how he could be out looking for Rachel instead of heading into Star Industries to have some sort of western showdown between him and Mr. Edwards. However, at the moment saner thoughts were not prevailing, but rather those filled with emotion appeared to take precedence. Jonathan proceeded toward the front door of the building. As he was walking he took a glance up at the behemoth skyscraper that was Star Industries, that now seemed like a castle that Jonathan was attempting to storm, so he could take down its reigning King. It was like some sort of medieval moment but it was far from the fluff of fairytale legends; this was a much harsher and unforgiving reality that could wind up with someone getting hurt or something unspeakably worse happening.

While these things were becoming clearer to Jonathan he still couldn't stop moving toward the door; like a deer in headlights he was frozen to one form of action. Except his form of action didn't involve being rendered stiff as some unidentifiable object came hurling at him, instead he couldn't help but dart at the incoming object head on. He walked through the glass doors; there were a few scattered suits throughout the lobby as usual. There was security at the front desk as Jonathan stood a few inches away from the doorway canvassing the room. He breathed in and out trying to play the scenario out as it unfolded before him. He continued to direct his attention toward the guards at the front desk, not moving anymore only staring; as a few people behind him came through the door while politely uttering "excuse me" passively letting Jonathan know that he was in the way. In fact he was standing right in front of the doors; then one of the security guards lifted his head and looked directly at him. Jonathan immediately broke eye contact and began to start walking. He was thinking to himself that the guard might somehow be on to him even though there was no proof of this other than the random look that he just received. He now thought he made himself possibly look suspicious by breaking eye contact with the guard. Jonathan reached inside his jean pocket; his hand was moist rubbing against the warm denim of his pants no doubt from his body heat rising from being anxious due to all the excitement. He grabbed his phone and put it to his ear pretending to be engaged in conversation as he made his way over to the elevator. He glanced up again to see if the guard was still watching him; to his surprise he wasn't. The guard had directed his attention to a pretty blue skirt that was passing by.

Looking up, Jonathan wondered if the cameras had caught him walking into the building, he felt like some sort of foreign terrorist on U.S. soil that at any moment, a special military task force would come jumping in to take him out. Although in this case, it wouldn't be a task force it would be hired guns; for all Jonathan knew this man might have someone gun him down right there in front of everyone. At this point Jonathan didn't put that form of boldness past Mr. Edwards; he had no idea what to expect. He got on the elevator waiting to get off at the 35th floor because you could only access the executive floors from that floor and you have to have proper ID to be cleared. Jonathan didn't have an ID but he figured that by now the security on that floor would recognize him and maybe let him up. There was no one else on the elevator while he rode up; it was unapologetically ironic how Jonathan was always surrounded by people he didn't want to be around in Winterville. However, now that he was in a City that was about 100 times bigger, he found that he was often having moments where he was completely alone. Although at the current moment Jonathan couldn't focus on that; he had to pay attention to the task at hand. He looked at the black digital screen in the elevator watching the red numbers continually go up, the elevator was passing the 28th floor, which meant that he still had a few more moments for his imagination to torture him. His thoughts refused to control themselves; because who knew what would happen to him once he got off that elevator. The whole theory of one of Mr. Edward's henchmen gunning him down as soon he got off the elevator was still a very real possibility. He still had no clue as to what he was doing, where Rachel was, and how he would find her, or if he would even walk out of the building in one piece.

It didn't matter now because he was out of time to think, the elevator was stopping; he had arrived at the 35th floor. He planted his feet firmly shoulder length apart, as if he were about to fight, he clenched his jaw and balled his right hand into a fist; while rubbing his thumb across his knuckles. He took a deep breath as the doors opened; there was the security desk that he remembered from his last visit. He also remembered that the particular guard who worked behind the desk was not a very nice guy; last time he acted like he was going to shoot Jonathan in the head. Except this time was a lot different, Jonathan had learned so much but yet learned so little at the same time. He took a step out of the elevator like an infant trying to walk for the first time and hesitated for a moment but he continued to move. He put one foot in front of the other and before he knew it, he was a few steps outside the elevator. There were actually a few people in the lobby this time around; if they were up here they were considered the top dawgs of the company. Besides, their suits gave them away and if that wasn't enough, their extensive corporate vernacular definitely did the trick. There were two separate groups talking in the lobby. Both groups were deeply engaged in their conversation almost as if nothing else existed outside of what they were talking about. As Jonathan looked around his eyes met the angry security man's cold gaze. He had been staring at Jonathan ever since the elevator doors opened up, however Jonathan was just now noticing it. Jonathan started walking toward the security desk; since he didn't have an ID card to get up he was going to have security let him up. It looked as if Jonathan's luck was running a bit dry today because it was the same guy who was there before. Jonathan kept his eyes on the security gaurd; he looked just as angry and annoyed as last time if not worse. By now, Jonathan had seen worse things than a grumpy security guard and he refused to be intimidated so he continued to stare back at the man now adding his own cold stare. The security guard was getting testy so he got up out of his seat, as Jonathan kept moving forward, "Can I help you?" asked the security guard which came out as more of a statement than an actual question. "Yea", Jonathan replied. "I'm here to..." then suddenly his phone began to ring, Jonathan awkwardly looked down and grabbed his phone; it was his mother's cell phone number on the screen. His eyes glanced back at the security guard as he was turning his back; he looked at the phone a bit confused. It was bad timing but subconsciously Jonathan was grateful for the interruption. He hesitantly answered the phone, "Hello?" "Johnny!" exclaimed his Mother. "Uh hey…Mom", said Jonathan as he tried to focus on the situation at hand. "Uh hey…guess what" she said, while mocking her son. This surely wasn't the time for guessing games and Jonathan certainly wasn't in the mood for one either. Again, he glanced back at the guard, all the while the guard was still staring at Jonathan as if he were about to fire two shots into his chest. Although now the guard was becoming increasingly more agitated with what was going on. "Hey, you need something kid?!" said the guard, in a tone that happen to penetrate some of the hard knock concentration of the big wigs that were standing around engaged in conversation. A few of them happened to look up at the guard and then direct their attention to Jonathan. Jonathan saw their eyes looking him over and he even recognized one of them it was that guy who Rachel worked with; Ronald Perkins. Jonathan remembered his name because he was a bit flirty with Rachel that night at the corporate party. The situation was getting ugly before it really even got started. "Johnny, you there?" asked Ms. Cross. Jonathan was a bit preoccupied making sure he wasn't about to get beat down by super guard behind the desk. "Uhhh yea, I'm here…I'm here" He replied. "Me too; surprise!!!" said Ms. Cross, there was a lot going on in Jonathan's mind; too much in fact. He didn't really understand what she was talking about, "What?" He asked. "I said I'm here Johnny, I'm in Edge City!" said Ms. Cross. Immediately, the room seemed to disappear and only Jonathan and his phone were present, everything else vanished in Jonathan's mind. He thought to himself that this couldn't be happening, what the hell was she doing here? Didn't this woman know how dangerous this place is? Does she have absolutely NO clue as to what's been going on in the last few months? He suddenly realized the answers to his unspoken horde of questions and these answers were really all the same, so in fact there was only one answer and that answer was NO. No, she didn't know what was going on, NO she didn't realize this was extremely bad timing for her to make an unannounced trip. Then again how could she? She was hundreds of miles away and Jonathan didn't call her and tell her that the CEO of the company he was working for was really some dangerous sociopath.

No, that wouldn't have been a pleasant conversation; so not only was he fearing for Rachel's life and his own well being. Now his mother could possibly enter the equation and be placed in unnecessary danger; it was too much! Without any form of verbal filter or structured thinking to keep him from blurting out, Jonathan instinctually shouted "No!" "Excuse me?" said Ms. Cross. By now Jonathan had managed to get the attention of everyone who was in the lobby, Jonathan looked over his shoulder and saw that the security guard was leaving his desk, presumably to walk over to Jonathan and straighten him out. "Uhh… I meant, I wasn't talking to you Mom" "Look, I'm at the office and there's a lot going on, just stay where you are and I'll head to the airport in a few minutes" said Jonathan; rubbing his head in glum and disbelief. "Oh sweetie I was just getting ready to tell you, you don't have to do that, a man from your office is already here to pick me up" said Ms. Cross. "What man?" asked Jonathan, as he felt what could only be described as an ice cold wave rush through his body meanwhile his stomach was starting to clinch up. It didn't take long for his mind to start coming up with a multitude of dangerous and unpleasant scenarios. Before he could respond, he felt an iron solid hand grab his shoulder and jerk him around; it was the nasty security guard except now he was up close and personal "Kid you got a problem?" asked the security guard , in a tone that suggested to Jonathan he better not give this man an answer that he didn't want to hear. He looked at the security guard straight in the eyes. Jonathan was now too worried about his mother to try and poke his chest up at this overzealous security guard. "No, no sir, I was actually just leaving" said Jonathan; as he noticed everyone was now focused on him. Possibly wondering if they were going to get a glimpse of an office beat down. "Yea I think you should do that", quipped the guard; while staring Jonathan dead in the face. The security guard was seriously annoyed to the point where he was breathing sharply through his nose. So hard in fact that the air from his nostrils brushed up against Jonathan's face and it was thick enough that Jonathan could almost taste the anger coming from the guard. It was indeed in Jonathan's best interest to leave, as Jonathan headed back toward the elevator he didn't say another word to the guard he just turned around and started walking. Now turning his attention back to the phone, "Mom…who…just please stay there, I'm on my way", said Jonathan; feeling very frustrated. "Johnny I'm looking right at the man" said Ms. Cross. Jonathan could now hear his mother talking to the mystery man. "What did you say your name was again, sir?" "Adrian was it?" Ms. Cross repeated.

That same overwhelming fear that Jonathan was feeling a few seconds ago only intensified. He managed to keep his mouth shut until he got on the elevator. He heard his mother over the phone "Johnny, are you there?" "Can you hear me, hello…Johnny?" asked Ms. Cross. Jonathan didn't respond, he couldn't he pressed the lower lobby button as the elevator doors closed. The call dropped once the elevator started moving. Jonathan stood there with the cell phone in his hand;

he was dazed, sick, worried, fearful, vulnerable, and upset; all of these emotions somehow managing to coexist within him at the moment. He was beyond the point of comprehension and was overtaken by his emotions; it was all proving to be beyond what he could bear. Then suddenly his legs betrayed him and they refused to stand any longer. He collapsed in the elevator and fell to his knees then to his face. Tears sprouted forth without his knowledge and his eyes and body began to weep uncontrollably without his mind's permission. Jonathan was far from in control, he had none at the moment. He cried as the elevator continued to descend; he worried about whether it might stop and reveal him crying uncontrollably. Tears were wetting the surface of the floor, his cries were already loud enough but were intensified by the fact that he was in an elevator which made the sounds of his screams amplified. They were so loud that it managed to get through to his brain and register what was going on so his mind could once again gain control of his body. Ironically the sounds of his own cries broke his body's concentration of despair; he recognized what was happening and he knew he couldn't just lay there and quit. He had no choice but to pull himself out of the moment…out of himself. He managed to push himself up with his arms, his legs however still tried to argue with his mind, refusing to move. However, he still pushed himself to get up. After all Mr. Edwards told him before that he had an animal inside of him, and in that moment his statement proved to be right. That animal refused to quit, it refused to die, it refused to back down, deep inside it didn't know how to. It commanded that Jonathan get back up and not only get back up but that he had to get back up swinging, he had to fight. Jonathan blinked and when he opened his eyes again he was standing upright fully aware and in control of himself. The elevator doors then opened and immediately Jonathan dashed out like a Lion springing from a cage. Knocking a few people out of the way, he was making a mad dash for the car, he knew he had to hurry up and get to the airport. He could feel his blood flowing while he was running to his car across the street, as he got closer he could see his reflection in the driver side window of the car. Even to himself he looked like a man on a mission, however he didn't have time to admire himself in the window; he had more pressing matters to take care of. He hopped in the car and burned rubber and as he peeled off the lot, he heard a sharp screech of the tires as they forcefully slid across the pavement. He pushed his foot onto the pedal as if he meant to go through it, it shot down to the floor as he heard the car's engine wake up and assert its dominance on the road. Traffic was light as he began to ride through the streets and the lights seemed to work in his favor as they continued to turn green without a red light in sight. Jonathan was still beyond surprised about his mother being here that he didn't even notice the fact that he had forgotten about Rachel. He felt his hands gripping tighter around the steering wheel as he reacted to the thought of Adrian being within even ten feet of his mother. Then suddenly his hands loosened up in response to another thought that joined the party. He started to replay the conversation with his mother in his mind.

She said that one of the men from his office was there to pick her up; he knew it was Adrian because he heard her say his name. What he didn't know was how in the world Adrian knew that she was going to be coming into town? It was a lot going on all at once; it was frustrating and felt like he always had questions, and when he did get an answer it often lead to an even greater question. He wondered what would happen next and then remembered that the call had dropped while he was in the elevator. He needed to call her back and make sure that everything was alright; it also occurred to him that she might not even be at the airport by the time he got there. After all, the call ended without Jonathan saying anything and she might have just decided to head out. Goodness, the thought of Adrian being alone with his mother was more than enough to send his blood boiling. He felt his foot press down on the gas even harder and his hands clinched the wheel yet again; he had to hurry up and get to that airport! He had to make sure that she was safe, it was only then in that moment that Jonathan remembered Rachel. With all the collapsing in elevator and surprise visits Jonathan had forgot all about his knightly quest of defending and/or rescuing the fair maiden. Although noble in nature, his mission for Rachel would have to be put on hold for the moment. Besides, he had no way of tracking her down and since their latest conversation; Rachel made it pretty clear that she didn't want to speak to him. But that didn't change anything in Jonathan's mind because he knew he still had to do something he couldn't just sit by and wait for something irreversibly bad to happen to her. It hurt but he knew that at the current moment he wasn't able to do anything for Rachel but there was something else he could do. He could call his mother back to make sure she was ok and wasn't dumped in the trunk of some car. He picked up the phone and redialed her number; he listened intensely as it began to ring. He was getting closer to the airport with every second that passed by. By normal standards he was about 30 minutes out from the airport but given the way Jonathan was driving he would be there in fifteen. The phone rang again for a few seconds until she answered the call, "Well goodness I was beginning to think that you wanted me to just hop back on the plane and go home" said Ms. Cross. Jonathan sighed to himself when he heard her say that because that was the honest truth. That was exactly what Jonathan wanted to happen; for her to leave and go home and not even so much as sneeze in the direction of Edge City. "No…no, of course not" said Jonathan. He tried to sound convincing, "The call dropped when I was on the elevator" he said. "You're still at the airport, right?" asked Jonathan; praying to GOD that she would say yes to that question. "Yes honey, I'm still here in this big fancy airport, I swear you could fit all of Winterville in here" replied Ms. Cross

"Mom" said Jonathan; in a calm but quick tone that seemed to cut Ms. Cross off while she was still speaking. "Is the man from my office still with you?" asked Jonathan. "Yea, he's here he's actually on the phone right now while he's waiting for my bags." said Ms. Cross. "Now listen Johnny, you know I don't really like to speak ill of anyone but that man is…well…kind of creepy looking" said Ms. Cross. "I mean goodness he kind of looks like…" before she could finish her sentence, Jonathan interjected "The Grim Reaper" he said; as a statement that was more matter of fact, than an opinion. Ms. Cross chuckled at the comment, "Well you said it" she said. "So where are you Mr. Edge City?" she quipped. "On my way to come get you" said Jonathan as he was maneuvering his way through the street; normally he wouldn't try to talk on the phone very long while he was driving but given the circumstances he was going to stay on the line. Ironically, Ms. Cross abruptly became aware of this thought and replied accordingly, "Well I would hope so 'cause I don't like you talking on the phone and driving Johnny." "Especially here, I'm sure the traffic here is nothing like back home", she said. "Mom believe me, nothing here is like back home" said Jonathan. "Well just call me when you get here" said Ms. Cross. She then hung up the phone, without warning. "No wait!" shouted Jonathan; he wanted her to stay on the phone with him until he got to the airport. He wanted to make sure she was safe and remained that way. His first instinct was to call her back but he knew she wouldn't answer the phone at least not until she was sure enough time had passed for him to make the drive over there.

He tried to keep his cool and take comfort in the fact that he had just spoken to her and she was ok. Besides, he was almost there it wouldn't be much longer. The rest of the way Jonathan didn't even blink; he was focused. Now wasn't the time to be preoccupied with worry or doubt with what might happen. He had to concentrate solely on the moment he was in, taking his eyes off the moment could easily result in somebody getting killed. When he finally got to the airport he called his mother back, he had no clue what airline she came in on and what gate she would be coming out of. He waited for her to pick up the phone but this time she didn't answer. It was the first time that

Jonathan had seen the Silver Edge City Airport. It truly was a sight to behold, however his wide eyed moment would have to be saved for later, this wasn't the time to stand around and gawk at all the pretty scenery. He needed to find his mother and make sure she was still in the same condition he left her in back at Winterville; safe. There was a sea of people, everyone all moving around going on about their personal lives each with their own personal mission for the day, so trying to find his mother was going to be like trying to find a needle in <u>two</u> hay stacks. He dialed the number again as he continued creeping along in his car hopeful to perhaps catch a glimpse of her safe and sound waiting curbside for Jonathan to come pick her up. Or at least that's what Jonathan wanted to happen. He was forced to keep driving past the baggage claim area; he had cars stacking up behind him with a few police officers directing the flow of traffic in front. He was forced to keep driving forward, he started to get a bit anxious but he saw the signs that were saying to keep straight and follow the road on the left and apparently it would loop back around, so he could pass back through baggage claim. As he steered down the winding left road he dialed his mother again, "Come on pick up" he muttered to himself. "Come on" "Come on" "Hey Johnny, you here?" answered Ms. Cross. Jonathan let out a sigh of relief which was Ms. Cross heard, it sounded like he was breathing heavily on the phone. "Well what's going on in that car?" she asked. "You ran a marathon before you got here?" asked Ms. Cross; in a very sarcastic manner.

By this time Jonathan was now coming back around; approaching the baggage claim area when he saw her standing outside on the curb. "Yea, I ran all the way over here just to see you!" Jonathan teased. He watched her as he steadily got closer; he pulled up toward where she was standing and felt something going on with his mouth. It took him a second to realize that for the first time all day he was smiling. For a moment, no matter how brief it might have been, he was happy for those few seconds. He was happy to see his mother alive and well, he watched as she smiled back and hung up the phone while watching him pull forward. Then suddenly a thick blanket of smog covered the atmosphere, immediately darkening everything else around it from its black ether. This darkness had a face and a name to go along with it; Adrian. There he was in his entire dark splendor looking like some sort of stealth assassin; he was dressed in all black to match his ever present murky demeanor. He locked eyes with Jonathan as he parked the car on the curb and put his hazard lights on. Jonathan broke there mini stare down session and focused his attention to his mother who eagerly made her way around to the driver side. Jonathan opened up the door and embraced his mother, "My guy!" said Ms. Cross. Normally Jonathan wasn't much for the whole sentimental thing but today he was and in full effect. He held her tightly silently thanking GOD that she was alright. "How you been?" asked Jonathan still squeezing her closely "Missing you" Ms. Cross responded. Finally, he loosened his grip enough for both of them to get a good look at each other. "You know Mom's are always thinking about their sons" said Ms. Cross. "Yea I know" Jonathan replied; meanwhile almost forgetting that Adrian was right there on the other side of the car staring back at the two of them. Jonathan turned his head to look over at Adrian and sure enough there he was like a plague lying in wait to strike its next population of victims. "Hey, why don't you come inside and help me with the bags" said Adrian. His voice carried over the car directly to Jonathan in a way that suggested that it was used to traveling to Jonathan' ears. Jonathan stared back for few a seconds before answering; he felt different and a little more in control of himself. He thought for a second and then responded "So tell me again, how you knew my mother was coming into town?" inquired Jonathan. Then he turned his attention to his mother to see if she could shed some light on the situation. "Well it was the funniest thing your boss's office called me and I spoke to a gentleman named Kane, I believe that's what he said he's name was" explained Ms. Cross but before she could finish   she happened to look down at her hand and notice the silver paint job that was underneath it. "Well wait a minute here!" she shouted; while looking at Jonathan with her mouth open. "Is this yours?!" Jonathan looked down and forgot all about the fact that the last time she saw him he was driving away in an old Chevy and now he was driving a car that cost as much as the home he grew up in.

"Uh…yea" he said reluctantly because he didn't want the sudden shock of the car to throw off the question he had just asked. "Yea it is, but wait a sec did you say Kane? You mean Mr. Edwards? He tried to get a sentence out but before he could his mother interjected, "Goodness Johnny, well where's the truck!?" "And have you seriously been making this kind of money?" "You can afford this?" asked Ms. Cross; firing off her intuitive round of questioning in rapid succession. Johnny glanced at Adrian, with his eyes saying that he wouldn't just slip out of this so easily. Jonathan didn't think of a response before Adrian decided to interject. "Our employer ma'am, the gentleman that both your son and I work for, saw to it that Jonathan have the proper tools befitting someone who worked for him." said Adrian. It was awkward to hear him talk like that, Jonathan was used to hearing "Mr. Death" over here sound like the walking undead. Usually only responding in short answers and unidentifiable grunts, it was almost unsettling to hear him attempting to be nice. His scratchy voice certainly didn't help the equation either, he sounded like a wild beast trying to say hello when it should be growling; it just didn't work.

Unfortunately Ms. Cross had no notes to compare like Jonathan did so she was able to take what Adrian was saying with virgin ears. She looked at Adrian then back at Jonathan. "So, you're saying this Kane man, your boss bought that for you?" questioned Ms. Cross. "Well yea, it's a company car is what I was trying to tell you" Jonathan quickly responded. "Yea this is definitely the big city. Where else do they give sport cars as company cars?" quipped Ms. Cross. That was enough talking about the car. Jonathan wanted to get back to finding out just how in the world Adrian knew to pick her up and why she was talking to Mr. Edwards. "But hey that's enough about me for right now" said Jonathan; while giving his mother another hug attempting to get her mind back on her seeing him. "Where are your bags?" asked Jonathan. "Oh, well we were still waiting for the bags to come on the conveyor belt inside." "They weren't done unloading the plane when I first got to baggage claim." she said. "So Mr. Adrian here said he'd wait for me and I'm glad he's here because I don't think my bags would fit in this new car of yours" said Ms. Cross

As they were talking a police officer walked up; Jonathan thought he noticed him first or so he assumed. Adrian had his back to the officer as he was walking up but immediately spoke saying, "He was just greeting his mother, she just flew in town; he won't be parked here long." said Adrian. By this time he had turned his head to look at the cop "We'll be leaving in a moment" Adrian furthered assured. He was staring the cop square in the face burning a hole in the officer's eyes. The cop had a stern look on his face as if he were about to cuss. Jonathan almost dared to smile, perhaps the cop might take a swing at the ole' grim reaper. That would make Jonathan's day and then he could grab his mother and leave but he would need to grab her bags first. "Hey come on Mom let's go see if your bags are here yet." said Jonathan; as he continued to watch Adrian and the officer with happy anticipation in his eyes thinking that maybe, just maybe something would happen. Jonathan and his mother walked into the airport when she put her arm around him, "I missed you, guy", she said and for a change Jonathan wasn't embarrassed by the show of affection, on the contrary he embraced it and placed his arm around her. "Me too" he said. He didn't notice as Ms. Cross slightly frowned and raised an eyebrow, "You missed yourself too?" she asked sarcastically. "I meant I missed you too" replied Jonathan, with a smile on his face. He looked back and saw Adrian still having a standoff with the officer outside. He continued to look at them through the glass as

Adrian took a step forward toward the cop; he said something with a semi blank stare with hints of anger on his face. Whatever he said had an effect on the cop, like a wounded animal he backed up and turned the other way. Jonathan grinded his teeth as he watched the cop scurry away. As he walked with his mother he wondered was there anyone who could stop these people? He turned around in an attempt to avoid locking eyes with Adrian. "So tell me again how all this came about?" Jonathan inquired. "Oh you mean my little surprise visit", said Ms. Cross. "Well it was the funniest yet divine thing really." "I was just going about my day to day" "And I had been thinking lately about coming to see you since I hadn't been officially invited in the several months you've been over here", retorted Ms. Cross; occupied with a guilt inducing glare aimed at Jonathan. "Well I was trying to get settled and…" said Jonathan but Ms. Cross interjected. "I'm just messing with you!"

With the two of them now waiting in front of the conveyor belt watching to see if her bags were there, "I know, I just wish you wouldn't" said Jonathan. With a wide grin that hadn't appeared on his face in months. "Ohhh-ha-ha-ha-ha, touché!" bellowed Ms. Cross. Jonathan looked at the bags coming down on the belt, "I see em." he said "How do you know those are my bags?" asked Ms. Cross, "Unless you went out and bought new ones you've been using the same set of luggage for the last ten years" said Jonathan. "But seriously, tell me about the trip"; said Jonathan, still unsettled about all of this. After all, an hour ago he was on his way to confront Mr. Edwards but now finding himself at the airport picking up his mother with Adrian. He couldn't make something like that up even if he tried.

Jonathan grabbed her bags which were heavy because his mother didn't believe in packing light. The bags were white ten years ago but over the course of wear and tear they've changed into more of a bone white with hints of brown from the dirt that had made its way deep into the fabric. "Oh yea like I was saying", continued Ms. Cross;

"I had been thinking about a way to come see you." "When about two weeks ago the phone rang and it was a lady from your office" she said "Well at least she said she was from your office" "What Lady?" asked Jonathan; thinking that maybe it could have been Rachel. "Oh goodness Johnny I can't remember, I think she said her name was Bridget or something like that." "You know, just a receptionist I guess" Ms. Cross explained. "Wait" interrupted Jonathan. "How'd they have your number?" he asked. Before she answered he thought about that question himself. Right before she spoke it dawned on him that when he initially got hired he put her down as his emergency contact. "That's the same thing I asked" said Ms. Cross. "But apparently you gave them my information" she answered, "Yea that sounds about right" said Jonathan; while regrettably wishing he had never done such a thing. Although, there was no way for him to know that all of this was going to happen; it was one of those hindsight moments being a painfully clear 20/20. Ms. Cross continued to tell her story, "So anyway, like I was saying…I was talking to the lady and she was telling me about how you were such a great addition to the team and that your boss, wanted her to give me a call" "So I'm sitting there like well gee, this is a nice surprise" Ms. Cross continued "So anyway, she talked for about another minute before she said her boss…uh Edwards I think she said wanted to speak to me"

As his mother continued on, he saw Adrian walk through the door. He began to directly hone in on their position and didn't need to look around for a moment to see if he spotted them. It was as if he knew exactly where they were the whole time and Jonathan knew for a fact that Adrian didn't look inside while he was talking to the cop. All he could do is chalk it up to his uncanny nature. However, the more he heard his mother speak in the background the less he actually needed to hear because by this point Jonathan was pretty much piecing the rest of her story together. He understood enough about Mr. Edwards to know that he liked being in control and didn't believe in loose ends.

So he figured he would gain absolute control over Jonathan by sending him a message. The message was now loud and clear if it wasn't before, first Rachel and now this. Mr. Edwards wanted to let him know that he could get to the ones Jonathan loved with very little effort; he proved that point with his mother. As for Rachel that was a slightly different message but a threatening one all the same; it was like he was letting him know that he was watching him at all times. Adrian approached the two of them, his eyes piercing as they always do but this time they were fixed on Ms. Cross. "At my employer's request he would like for the two of you to join him for dinner" informed Adrian. As soon as he said this he looked directly at Jonathan quietly daring him to try and refuse the offer. Jonathan shockingly took the bait to defy Adrian. "Well, I know mom's probably tired from the flight besides I'm sure she's eager to come see her son's new pad", replied Jonathan. Jonathan was hoping to throw some bait in front of his mother by mentioning his apartment; knowing that she was a sucker for stuff like that. However, the evening seemed to be full of surprises. Just as Jonathan bucked the expected normalcy of Adrian's offer; so did Ms. Cross with Jonathan's offer. "Oh honey no, dinner actually sounds like a great idea!" "I'm good and hungry from that flight, plus I'd like to meet the man who hired my boy." said Ms. Cross. "Heck, maybe he'll give me a car!" exclaimed Ms. Cross; laughing at her own joke but Jonathan wasn't laughing because none of this was funny to him at all and for good reason. He didn't want his mother anywhere near that mad man. It was bad enough Rachel was still M.I.A now his mother was duped into joining this nightmare. All of this was anything but humorous but nonetheless, Jonathan was doing a good job of holding himself together. He had to, there was too much on the line for him to lose it. He had his moment back in the elevator at Star Industries but that was about all he could afford for now. "Well then, he'll be pleased to know that you accepted his invitation" said Adrian. They all left the airport. Jonathan drove his mother of course, he refused to have it any other way and they followed Adrian as he took the lead in a black SUV carrying Ms. Cross' luggage as cargo. Adrian informed them Mr. Edwards had already taken the liberty of picking out a restaurant and was patiently awaiting their arrival. Jonathan didn't like this at all but there wasn't much he could do at the moment. However, that didn't keep him from contemplating taking his mother and driving as far away from Edge City as he could. He thought about it the whole time he trailed behind Adrian. All the while having to engage his mother in the routine I-haven't-seen-you-in-a-while-so-tell-me-everything conversation. Jonathan remembered that when he spoke to Mr. Edwards earlier in the day he wanted him to come by the office to talk to him. Obviously it was another lie, another way of getting further in Jonathan's head and far under his skin; by this time Mr. Edwards was probably halfway to Jonathan's bones. It was some sick poetic story, he had been trying to get ahold of this man almost half the day and this is how he's forced to meet him; over dinner. It definitely put a damper on the whole showdown scenario Jonathan had thought of earlier. By now it was a little after six and the sun was beginning to set. The sky was burnt orange with flares of purple coming from the outer edges promising another adventurous night in the city. But the truth for Jonathan is that it was an undesired signal, warning him to go home. So far nothing good ever came from a night in the city, they were becoming marked with distasteful images and troubling memories. By the time they had arrived to the restaurant it was about 6:40 p.m. The parking lot was pretty crowded; it was an expensive restaurant. He could tell by the way it looked; an old rustic building, the old bricks gave it character and charm. It gave it a subtle yet direct statement of elegance. It wasn't hard to see why a place like this would be attractive to Mr. Edwards. The restaurant was surrounded by a collage of automobiles most of them more in tune with the reflection of their no doubt affluent owners. Jonathan watched the back of the black SUV Adrian was driving; the tail lights erupted bright red as Adrian put his foot on the brakes. The reflection of the light traveled through the windshield and landed on Jonathan's face. It was also a signal to Jonathan that the real fireworks were about to begin; sitting in that restaurant was the very man Jonathan knew he had to deal with. For obvious reasons, it wasn't the best scenario for Jonathan because this wasn't the time nor the place to try and challenge him. In addition, given the fact that his mother would be present and now counting her as a factor in the equation; it just wasn't a move he was willing to take.

"Oh this looks like a nice place, Johnny" "Have you been here before?" asked Ms. Cross. "No" replied Jonathan; he looked around the parking lot. His peripheral vision watching as Adrian pulled into a parking spot near the front door. "Yeah really nice" repeated Ms. Cross. "Yea it definitely suits him" said Jonathan with a faint tone of voice hardly audible under his breath. "Did you say something?" asked Ms. Cross, as she looked at her son awaiting his reply; "Oh no…I was just agreeing with you." he quickly responded. Jonathan wanted to peel off the lot and get his Mother out of there but at the same time he wanted to stay over for dinner so he could possibly fish for some information from Mr. Edwards. Although reality could care less as to what Jonathan was feeling or contemplating because when it came down to it he was about to go in that restaurant and share a meal with this man regardless of how he felt.

He parked and got out of the car. The moment was here and the night was rapidly approaching and he could taste it in the air. It was like the moon was waiting for its chance to come out; a chance to make the city morph into its primal state. It's just like what Jonathan was thinking about earlier how no good things come from a night in this city. Something spectacular would have to happen in his favor to prove otherwise. It was the distasteful truth at this point, one that wasn't pleasant to swallow. However, for Jonathan's sake he was hoping and praying in the back of his mind that maybe things would prove to be different tonight but only time would tell. He strolled toward the door with his mother within arm's reach on his left side. He kept his eyes on Adrian as the two of them walked up. Jonathan was uneasy but he was learning to get a handle on his emotions. This wasn't the time for him to be ruled by his feelings; he needed to be sharp going in there tonight. Displaying fearful behavior now was like blood in the water. A signal to lurking sharks that there was a meal close by waiting to be devoured. There was a thick and pleasant aroma seeping through the walls of the restaurant and making its way to the parking lot. The scent of fine steak and premium ingredients loitered in the atmosphere. "Oh wow, you can smell the food already" "So far I must admit I'm liking this boss of yours" said Ms. Cross. Jonathan didn't respond, for her sake he merely looked at his mother and gave a simple smirk to briefly entertain her comment. He didn't want her to get the impression that something was wrong. "Just give it time" was what he really wanted to say to her but his tongue remained silent. Adrian walked ahead of them toward the front door and looked back as the door opened behind him. The opened door revealed the source of its magic, a gentleman dressed in a slim fit black suit greeted them. "Welcome to the Iron House Grill" said the gentleman. Ms. Cross smiled and replied, "Oh Thank You" Jonathan didn't even acknowledge the man since he was too distracted in trying to stay aware of his surroundings. He was trying to see if his vision could peer ahead into the restaurant, perhaps catch some glimpse of what was going on inside. Maybe he could get some kind of clue as to what the rest of the night held in store for him. "Umm… have we forgotten our manners?" asked Ms. Cross, referring to Jonathan's rudeness towards the greeter. "Oh…thank you sir" Jonathan finally replied; still not making eye contact with the man; there was no time for pleasantries tonight. Adrian again, stayed in front of them serving as their unwanted guide for the evening. The lighting in the restaurant was mild but well lit enough for one to clearly see all that was happening. The tables were adorned with white table cloth, and filled with people eating and conversing. By the looks of it each table actually had its own waiter, not three to four tables per waiter. Adrian led them to the back, to one of the private dining rooms. Jonathan felt a funny sensation in his stomach as he walked into the room. That same feeling one gets when their riding a roller coaster and it suddenly drops. Adrian opened the door and there he was, Mr. Edwards in the flesh. He was dressed down compared to his previous ensembles. He was wearing a dark brown cardigan, probably cashmere by the looks of it. He had on a pair of dark slacks, accompanied by dark brown loafers. He almost blended in with the room, almost like a chameleon but chameleons were too docile to be compared to him. He was more like the lion on the plains of Africa who blend in the tall grass as it stalks its prey.

Jonathan clenched up for a moment and unknowingly began balling his left fist. He then took a deep breath while his mouth was beginning to get dry; he was obviously nervous. Mr. Edwards stood up and immediately made his way over to Ms. Cross, "It's more than my pleasure and prestigious honor to meet you, Ms. Cross" said Mr. Edwards as he gently grabbed her right hand and kissed it. Jonathan rolled his eyes and watched his Mother's reaction; there was evidence of her blushing all over her face. "Oh well aren't you the charmer?" said Ms. Cross. "Indeed he is" said Jonathan; now realizing he had been thrown into the lion's den, tonight he was going to have to fight if he wanted to survive but he was going to fight his way; not the way Mr. Edwards wanted him to nor in a way that he would be expecting. Mr. Edwards looked up, as he stood upright still holding onto Ms. Cross's hand. "You've raised an exceptional young man Ms. Cross, you should be proud" he said; all the while looking at Jonathan. "Oh please call me Mary" responded Ms. Cross and although he was a bit nervous Jonathan didn't look away this time. He was calling on that animal inside of him hoping it would kick in again like it did in the elevator. He smiled back at Mr. Edwards playing along with his little cat and mouse game, for now. Jonathan turned his head and glanced at his Mother; she was still smiling. Mr. Edwards let her hand go with his left and now extended his right hand to Jonathan awaiting a handshake. Jonathan smiled and replied with a firm grip "Always a pleasure sir, thank you for inviting us" said Jonathan. "I must admit this was a very pleasant surprise" said Jonathan; as he began to loosen his grip; he felt the firmness of Mr. Edwards hand remain, he wasn't letting go just yet. "Not a problem in the slightest, in fact I'd accept nothing less" Mr. Edwards replied; looking directly in Jonathan's eyes. That simple eye contact had so many hidden innuendos it wasn't even close to being funny.

After a few delayed seconds, Mr. Edwards giving time for his subtle comment to marinate with Jonathan. He let go of his hand, "Well if you would be so kind, please have a seat." said Mr. Edwards. "I trust my associate Mr. Adrian was more than longsuffering for the both of you", he said. "Yes of course, Adrian's the master of suffering" said Jonathan; while taking his seat he managed to make brief eye contact with Adrian. Adrian didn't flinch, in some sick way he looked as if he openly welcomed the comment. As if he wanted to say "And don't you forget it!" Mr. Edwards looked over at Adrian for a second halfway smirking but not enough for an untrained eye to see, only those who've become familiar with these two gentlemen would catch anything. So in this case that someone would be Jonathan and which also meant that if no one else saw it, then it really didn't happen. "Well I'm glad to hear that he took good care of you" said Mr. Edwards. "Oh yes, he was a complete gentleman, he stayed with me until Johnny got to the airport and helped me with my bags and everything" said Ms. Cross. "He did great" she further complimented. "Glad to hear it, Adrian always accomplishes his mission; as do I" said Mr. Edwards; now redirecting his attention onto Jonathan. "Nevertheless, this is where Adrian makes his departure for the evening" said Mr. Edwards and on queue; he gave Adrian a nod as if he were a general relieving a soldier from his post. Adrian was standing back from the table toward the right of Mr. Edwards' shoulder which made sense from his standpoint. He could see everything that was going on in the room; he also could see anyone coming if they tried to walk in. Jonathan pictured a silencer tucked away inside Adrian's coat pocket locked and loaded, ready to go at a moment's notice. He had no proof of this but given Adrian's less than admirable track record, it wasn't a far-fetched idea. Adrian took a few steps toward the table, "It's been a true pleasure Ms. Cross" said Adrian. "You don't have to call me… we'll thank you." she said. "It was my pleasure as well" Ms. Cross replied. Jonathan wanted to throw up at the mere words that were being exchanged between the silent henchman and his mother. He didn't care whether or not she realized how bad this guy was or the both of them for that matter; it was still beyond disturbing. He was more than relieved to see that Adrian was leaving, one mad man gone one to more to go.

One of the waiters walked over and asked them what they wanted to drink. Mr. Edwards; still being in the early stages of his wine glass, didn't respond. "I'll have a club soda." Ms. Cross answered "Oh and could you bring me one of those little bowls with some slices of lime instead of lemon. " she said , "Yes, ma'am of course" replied the waiter. "And for you sir?" asked the waiter looking wide eyed at Jonathan awaiting his response. "I'll have the house wine, with water on the side. There was a moment of silence that seemed to rush itself into the room. Jonathan instinctually felt the need to look over at his mother. Her head cocked to the side and her mouth was partially open, "Well…goodness you move to the city and you pick up the taste of alcohol" said Ms. Cross. Although she wasn't really upset, she still enjoyed giving him a bit of a hard time. "Guilty" said Jonathan. "I'll have to admit that I've picked up some bad habits here in the city" said Jonathan. Ms. Cross rolled her eyes jokingly, turned to face towards Mr. Edwards, "Are you corrupting my son?" she asked. Suddenly, a bead of sweat forced its way through the pores of Jonathan's skin on his forehead and rolled down to the left side of his face but invisible to the rest of the table. "You have no idea" replied Jonathan; using it as a mild joke to throw off any impropriety between them. Ms. Cross responded with a smack in Jonathan's arm and a motherly look towards Mr. Edwards. "Johnny has always been ahead of the curve from the rest of the kids back home" explained Ms. Cross. "Sometimes his overzealousness could cause him some problems" she explained. "I just wanna make sure he's learned from his past mistakes and that he doesn't do anything that's going to get him into trouble out here", said Ms. Cross; followed by a smile. She wasn't actually worried about Jonathan in the sense of his moral compass, merely letting her maternal two cents be thrown into the equation.

"I assure you, Mary he's in the best of hands and under the most watchful of eyes in and out of my presence" stated Mr. Edwards; his eyes fixed on Ms. Cross but the meaning of his words were hurling at Jonathan's face while violently making their way into his mind. That picture revealed who was in control; an iron fist in a velvet glove; the unassuming strong hand that Mr. Edwards had in his arsenal. It was a battle of innuendoes that night, with the presence of innocence being represented by Ms. Cross, being unaware of the silent battle taking place in the deep undertones of the conversation. "I'm just pleased you could make the trip" said Mr. Edwards, smoothly turning the tide of the conversation. "Yea, me too it is an unexpected change of pace" said Jonathan, chiming in with a kind lie; he didn't want his mother anywhere near Edge City. Or even worse, having dinner with this man who has now introduced him to a dangerous side of living. "So how long are you here?" asked Jonathan. "A whole month!" exclaimed Ms. Cross. Jonathan began to choke on a sip of water that he had just taken. "Oh, I'm just teasing" said Ms. Cross. "I wouldn't do that to you" she said. "Although I'm sure he wouldn't mind the homemade meals" she said while glancing at Mr. Edwards. Jonathan coughed to clear his throat as he took another sip of water, he was starting to get eager for the arrival of the glass of wine that he ordered. "Only till the weekend, don't panic" said Ms. Cross. "I'll admit you had me there for a second" said Jonathan. "Well enough about me" said Ms. Cross "I want to hear more about you" she inquired. "Now Mr. Edwards, you seem like a strict business man, but I hope you're allowing my boy to have a personal life" said Ms. Cross. "Yes to both the former and the latter" replied Mr. Edwards.

"Good" said Ms. Cross. "So my next question Johnny, is have you met anybody while you've been here?" Jonathan took a sip of his wine that finally made its way to the table, but shaking his head slightly before doing so. "I know what you're getting at" he said. He knew she was really trying to get to see if he's started anything that even resembled a love life. "Well if you must know there is this one gorgeous girl" said Jonathan. Ms. Cross leaned back into her seat with both excitement and anticipation occupying her face. "Well does this gorgeous girl have a name?" she asked. "Yea, her name is Rachel" replied Jonathan; if he was going to have to sit here and play dinner party with the villain, he would at least try to play the game well. He hoped that at the mention of Rachel's name that would maybe throw Edwards off his game. However, it undoubtedly proved to be a naïve notion on Jonathan's part, Mr. Edwards resolve was too perfected and steadfast for that. This wasn't amateur hour for him, in fact he played along. "Ahh, Ms. Monroe, take your son's description as very accurate; she is indeed a gorgeous young woman" said Mr. Edwards "But beauty is fleeting, she's got fight, something you need in this town." He said, taking yet another calculated sip of wine and not even looking in Jonathan's direction. Jonathan wanted to know if Rachel was okay but it was useless to try and keep this up. Mr. Edwards was unshakable. If he was going to divulge any information it would be completely on his terms, not because of a young kid from Winterville made him play his hand.

The night continued on with Mr. Edwards in the lead of whatever game this was supposed to be. There was no point, Jonathan tried to throw a few things out in attempt to bait him but it was to no avail. So he subsided after a while and retreated to his mental corner to lick his wounds. He just wanted to finish out the meal without some other disaster taking place. Fortunately for Jonathan, nothing bad or painfully unpleasant reared its head; he didn't have to go toe to toe with the champ like he had replayed over in his mind earlier. The atmosphere remained civil, Mr. Edwards only saying a few things to Ms. Cross to fool her of his illusions. Like the fact that he mentioned he owned the restaurant that they were eating in, or that Star Industries was pleased to have Jonathan on the team. All of these things added to the recipe of deceit that Mr. Edwards was serving that night. It was indeed a cold dish, one that Jonathan didn't care to have any of, but for the sake of innocent blood at the table, he pretended to take bites. Only to spit them out in his napkin of reality. They stayed up until almost 11:00 p.m.; the rest of the guests had all gone home. Only the staff remained, as they wiped down tables outside of the private dining room, doing the usual closing down shop routine that all businesses do after hours. Finally the time came where the meal came to a close and Mr. Edwards released his invisible grasp over the evening. Mr. Edwards was still inside the restaurant when Jonathan and his mother left, the parking lot was now empty, the dark concrete reminded Ms. Cross of the ocean at night. She said that it was the way the city lights bounced off the ground gave it some sort of distorted but beautiful look. They were both tired by the time they got in the car, apparently Adrian was instructed go ahead of them to drop their bags off at Jonathan's place at the front desk. This came up toward the end of dinner when Ms. Cross suddenly remembered that her bags were in Adrian's car. When they arrived at Jonathan's place Ms. Cross was too worn out from the evening to make a big fuss over Jonathan's new place. He showed her to the guest bedroom that had minimal furniture but the bed was fully made. He had left the shades up earlier so he could see the night's sky staring back at him through the window but it was dark, there were no stars tonight. "Night Johnny boy." Said Ms. Cross as she climbed into the bed, "Night." Said Jonathan as he closed the door. He stood outside the door for a minute and took a deep breath. He was glad that nothing too crazy happened tonight. For him this was one of Edge City's tamer nights. The loft was dark and he had the lights dimmed, he was ready to climb into bed. He began to unbutton his shirt as he made his way to his bedroom. Hearing the quite sound of his shoes walking on the hard wood floor. He actually looked down to watch his feet move as he walked. As he reached the doorway of his bedroom, he heard a knock at the door. It wasn't a loud bang but it was enough to disrupt the still silence that had blanketed the entire place; enough to make Jonathan jump a little. He turned around quickly; it was far too late for a house call. He walked out toward the living room and glanced at the guest room to see if his mother was going to come out, but she must have been asleep already because the door handle didn't move. He dashed quickly to the kitchen grabbing a large butcher knife from the new set of knives he had bought months ago. He made his way to the door, moving cautiously. He inched forward waiting to hear another knock but instead he was meet with silence, which made it even more disturbing. He was prepared for the worst, he thought about why he hadn't bought a gun, no reasonable response came to mind. He reached for the lock on the door; he turned the knob slowly, his moist hands almost slipping around the handle as he tried to get a good grip. He was trying not to alert whoever was on the other side of the door, so he could maintain the element of surprise. He flung the door open aggressively with the kitchen knife in his other hand waiting to strike, but he couldn't because standing in the doorway was the woman he loved; Rachel.

CHAPTER THIRTEEN
THE MIRROR IMAGE

The air coming from the vent was chilly; it blew directly on her dark hair, causing it to move as the air pushed against it. She didn't take notice of something like that; right now it wasn't important. However, it didn't stop Jonathan from noticing but that really couldn't be counted because he noticed everything about Rachel. He noticed whether or not she was wearing more eyeliner than she did the day before or when her nails carried the scent of a fresh polish signifying that she had just gotten them done. As always, she had his full attention and this time he held a greater weight of compassion for her. He had been looking for her all day and now here at 1:15 AM, she was sitting at his kitchen counter; legs crossed with her arms folded for her own comfort. Jonathan could tell it was a safety mechanism for her without her saying anything. He knew this about her because he found himself often wanting to hold himself in the same manner she was currently demonstrating. She confided in him with the absence of tears. She was shaken up a bit but she wasn't going to cry. It was contrary to who she was to do such a thing; she never wanted to be perceived as a little girl in the big city. She was tough and beautiful; the kind who possessed a frailty on the inside but refused to be broken on the outside. She was better at hiding her feelings than Jonathan was; nonetheless the fact that she was there was enough to show Jonathan she didn't have a stony heart.

"I didn't know where you were." "I just didn't know what to do", admitted Jonathan in a very exhausted tone. "But believe me when I tell you I couldn't stop thinking about you; I refused to", he said. Rachel only looked up at him when he said this, no words left her mouth. Her soft eyes did all the talking and if their message could be deciphered they would say thank you and how she wanted to stay there for the night. "I just couldn't believe or didn't want to believe that this happened" she said. Her voice was tired, her vivacious personality suppressed by the shock of what happened. "I'm just glad you weren't there" said Jonathan. He started to say, "If you had been there…" but was unable to finish his sentence. Her apartment had been broken into; it looked like a hurricane had blown through there. The door was hanging off the hinges, furniture was ripped, the whole nine. "I can go to the police" stated Rachel. "Can you though?" asked Jonathan. "I mean really, this guy seems to know everything everyone is thinking and doing before they do" he said. Suspiciously, he then looked over across the dim lit living room looking at the guest room his mother was occupying. Trying to make sure he kept his voice down, the last thing he wanted right now was for his mother to come traipsing out of her room and into the midst of something else she had no business walking into. "Look I'm not getting sucked in to your little sick game with this guy" said Rachel. "Sick game?" replied Jonathan "Wait, you think this is funny?" "Like I like what's going on?" "I'm out here running scared for my life just for the hell of it?!?" snapped Jonathan. "This isn't some game Rachel!" asserted Jonathan; once again looking at the guest room door. "Besides you were in, the minute he decided to wrap his hand around my life." said Jonathan. "Look I'm sorry, trust me I am" sighed Jonathan. He walked over to the dining room table and took a seat. "Nothing went the way I planned for it to go." "None of this was part of the plan." "I didn't plan on getting beaten to a pulp in a parking lot." I didn't plan on working for a Psychopath." I didn't plan on having my life spiral out of control" I didn't plan on my mother being in danger" "I didn't plan on falling in love…" he said; in a highly frustrated yet suppressed voice where the words had a deep presence once they left his mouth. They stayed in the air for a while before they became a reality; a living and breathing existence. A tear made its way down Jonathan's face. Rachel looked on as he sat there all but broken at the table. He was hurt, she was hurt they were in pain together. They needed each other, whether they knew it or not.

They ventured into his room as not to wake his new found visitor in the guest room so they could stay up for a few more hours trading sad eyes and heart tugging words. After they talked some more she fell asleep in his bed and Jonathan wasn't about to wake her up so he quietly slipped onto the couch in the living room. It was exhausting but deep down he didn't care, he was glad that she was ok. Besides he'd rather her there talking to him instead of her being out there somewhere where Mr. Edwards could reach his hand out and manipulate her circumstances. Although he knew that Mr. Edwards could come knocking at his door if he really wanted to at any moment. At least this way they would face the knock together. Though Rachel hadn't been as vocal to Jonathan about her feelings in the past, she sent a message loud and clear last night by choosing to come to him for comfort.

Jonathan had spent the night on the couch, normally he wasn't a light sleeper but his present frail sleeping habits seemed to intensify the more nights he spent in the city. He heard the squeak of a door's golden bolts and screws turning in unison. His eyes opened from a much needed deep sleep; his body wanted more of that level of rest that he had been deprived of lately. He propped his head up over the back of the couch so he could see. "Morning" said Ms. Cross. "Good Morning" Jonathan replied. His mind catching up to what he had just said, "Wait" he exclaimed fidgeting noticeably and looking at his door. He just remembered Rachel was in his room and no doubt the question that he didn't want to hear asked was about to be asked. He tried to recover from his fall of obviousness and rebound his composure and quickly; got up from the couch, "Hey, good morning" "How'd you sleep?" he asked, while trying to steal a look at his closed bedroom door. "It was good; sweet goodness I was tired, "I swear I hit the bed like a ton of bricks" confessed Ms. Cross; as she made her way to the refrigerator for a morning snack Jonathan moved toward his bedroom door. As she pulled the door handle open, Ms. Cross sarcastically added, "Please tell me you have something other than take out in your fridge" Jonathan stood back a little bit staying as close as he could to his door. He still had sleep in his eyes as he rubbed his finger in his right eye. He looked at the gold door knob as if it were some forbidden fruit but perhaps in this moment it might has well been. Because behind that door was forbidden fruit sprawled out across his sheets. The last thing that he needed was for his mother to see a young woman in his bedroom. Even though he was out of her house now, that level of embarrassment wasn't something he wanted to experience at the moment. "Jonathan Cross!" exclaimed Ms. Cross. This startled Jonathan and he jumped and turned around. "Yea, what…what is it?" asking as if he had been found out. "I taught you better than this" she affirmed. "Is this ALL you have in your fridge?" she asked; with disappointment floating around her lips. To her credit she was right there wasn't much in there but some take out boxes of Chinese food, scattered sodas and remnants of a few steak dinners. "Oh yea I just… I just haven't been to the store yet" he replied. He distanced himself but not too far from the door taking a few steps forward. It wasn't even a few minutes into the morning and he'd already found himself in a predicament. He watched as his mother dressed in a sky blue night gown went rummaging through his refrigerator. The back of his neck was starting to collect sweat as he thought about the worst case scenario. Rachel could come traipsing out of his room at a moment's notice dressed in his clothes. He really didn't want that to happen. His mother raised her head from the shallow space in his refrigerator and closed the door. "Ok, I see I'm gonna have to go get some food" she said shaking her head. She turned to look at Jonathan and then looked behind him at the closed bedroom door. "Wait" she said, with the look of confusion starting to move across her face. "Why were you sleeping on the couch?" she asked

"I couldn't really sleep last night, I tossed around the bed and then decided to come out here and watch some TV" he cleverly responded. "And I guess it ended up watching me." Ms. Cross, accepting his answer had an unexpected surprised look make its way onto her face, as if she had just thought of something. "Oh, and I meant to tell you this last night but I was just dog tired." "I'm proud of you Johnny, your place is wonderful!" blushed Ms. Cross. "But not just because of your place but everything." "You came to the city like you wanted." "You left Winterville like you wanted." "And you even landed a job like you wanted." "So like I said, I'm proud of you Johnny." "You done good kiddo" Ms. Cross proudly shared. "…Minus the fridge of course." she teased. "Thanks" Jonathan replied. "But you still owe me a tour." she said, "Well let's see the bachelors headquarters" said Ms. Cross; as she began to make her way over to Jonathan's room. She appeared to almost glide across the floor heading for Jonathan's room. "No wait…uh I have to straighten up" said Jonathan. "Oh please just let me see…" insisted Ms. Cross. "When will this end?" mumbled Jonathan; trying to let some suppressed frustration out. Right as Jonathan stepped in the way of his mother to keep her from opening the door, the doorbell rang. It caught both of their attention as Jonathan looked at his bedroom door and then at the front door. "Well goodness, it's not fully nine o'clock yet" "Were you expecting somebody?" asked Ms. Cross. She was right it was early; too early for someone to be making a house call. "No" Jonathan replied. "Let me go in the room, I'm not even dressed" said Ms. Cross; as she made her way back to the guest room, fixing and primping herself along the way. Jonathan started to open his bedroom door and check on Rachel but the doorbell rang again. He walked to the front door, as he vowed to himself to put a peep hole in the door. He had grown weary of being surprised like this in his own home. "Who is it?" he asked when he approached the door. "Just open the door, boy scout." He recognized the voice even through the door. "Rachel?" he asked in a perplexed tone as he managed to keep his voice down. He opened the door and there she was yet again standing in his doorway. He stood there in his pajamas, which he realized were nothing more than his boxers and a white undershirt. He felt the embarrassment hit his face but it didn't stay there long because he had other emotions vying for his attention; one of them being anxiety as he wondered how and when she left. The answer he sought came without him even asking, "I got up early and tip-toed out" she said. "I just had to get some fresh air, think a bit and I called the police." "I'm filing a report" "I'll let them come to the conclusion, if any about who could've broken into my apartment" Rachel said.

Jonathan didn't speak, only responded with a nod letting her know he understood where she was coming from. She was taking a chance of rolling the dice in an unpredictable and dangerous game so he chose not to argue with her, besides he knew that would only prove to be a losing battle. Instead he offered a shoulder to lean on and in this case an overnight place to stay. "Well come in you don't need to stand outside like that" said Jonathan; realizing that inviting her in now wasn't anything that would be considered out of place. Although his mother would undoubtedly bombard her with questions, this was still better than the alternative. Rachel walked in and sat down. She was wearing a different outfit than last night. She had on a white sleeveless blouse with denim leggings. Jonathan was happy to see her as he always was, but neither one of them could take their minds completely off their new found troubles. The pace of this life was real, everything was tangible. Although he had to admit at time things seemed too outrageous to be real. However, he could touch the melancholy that made its way into both of their lives. Its fatal aftertaste lingered on his tongue after he uttered his sentences. He smelled lurking defeat rising from the ground. He could see the frustration building around him like a cloud of smog.

"How long is your mother planning on staying in this city?" Rachel asked; in disbelief that she was even there in the first place. She cared for Jonathan but she questioned his judgment. What she really meant behind her smoked screened question was "How could you let her come into this?" Jonathan picked up on the disguised overtone. He explained his case laying out as much detail that pertained to the point as possible, trimming the fat off of his answers. He kept his voice down as much as he could without looking like a child to Rachel. "Have you even figured out why that money was in your account? she asked "Like where did it come from? " she further inquired. "I know where it came from" Jonathan replied. "I don't' mean the direct source." said Rachel. Her attitude was still sharp and she had a way of being lovely yet blunt. "I mean what was the purpose behind him doing that?" "What's his endgame with all of this?" "I'm not sure if there even is an endgame with him" said Jonathan in a relaxing voice, choosing to stay calm. He knew he had to stop being so rattled all the time since that wasn't going to solve his problems. "I still don't' know why he did it" "But then again, do I ever really know why he does any of the things that he does? Jonathan knew he wasn't even an inch closer to getting answers for all the questions that he had. He had to buy some time so he tried to deflect his attention back to Rachel, "I know who he sent to trash your place" confessed Jonathan. "Excuse me?" said Rachel; fidgeting in her seat as if she were about to jump out and grab Jonathan's neck while demanding that he tell her everything he knows or thinks he knows. "He has a strong arm he uses when he wants to reach out and touch somebody so to speak" said Jonathan. "Wait, you mean juggernaut?" asked Rachel. "Jugger what?" asked Jonathan. "That's what some of the girls at the office call him, that's not his real name" she explained. "Percy" said Jonathan; attempting to take another crack at figuring out who she was talking about. "Yea, sounds like something you'd name a bulldog" she said. "Well it fits" agreed Jonathan. "I think the name matches the occupation" he said. They both continued to talk a while longer trying to figure things out and assemble what pieces the other might have been missing.

He asked if she was going to stay over again but she declined opting to stay at a girlfriend's house instead. Jonathan knew that was a wiser choice, in case Edwards wanted to send "Juggernaut" over his way. He'd be able to kill two birds with one stone, although Jonathan doubted that Mr. Edwards would take that route. He wanted Jonathan around because he wanted him to be in the fold but that was about all Jonathan knew. He noticed his mother never came out of the room, he thought that was odd but he didn't focus on it. The other woman that he loved was right in front of him, there was no need to split his focus Rachel had his undivided attention. Rachel had a bit of a tough shell that Jonathan had worn down even though he didn't realize it. She walked over, and hugged him, placed her head on his chest. He squeezed her a little tighter; he could not let anything happen to her. He would never be able to forgive himself if something did. She quietly left after they embraced, he watched her as she walked with elegance even in a tough time like this.

As she closed the front door, he simultaneously heard the sound of another door opening. "Was that your lady friend? his mother asked. She had a wide grin nested tightly within her face as she walked out. She had changed into a sundress, white at the top with multicolored flowers toward the bottom. Jonathan looked at the door then back at her "I had wondered where you went" he said. "I thought maybe you fell asleep and couldn't get up" he jested. "Ha…ha… that was remarkably unfunny my son" Ms. Cross responded. "Well you're a young man, young but still a man so I thought I'd give you some space" she said. "I'm sure you didn't want your ole mom coming out and causing you to lose any points you might have accumulated with Ms…." "Rachel" said Jonathan. "Oh! That's right!" "That's the girl you told me about last night!" Ms. Cross exclaimed. "Well I guess a thank you is in order" said Jonathan. "For what, not messing your game up?" she replied. "Well yes, actually that's exactly what I meant; not messing up my game" said Jonathan. "You've been reading those teen magazines again haven't you?" he said. "No I just realize that my Johnny is turning into Jonathan, you're not so little anymore" his Mom said; as she looked him over, then glancing over the place. "Like I said before, you've done well kiddo" "I'm proud of you and you should be proud of yourself" she said. It was difficult for Jonathan to accept what she said. It was understandable to look at it from her point of view and why she would say such a thing. All she saw was her son who moved out of a small town, landed the right job, got the nice place, got the girl, and seemingly putting his life together. She was on the outside looking in but Jonathan was too deep on the inside to hear anything that resembled a shell of the fantasy that he was in original pursuit of when he left home. That all sounded good and well but there was no way Jonathan could be proud of himself after all that had gone on in this concrete jungle. He experienced things that he never thought that he would. Was he proud of himself? He couldn't be, at least not right now. He was too overtaken by guilt and disappointment in him succumbing to the entrapment of pride instead of upholding his moral foundation. So much that he only could muster a, "Thanks mom, I appreciate it."

Before Jonathan could come up with a distraction to change the subject of how-well-he-was-doing-when-he-really-wasn't, his phone did the job for him. He heard it blaring through his bedroom door, reminding him that he turned the volume all the way up on it earlier. "You're just Mr. Popular this morning", quipped Ms. Cross. Jonathan moved briskly so he wouldn't miss the call. "I'm Mr. Popular EVERYDAY" he said; continuing to keep the mood light. He opened his door, it was the first time he had opened it since yesterday. The sound of the ringing intensified once he opened the door; it was like an infant screaming to be fed; crying out for the attention it needed. The caller ID said it was coming from Star Industries. He knew who it was; he turned to head out the door pausing as the phone kept ringing toward his back. He ignored the call. It stopped, but he knew that it would just lead to another call so he didn't move. Sure enough the phone rang again. "Are you going to grab that or not Mr. Popular?" heckled Ms. Cross from the living room. He snatched the phone off of the night stand by his bed; he answered it and put it to his ear first without saying anything. "Hello Jonathan, how are you this fine Edge City morning?" asked Mr. Edwards. There was something in his voice that affected Jonathan's inner most being and had the power to send him into a state of dismay like a pollutant in the water, he could taste it. He might not be able to identify what exactly it was but it was there. He looked at his bedroom door standing open, this wasn't the type of call intended to be overheard. So he was about to head to the bathroom before he caught a faint whiff of a calming scent. It was Rachel's perfume still lingering around in his bed from the night before. It chose to stay maybe perhaps having a mind of its own in an attempt to communicate with Jonathan in Rachel's stead. It talked to him briefly but its message was clear. It calmed him and gave him strength to stand on; Rachel did more for him than she realized. Her perfume placed her visage in his mind, which gave him the calmness and the yearning to protect her from which he drew the strength. He walked into his bathroom and left the door slightly ajar; enough for one to overhear the conversation yet absent from any distastefulness that might occur during the exchange. "Isn't it a bit early for the cat and mouse?" asked Jonathan; it was the first time he had demonstrated any hostility towards Mr. Edwards. "Not if the old cat hasn't had its breakfast" replied Mr. Edwards. "You know what?" "How about you enlighten me on what exactly it is that you want from me?" Jonathan demanded; with sharpness in his voice from the crux of bitterness now nestled deep inside. "I want to show you who you are Jonathan" said Mr. Edwards. "Because it's evident that you haven't the slightest-clue" "I could tell that you were searching for yourself when I first met you" "You've always been searching." "I can show you…*You*" he said. "So, smoke and mirrors are going to tell me about myself?" "Hmmm, that's interesting; I   thought those were used for illusions?" Jonathan sarcastically asked. "Biting the hand that feeds you leads to starvation, Jonathan." "I remember a certain someone who told me that they were more than just merely hungry for life but that they were starving" Mr. Edwards cleverly rebutted. "You don't want to stop eating, even if you think you do." "I'll tell you why", Mr. Edwards continued; his voice penetrating Jonathan's mind like a virus entering its host. "If you stop eating you get weak and become malnourished and malnourishment leads to death" said Mr. Edwards. "So you see, you have to eat...we all do. Eating is in a person's best interest" Mr. Edwards further explained. Jonathan clenched the phone tightly until the veins in his hand began to become visible. He wasn't stupid he heard the blatant threat that Mr. Edwards tried to disguise with metaphors. "You know pride is dangerous" said Jonathan; aiming to keep his wits about him. "The mere fact that you would fix your mouth to say something like that lets me know that you're in need of my help" responded Mr. Edwards. "Pride is not dangerous Jonathan, pride is essential." "Without pride in oneself, you wouldn't see the need for self-preservation because you'd have no self-esteem." "Without self-esteem you would see no need to better yourself and hone your skills." "And without being skillful, success in life would be highly improbable." "Boy you're in dire need of assistance" said Mr. Edwards. "Which is why I want you to come by the office" "We need to talk, Mr. Cross." Jonathan didn't want to say anything but he did, he couldn't run if he wanted to. This whole stunt he pulled with his mother and now with Rachel was proof that he could stretch his hand out anytime and touch or break anything he wanted, when he wanted. "When?" snapped Jonathan; peeking out of the corner of the bathroom to make sure his mother wasn't too close to his bedroom door. Although, its wasn't like she would be able to hear anything Mr. Edwards was say-ing or even know who Jonathan was talking to for that matter. But still he didn't even want her to remotely hear anything he was talking about; it was bad enough she was in Edge City to begin with. Even Rachel commented on it earlier. It wasn't good for her to be there, it wasn't good for either of them to be in the city. This was Mr. Edwards territory, his playground, his home it was like he could be everywhere at the same time. Jonathan never knew when he was being watched but he knew he'd need to look over his shoulder at all times if he didn't go into the office. He was already looking over his shoulder enough as it is and he didn't need to add anything else to what was already a complex situation. "There's no time like the present, acting in the mo-ment generates results" responded Mr. Edwards." "And I trust you're not too busy at the moment" said Mr. Edwards. Jonathan caught a glimpse of himself standing in the bathroom, holding the phone. He locked eyes with himself, staying focused on his own eyes. He wanted to look within since he had always heard about eyes being the win-dows to the soul. He wanted to get a look at his. He wanted to see it, hoping that he would find that animal again; that animal that he had no name for. The one he never even knew existed before he came to Edge City. It was a tough thing for Jonathan to admit but what Mr. Edwards said might hold some truth. Jonathan didn't know everything about himself; he was still discovering who he was. This city managed to cause things to rise out of him that he didn't even know were there. So he looked in the mirror watching himself look back, he was trying to find out who he was, he was trying to find out what was on the inside of him. He was ready for answers. "No of course not, I wasn't do-ing anything important" Jonathan replied; with sarcasm and defiance taking refuge in his voice. They both hung up the phone almost in unison. Jonathan placed the phone down by the sink; he laid his hand down and hung his head slightly as he felt his chest breath in and out trying to collect himself. Though this time around he wasn't about to sob his way to the floor and pout his way to Star Industries. He was getting his mind right because he knew he would be going behind enemy lines. He was going to do what he had to do; have some face time with the enemy. He was oddly eager this time around; perhaps that animal was making its way back again after all.

He closed the bathroom door and hopped in the shower. He needed to energize himself for what was ahead. The water always helped him get ready for the day; he needed something familiar to help him tackle the unfamiliar. He got himself dressed and started to do something he never thought he would ever do in his life. He started thinking about Winterville and how he used to act when he was back home. Although he never boasted in arrogance, he did walk with a sense of self-worth. He carried himself differently because he knew deep down inside that he was a big thinking fish in a small thinking pond, so he acted differently because he thought differently. However, his actual size never changed, he felt bigger because he thought bigger. Back home anytime something ever rose up that presented itself as a problem, Jonathan would never sweat it because he knew that he could overcome it since he knew who he was in that situation. He was a bigger thinking fish dealing with a problem coming from a smaller thinking environment. He started to realize that's how he dealt with things back home, it wasn't a matter of his size it was a matter of his mentality. That's what the issue was; he kept thinking that he was so outmatched against this problem. What he needed to do now was begin to think bigger; even bigger than Mr. Edwards. He always noticed that Edwards seemed to be a step ahead of him; like a highly skilled chess player always thinking at least several moves ahead. That was a start and a clue as to what Jonathan needed to do, he needed to do the same. Truthfully, he looked at Mr. Edwards as more of a great white shark than some run of the mill fish. Perhaps that could prove to be his downfall; maybe there was a way for Jonathan to think of something that Mr. Edwards didn't or simply overlooked. But he had no idea where to start or what to think of but now he knew that his mindset had to change if he was going to have a fighting chance of survival. He was playing in the major league and he was still swinging like it was T-Ball; he had no choice but to step his game up. So he got dressed and put on a suit but not one of the cheap suits he came to the city with. Over the last month or so he managed to buy a few nice and more expensive, form fitting suits. It made him looked like he belonged amongst the higher circles of society.

He left the apartment explaining to his mother that an impromptu business meeting had been scheduled and he got called into the office, which happened to be the truth. He tried to offer her his car and take a taxi that way she wasn't stuck in the loft all day. She refused and told him it was unnecessary, she didn't mind taking a taxi or even going on foot if she had to. The truth of the matter was Ms. Cross was having a semi-adventure of her own just by being in the city. Also, she might have been a little nervous driving Jonathan's new car, at heart she was still a Winterville woman so she didn't want push the envelope too far, even though she would never admit that. By the time he walked down to his car the sun was seated high in its position. It was just after 10:30 am. The city was awake and its veins; being the people were flowing throughout the body of the city. Edge City was alive with a personality and its own set of rules; it kept itself in constant rotation. This explained why events never happened the same way twice in the city. He drove on that ole familiar road he had driven too many times before, it was like his hands and his feet remembered the route for him without the assistance of his eyes or his brain. It was almost as if he didn't need to pay attention to the road and could allow his body to guide him there if he had to. That's how it felt as he passed by the familiar surroundings until he finally saw that dreaded silver tower. It stood there like an erect monument telling a man's story. A testament to the fowl king that was Kane Edwards, it further reminded Jonathan what he was really up against. This man wasn't dusty back roads and old timber wood ways. He was skyscrapers and caviar tastes with a sinister intellect to guide him. Was it even possible to out think him? Jonathan didn't fully know the answer to that question. He knew what the answer had to be, not what it actually was or what it could be. He would have been lying to himself if he said he wasn't starting to have second thoughts trying to figure out what it was he could do to catch this man by surprise. He knew that if he was going to do that, he was first going to have to believe in himself and that he was capable of beating him. But was he? Was he fooling himself to think that he had a chance to overthrow the king? History has always taught us that it's not always easy to force a monarchy off their throne. Not to mention the fact that situations like that often end with one of the battling parties losing their lives. He was a young man trying to play for keeps with a man who didn't play by anyone's rules. He always stared high in the sky when he stood in front of the Star Tower; it was a twisted feeling being in that position. Even after all that he had been through in the city, there was a part of Jonathan that still stood in awe of his surroundings. It wasn't in the way that he expected but he had still come a long way. He never quite imagined it being like this; there he was in his $1,200 suit still finding himself playing the outsider role. It was a cruel irony that didn't want to let up, he had to travel that far and go through all of that only to find himself in the same emotional position he was in when he left Winterville, but even that was a lie. He wasn't the same nor was his position on the emotional spectrum; that would almost be considered a compliment compared to where he was now. At least back in Winterville he wasn't caught up in some extended wind of calamity.

His attitude was crisp and ready, he felt sharper as he became keenly aware of what was going on around him. He steadily observed the hustle and bustle of people who were going to and fro from their daily activities. He felt the slight encounter of people who minutely bumped into and brushed up against him, from their lack of attention to what was going on; they were too busy on their smartphones and preparing for their next meeting. Now he could understand why all these worker ants acted the way they did, he could relate to what it meant to be at the disposal of the Queen or in this case the King. He walked in, through a sea of worker drones all going about their own lies, instead of lives because they didn't know that they were pawns being used for the corporate endgame for others. All the way up he took short breathes as if preparing to submerge himself under water. Like an athlete prepares before performing, it was game time and there was no choice but to show up and perform. Now how he would perform was up to him, this wasn't the time for fear, there was too much at stake for Jonathan to make this about himself.

When he arrived to that familiar sanctum he saw that same receptionist that was there when he made his first trip to Mr. Edwards' office. She had that bright red lip gloss on again; it was what stood out the most and what she would be remembered for. It distracted one's eyes from noticing anything else. "Mr. Cross, so good to see you, Mr. Edwards is expecting you" she said. Jonathan had never walked around the whole top level but there were a few other offices on the floor. They were all impressive spaces fit for other expensive important people. But there weren't as many offices like there were on the other floors, it was only a few people toward the upper part of the ladder at Star Industries. He fixed his tie and buttoned the middle button of his jacket. He made his way to Edwards' office; he paused for another second, looked down and noticed that the door was already cracked open. Not entirely cracked however, it looked as if it were completely closed if someone wasn't paying attention. Jonathan had to pay attention, right now he couldn't afford to miss anything; the price could prove to be detrimental. He grabbed the door knob and tightened his grip, he closed his eyes for a second and clinched his teeth; he was about to enter into the lion's den. He pushed the door open with his hand still wrapped around the door knob tightly. The office was always imposing, it was so regal, so powerful, and it was an extension of its owner. There was an eerie quietness that floated in the room, like a monster in the dark that tip toed around the office, imposing its invisible fear. Jonathan looked straight ahead at the giant windows that acted as glass walls which ran from top to bottom. Giving anyone who looked out of them an instantaneous feeling of sovereignty; with such a view of the city it was almost impossible how anyone could stare out of it on a daily basis and not begin to develop some sort of complex. In the midst of all of that, there he was staring out the massive floor to ceiling windows with his back toward everything else including Jonathan. He was wearing a navy blue suit. Even his clothes could be deceptive; the suit presented itself to be black however with a closer look its true color would be revealed.

"Scotch?" asked Mr. Edwards holding it up with his right hand. The light from the sun pierced through the glass, making the scotch look like liquid gold. "You know I'm not really in the drinking mood" said Jonathan sarcastically. In the seam of his sarcasm there was anger and frustration waiting in the wings "Do you remember the first thing that I told you, when you entered this office?" he asked. "I don't know Kane, do you?" Jonathan boldly replied with sarcasm but this time with more anger and frustration in the forefront of his voice. "Don't play games with me boy!!" Mr. Edwards shouted as he turned around violently almost tearing his suit as he moved like a sidewinding viper. Jonathan stood his ground in the flesh but on the inside he was afraid, he was trying not to be but he didn't know how all of this would end. He couldn't be too surprised, he knew that there was a possibility that he would tangle with the beast. "Don't toy with me, I own this city and everything in it!" "I've got it by the jugular and if I decide at whatever point in time to snap its neck or slit its throat I can do just that!" "Boy I can outstretch my arm and break you at a moment's notice!" "I AM POWER, I AM INFLUENCE!!" "So I'll ask you only one-more-time, do you or do you not remember what I told you before?!?" Jonathan knew he was in the presence of a wild beast, like one of the big cats in the wild. He had to maintain eye contact which proved to be increasingly difficult, especially as Mr. Edwards inched his way closer to Jonathan as he was shouting to what sounded like the top of his lungs. However, he couldn't look away and run, if an animal runs away from a predator in the wild, it has permanently labeled itself as prey. "Never insult prestige" replied Jonathan; he said it firmly without wavering. Mr. Edwards stood there with the glass still in his hand after hearing Jonathan's response his anger subsided and he reverted back to his normal state. He took another sip of his Scotch. "You know why I chose you?" asked Mr. Edwards "No" responded Jonathan. "Wait, what do you mean you chose me?" asked Jonathan. Mr. Edwards took yet another sip of his fading glass of Scotch. "When you came up to me that night at the museum, you made a decision about me and I made one about you." "I saw it in you" said Mr. Edwards. Jonathan was beyond bored and irritated of hearing these loose riddles. "You saw what?" asked Jonathan in a more demanding tone. Mr. Edwards smirked, still insulting Jonathan by not answering the question straight forwardly. "I saw something that I haven't see in anyone that I've come into contact with." "There were those who got close a few times but only to discover they were counterfeit." "I saw me Jonathan; I saw myself in you." "I saw my mirror image so to speak" said Mr. Edwards.

Jonathan was disgusted by that comparison. "I'm nothing like you" he stated, "Oh but you're everything like me, Jonathan." said Mr. Edwards. "I asked you want you wanted in life on the first night we met" "And you gave me the answer that I give myself on a daily basis; everything." "You said you wanted everything." "As do I Jonathan, as do I." Said Mr. Edwards "Right then, I knew what I was looking at." "I was looking at myself occupying another body" said Mr. Edwards. "That's not something a man gets to see every day and when he does, he has to seize that opportunity of immortality." As he was speaking there was a sadistic sparkle dancing around his eyes. "I thought you had it but I had to be sure, so I tested you even further." "Your will and resolve boy is second only to myself." "Who do you think orchestrated your little tussle that night back at your old apartment?" asked Mr. Edwards; as those words left his mouth, it felt like a vehement rushing wind hit Jonathan dead in the chest. His palms moistened almost immediately to the point that a few drops of sweat hit the floor. He felt his throat almost close in on him; his body and his mind were both in shock. "Wha…What…what did you say?" asked Jonathan; his voice now shaking from the amount of adrenaline rushing through his veins. His mind going back to the agony he felt lying on the cold pavement after he had just got the life almost completely beat out of him. Then his mind took him back to the last time he was in Mr. Edwards house, back when he witnessed the man tied to that chair who barely escaped with his life. Then he remembered there was a man who was there who had these piercing, cold eyes. Jonathan remembered that he looked familiar to him but he couldn't quite put his finger on it. Now he knew what it was, it was those eyes, they were the same eyes he saw that night in the parking garage through the ski mask. He was obviously some hired gun that Mr. Edwards had used to do his dirty work. "You son of a…" yelled Jonathan. "Don't…don't be so emotional boy, it clouds your judgment makes you feeble", replied Mr. Edwards; who had now taken a few more steps toward Jonathan like a lion going in for the kill. "You don't need the heavy weight of emotions clouding up your judgment; you already have that pretty Ms. Monroe distracting you enough". "You know you should be on your knees by now thanking me" he continued. By this time he had moved up even closer and was now in Jonathan's face. He was close enough to see Jonathan's eyes starting to swell but he refused to let a single tear flow from his face. "You should consider yourself and Ms. Monroe lucky." "Lucky I didn't send Percy over there while she was home, I could have had him snap her pretty little neck at a moment's…"

But before he could finish the last part of his sentence, that animal in Jonathan caused him to do the unthinkable. Jonathan introduced Mr. Edwards to his cousin right cross. He struck him as hard and fast as he could with one good solid punch to the face. It didn't register what he had just done until his fist had followed through with the punch. Jonathan took a step back and put his hands up as if he were a boxer ready to strike again. "You see that's what I'm talking about, it's in you, I'M in you" said Mr. Edwards. He still managed to keep his balance and hold onto his glass of scotch despite the fact that he had just been pelted by a young man half his age. Then he quickly dropped his glass and backhanded Jonathan, although Jonathan had taken a step back, he was still within reach. Jonathan stumbled slightly before he caught his footing. "What do you want?!" screamed Jonathan. "YOU, if you would stop acting like a child and get focused I can mold you into my image!" responded Mr. Edwards. "Everything I have can be yours and together we can build and conquer more!" "It could be Edge City today and tomorrow the WORLD!" "You have a choice to make boy and I'll expect a final answer by tomorrow" "Percy will see you out" said Mr. Edwards. With tears still fighting to be released he turned around and there was Percy, the juggernaut himself.

He stood 6'4 solid as a rock, arms cocked to the side ready to snap anyone in half who dared to challenge his alpha male existence. He was a man of few words and this moment was no exception. His giant muscular body language suggested that Jonathan get out now or suffer the lethal consequences. He wiped his mouth and walked out the door with Percy towering behind. "Oh and Jonathan" said Mr. Edwards. Percy then moved out of the way so Jonathan could see Mr. Edwards when he turned around, "I'm sure by now you realize that I don't take no for an answer" said Mr. Edwards; Jonathan stood there letting his silent anger do all the talking. Then he thought about something more calming but yet still perplexing, he promptly remembered the fact that he had a million dollars of Mr. Edwards' money sitting nicely in his account. Seeing as to how they had just had such a heart to heart encounter, there was no harm in asking one more question. "The money…what was it for?" asked Jonathan, in a quiet tone it was only a few decibels away from a whisper. He was too drained to say it any louder. Mr. Edwards shook his head and knocked off the last drop of scotch from his glass. "Insurance" he replied. He then turned around returning to another day in the life of an Edge City Kingpin. Percy resumed his foreboding presence and saw Jonathan out. Jonathan made his way through the building in complete silence. He was speechless, and emotionally burnt out from that overwhelming experience. He licked his wounds all the way back to his car; he watched his reflection in the driver side window as he opened the door. Seeing himself, he couldn't help but ask if all this was real and if any of that actually happened. The answer was yes to both questions. He then got in the car and sat down. He put the key in the ignition and started the drive back home; it would be a long ride with nothing but his thoughts and recent memories to keep him company. As he drove off, the truth rode with him. He had challenged the monarchy and he was found wanting. After all, if Kane Edwards was like a chess player thinking at least several moves ahead, Jonathan was faced with one question glaring at him for the rest of the ride home. What's a pawn to a King?

CHAPTER FOURTEEN
THE BEGINNING

<u>3 DAYS LATER,</u> It was only minimal, not substantial enough to measure. The few days that went by purchased Jonathan only a little time to ponder, just enough to throw around a few ideas of how he was going to do it. How was he going to escape? How was he going to run? Could he rise from under the strong hand of his oppressor? It was beyond time to leave the stone hearted puppet master. His mother was gone, she was safely and mundanely nestled back home in Winterville. Home was the safe haven, it was the last place he thought he ever wanted to be but now it didn't seem as bad as Jonathan thought it was. After all the things he had been through in Edge City he could use a nice stretch of normalcy. He had signed his verbal contract with Mr. Edwards two days ago; he told him that he was in. It was pointless to attempt to say anything but what Mr. Edwards wanted to hear. After their intense rendezvous two days ago, it left Jonathan with an uneven; bitter taste in his mouth. It was like he was bleeding on the inside of his mouth, and the blood was spilling onto his tongue. Blood and the tinge of its unpleasant copper aftertaste filled his mouth. The brain always registers that taste as an alert; that something was wrong. That somehow along the way the body took a hit somewhere and caused the life source of the body to flow freely.

From their last encounter things had started to come into a raw focus, details had begun to emerge from the deep and they brought pain with them. Jonathan still struggled with the knowledge of knowing that Mr. Edwards had orchestrated his private beat down session in the parking deck of his own building. It was enough to sit him down quietly in his loft with the lights off and his brain on. This man was beyond anything he had ever come into contact with. It was past Jonathan's rationale the things that Mr. Edwards had put him through. It was more than enough for Jonathan to give the words that were spoken to him a few days ago, brief unwanted credence. It made him think and occasionally go stand in front of his mirror. Was there even a hint of truth to what Mr. Edwards had said to him? This is what reluctantly replayed over in Jonathan's mind. After all he had to admit to himself that it was his tenacious hunger for more that caused him to move to Edge City in the first place. He had a burning desire for more when he approached Mr. Edwards that night at the museum. These things combined took up some space in his subconscious. Was it possible that he somehow did this to himself? Was there really a possibility that Jonathan had something in common with Mr. Edwards? Jonathan thought about it for a moment; he received some inner comfort because he knew he could never do some of the things that Mr. Edwards had done. Jonathan knew he couldn't have sent someone to break into the Mayor's house to plant evidence in order to make sure that the person stayed either in his pocket or out of his way. Either way it didn't work for him, to do such a thing, it was already becoming too taxing on him to be constantly looking over his shoulder just from working with the man. He didn't even want to think about how he'd have to watch himself if he were the main figurehead. He didn't want to have to deal with any added trouble; he had enough of that for himself. This wasn't the time for uncertainty he had to make a move; he just didn't know how to go about it. He was in his bedroom and spent a nice amount of time in the same spot for the past few days. He spent time with Rachel here and there but for a change she wasn't the sole thought in his mind. This was about him and nothing else; anything extra came with a hefty price tag. During the last few times that the two of them had spoken, he managed to contradict his previous thoughts by suggesting that Rachel leave with him. Mr. Edwards had given Jonathan a twisted offer; it was the most narcissistic thing that

Jonathan had ever heard of. He had been around Mr. Edwards long enough to know that he needed to look below the surface. He didn't just want to pass Jonathan the iron throne; this was a chance at immortality for Mr. Edwards. If he taught Jonathan all that he knew and raised him up to take over his empire, it would make him immortal so to speak.

Jonathan got a glimpse of the future during one of his little think tank sessions that involved him staring out of his windows for hours on end. During one of the sessions Jonathan saw himself in a sick version of the future, if by some insane chance he really took the lunatic's deal. He saw himself as an older more unruly man with a heart of stone. He had dull evil in his eyes from being overrun by all the hate, perversion of power, and pride. It was now him who ruled with shadowy methods. By then he would have surpassed Mr. Edwards's territory and ran all of Edge City, he had his hands in the surrounding states looking to expand and possibly take over the country. Nothing was off limits from his now debased mind, illegal gambling, drug smuggling, racketeering; the works. Everything was permissible, all desires snatched with a vengeance. By this point, Jonathan was now older so his mother was long gone. Rachel was lost forever, she would have represented the last real connection with anyone he had and proof that he was once a real human being. He was alone, just him and his black kingdom built on blood, intimidation, fear and any other device that could be used against someone to get what he wanted. What kind of life was that? What kind of existence would this prove to be? It was simple really, none that Jonathan wanted to be a part of. It made him physically sick for him to even think about it for longer than a minute; this proved to be actually true and not just metaphorical. He had actually thrown up the other day while trying to imagine this alternative world where he wasn't a man who he had chosen to be, but was a man that someone else told him to be. That version of himself wasn't a man of power, not by a long shot. Jonathan knew the opposite to be true; he knew that he would only be acting like a trained animal in the zoo. Only acting out a routine that the trainer taught him and he refused to go out like that. He still believed in himself too much to settle for some vile version of what he dreamed about all the time back in Winterville. This wasn't how he was going to end up; he would rather die than to be that person. Jonathan had to be who he wanted to be. Even after recent events, he still found himself wondering what that man was like. At least now he knew one thing for sure, the kind of man Mr. Edwards wanted him to be wasn't the kind he wanted to be. In the back of his mind he wondered if he could still attain the same dream he wanted if only he could wake up from this nightmare and pursue the real thing. The real fulfillment that he originally hoped for, this mode of thinking alone caused him internal problems. Here he was in a situation that started from him chasing a dream, even though in his current circumstances things had gone awry, he still wanted the original dream. The think tank sessions showed themselves to sometimes be unkind to Jonathan's mind. He would still flirt with the notion that Mr. Edwards was right about a few things. Did he see something in him that Jonathan didn't see? If there was something there, was it something that could cause him to turn out like that deranged man?

It wasn't a good road to try and go down; he didn't need to think about the road he just needed to get off it. Despite the anxiety he knew that he had to leave, there was just no other way around it. Silver Edge City had become a place he no longer wanted to be, or at least as long as Kane Edwards lived in it. For it to be a place of opportunity and higher heights it felt like he had been duped. Perhaps it was immature of him to blame a city for his mistakes or his ongoing sense of naivety. Either way, things didn't pan out the way he wanted them too, it was ugly but true. He would go for walks down the street by himself. He always liked to walk during the day possibly subconsciously he was avoiding walking alone at night due to that beating he took in the parking lot. It was still an unreal feeling to discover that the man he was working for and thought could show and teach him many great things of life could be capable of such treachery and dark hearted evil. That in itself was mind blowing; it was the kind of person that Jonathan had never seen before. He read about people like that in books or maybe a TV show or something but the reality was more gruesome. He discovered that Mr. Edwards had an invisible presence about him that could travel beyond his own body. It was like he had a way of being around a person even if he wasn't really around. He could take up residence in the thought life of other people; it was a dangerous skill that he had mastered. Jonathan was experiencing it at that moment by worrying about the situation. It was like he was walking with him on the street corner during the day; so Jonathan closed his eyes and thought of himself somewhere else. He stopped walking so he wouldn't walk right into an oncoming car. It looked odd to those around him watching a young man suddenly stop on the sidewalk and close his eyes. It didn't matter; he couldn't worry about how he would be perceived by people that he didn't even know. He had to do what he had to. He could feel the warmth from the sun hitting his body as he heard the sounds of the city talking in his ear. He heard the sound of a young child walking with their mother. "What's that man doing mommy?" "Come on just keep walking honey." He overheard their interaction but he still stood there with his eyes shut. He heard even more footsteps walking around him and the sound of cars driving by, brakes squeaking, horns honking, and a few occasional birds chirping and flying overhead. The city kept speaking but he kept focusing on how he wasn't going to let Mr. Edwards get the better of him. Mr. Edwards wasn't invincible; Jonathan knew that it wasn't impossible to get out of this, but it proved difficult. Then without warning everything got quiet and for a few moments he heard and saw nothing. Then he heard Rachel's voice began to echo in the back of his mind, with every passing second he could hear her more clearly. This wasn't a mushy dream sequence taking place he was remembering when Rachel told him something about Mr. Edwards. She told him about how Mr. Edward's childhood and earlier years were somewhat of a mystery, nothing beyond general information. Maybe there was something there for Jonathan to use, it might prove to be a long shot but he needed some sort of shot at this point. "Really kid?!" a man shouted as he bumped into Jonathan, Jonathan opened his eyes it was another business man wearing a suit and tie like the rest of the blue collar army that marched around the city. He looked Jonathan up and down in disgust wondering what his problem was, as he turned around and went about his daily grind in the city. Jonathan collected himself and looked around; he noticed things around him didn't stop moving just because he might have. Life kept going, this was an indication that the world didn't revolve around Jonathan and the world certainly did revolve around Mr. Edwards or Silver Edge City for that matter.

If he was going to break away from the iron fist, first he needed to face it head on. He pulled out his phone and scrolled to Adrian's name; he stopped and looked at it for a moment he didn't know what he was going to do. What was he thinking? Was he even thinking at all? It's not like he was going to pick up the phone and tell Adrian to go screw himself and that he was just going to ride out into the sunset. Although nobody referred to Mr. Edwards as The Don, that still didn't mean that they didn't have that mafia mentality, so he needed to be careful. That much was already made perfectly clear, he had enough threats and shady side missions to last him for the next twenty years. All he needed was a black jacket, a silencer, and a moody demeanor and he could fill Adrian's spot. He put his phone back in his pocket; took a deep breath and headed back to his apartment. He continued his observatory session as he headed back. His mind still going ahead of him down the highway of seemingly endless thoughts. Was this the last time he was going to walk down these busy streets? Would he ever again look up in awe of the towering metal giants that planted themselves all over the city? Would he leave Edge City and never look back? Then his mind while still riding down the expressway of thoughts decided to change lanes. What did Mr. Edwards mean, when they spoke a few days ago and he said something about the money deposited to Jonathan's account was for insurance? Insurance for what? That man could often speak in riddles, leaving Jonathan to try and figure out the solution to the puzzle. That's why this all must have been a game to Mr. Edwards but then again passing his business empire to someone else; one would assume was serious business for the King Pin. Back at Jonathan's place, it was quiet, it was nice to look at with all its furniture and the decent view but it was dead. Maybe that was an invisible yet tangible reflection of its owner. Even Jonathan had to admit that in light of recent events he did feel a bit on the zombie side. He supposed that it was an inevitable feeling; the place wasn't really dead but it was his perception being projected onto his surroundings. His perception was all foggy at this point, everything around the corner felt like gloom and doom. He closed the door and like clockwork he heard that old familiar sound, his phone was ringing at the top of its volume meter. It was Rachel's name that came up on the caller ID. He had to admit he was happy that she called. "I could use a friendly voice" he answered "Hey where are you, are you at home?" she asked "You know I'm not sure if I'm comfortable in still referring to Edge City as my home" he said. "It hasn't been the most welcoming of places" "I'm serious" said Rachel. "Yea…yea, I just got in what's up? "I'm on my way up" she said. "What?!? Rachel seriously come on we talked about this" "It's not the best time for you to be here right now" he said. She hung up the phone after he said that. "Rachel... Hello?" "Great", he mumbled to himself as he tossed the phone over the back of the couch in the living room. He aimed it right so that it wouldn't hit the floor. The next thing he heard was a knock at the door, the sound came in like a loud thump. It almost didn't sound like it was complete; Jonathan ran his right hand over the back of his head. "That was fast" he said under his breath as if she might've heard him if he said it any louder.

He opened the door; he could smell her perfume wafting into the room as he continued to pull the door open. "Well, I'd say this is a pleasant surprise but it's neither pleasant nor a surprise", said Jonathan. This was the first time he felt any emotion toward Rachel other than the normal blushing crush that made him feel like a little boy at times. This emotional perplexity wasn't solely the work of Rachel; the city accompanied by a certain turn of events had something to do with that as well. She was dressed down in a white shirt and grey sweatpants, hair in a ponytail with a pair of white sneakers that looked as if this was their first stroll out of the box they were purchased in. This was the least glamorous Jonathan had seen her since he met her, although he was too irritated to comment on it he still noticed. "Why are you.." She walked in and politely brushed passed him interrupting what he was about to say; in the middle of his sentence. "I have to talk to you" she said. He looked down the hallway as he closed the door making sure there were no henchmen behind her, lying in wait. He was about to ask her if she had been followed over here, then he realized that it didn't matter. He could rest assured that Mr. Edwards was probably very much aware of the whereabouts of the two of them. He had already proven enough that he had eyes in the sky. "You want to talk about what Rachel? he asked. She had a big sized burgundy handbag with her; she sat it down beside her as she plopped down on the couch, and immediately tucked in her legs as she got comfortable. A part of him was glad to see her but he wasn't going to allow himself to be overrun by his feelings for her, not today. "Just listen you're going to want to hear this" she said, "Really, Rachel do you have some sort of death wish? Your apartment wasn't enough for you?" "You want Percy to sling you around like some rag doll" he said. "Ok really Jonathan, I come see you and you act like this?" replied Rachel in a swift tone of voice. "Look I'm here so can you just talk to me or do you really want me to go?" she asked. She stared back at him and waited for his answer. Her eyes were like a dark emerald field awaiting its landing. She wanted to hear him tell her to stay. Jonathan sighed, and put his hands on his hips as he hung his head looking at his shoes. "No, stay" he said as he looked back at her in her eyes. "You're already here now, so just…" "Like I was saying" Rachel interrupted. "You're going to want to hear this" she said as she pulled out a manila folder from her purse. Jonathan walked over to the couch and sat down next to her, the couch was soft; Jonathan leaned back so he could rest for a moment. He opened up the folder and it was a picture of Adrian and what looked like a printed out copy of a birth certificate. He picked up the pieces of paper and sifted through them for a swift overview of each page not fully looking at what was on each one. Another page was a copy of Adrian's driver's license. "What is this?" he asked looking at Rachel confused. "I started to do some digging and called in a few favors that were due" she said. Just by the look of her there was something behind her eyes and voice like she knew something "And?" asked Jonathan. "Jonathan, Adrian isn't all who he says he is" she continued. "There's more to his and Edwards' story than they let on" she said. She was now leaning forward as if she was in anticipation for something. "For starters that's not his real name" said Rachel. Jonathan held the page that was a copy of his driver's license. It showed Adrian's mean stiff mugged face and his name, Adrian Daniels. "How do you know that?" asked Jonathan. "Like I said I called in some favors" "I had a few reporter friends in who in turn had a few other friends that helped me obtain some information." "I had to dig real deep, hospital records, cross checks, the whole nine" she said

"They traced that name back and it only went back ten years" she continued. "What do you mean?" asked Jonathan. He held the paper and then looked at Rachel. "So Adrian isn't his real name?" asked Jonathan; trying to understand where she was going with this.

"Well that's what I thought too at first." She said "Then I did some more digging" Rachel said. "You know how Mr. Edwards never really talks too much about his past" she said. "Yea" replied Jonathan; still wondering where she was going with all of this. "Well, I found his birth certificate" she said. "He was born in Harbor Stone, as Kane Emil Edwards." Harbor Stone was another big city located a few states up north. Jonathan had heard of it before but barely recognized the name. "He was born to Ivan and Cassandra Edwards in 1956", she continued as she rattled off newly discovered facts. Jonathan grabbed the corresponding pieces of paper to both match and keep up with what she was saying. "They died in 1974 from a tragic yet mysterious fire at their home", she said. "But here comes the interesting part" she proclaimed. "They were a big well to do family, I mean completely loaded" "In the event of their untimely death, their $75 Million Dollar worth of assets was to be split between their two children" she said; looking at Jonathan with a soft yet intense look on her face, waiting for him to catch on. "Wait, what did you say?" asked Jonathan; his face squeezing together and contorting making his invisible confusion now visible on his face. "What do you mean two children? he asked. "So you're saying he has a…" Jonathan looked at Rachel and then back over to the manila folder filled with white paper that contained the long and forgotten history of what probably at one time seemed like a normal family. These pages held hidden secrets that once put together told a very vivid story; it wasn't for the faint of heart. His eyes continued to look over the black and white pieces of the puzzle, turning each page while developing a growing devotion to each one as he flipped through them wanting to see what they had to say. He paused realizing that familiar silence was back but was it really familiar? Something about it was different; that same eerie presence void of sound. This silence wasn't built on an awkwardness that Jonathan had grown accustomed to. This silence was built on the foundation of revelatory knowledge that rushed in like a titan wind. It filled the room and those who were in the room had to keep quiet to marvel at its wisdom. Until finally the side effect of its revealing truth wore off. "Adrian is his brother" said Jonathan, his eyes now widening. The piece of paper he held in his hand was a copy of Adrian's original birth certificate; he was born in 1961 as Carl Alexander Edwards. "So he's his younger brother" said Jonathan. His mind started to pick up speed while still on a high from the new information. "Wait, you said something about a fire when they were kids?" asked Jonathan. "Yea, according to the report from the fire department they ruled out arson but they never really determined the source of the fire", she further explained. "But one of the lead investigators went on record saying he wasn't completely convinced that foul play wasn't involved" she commented. "Well, what happened to him?" asked Jonathan. "I tried to track him down but the trail was ice cold he disappeared years later after that case; drove his wife nuts" Rachel replied. "If he didn't die somewhere back then I'm sure he's probably dead now", she said. "That was so long ago, Edwards was eighteen years old so that means Adrian...or should I say Carl was..." "Thirteen" said Jonathan. His mind had learned a new method of thinking while he was in Edge City; it was operating differently but in a good way.

"Wait" said Jonathan. "I remember seeing Adrian's hand back at the office" said Jonathan. Now it was Rachel's turn to be enlightened, "Ok you saw his hand" she said sarcastically. "No, seriously have you ever noticed his left hand, it was severely burned" "He was obviously there the night that it happened" Jonathan concluded. Rachel paused for a moment. She then reached for the manila folder. "You know now that you mention it, I did remember reading something about the injuries he sustained that night, and yea they were both there" she said. "I've actually never noticed his hand" said Rachel. It wasn't hard to believe really, she wasn't around Adrian that much and who could blame her, he wasn't the friendly type. Besides that, Jonathan noticed that from time to time Adrian would wear black gloves. It added to his already stony demeanor. "That's it!" exclaimed Jonathan; his eyes lit up like a child on Christmas morning. "That's his weakness, his weak link in the chain" said Jonathan. His eyes glaring off into the distance staring at something he thought he would never see again…hope. Rachel looked confused but intrigued as she sat next to him; studying over the face of the man she had come to love. "What do you mean?" "What are you talking about?" she asked inquisitively. "The signs were there but there was no way I would have even known they were there" he said; in a rambling manner. "Jonathan?" asked Rachel, "What are you talking about?" she asked still puzzled. The conversation had changed gears so to speak it and it was now Jonathan's turn to share. "Adrian is his weakness; his Achilles" Jonathan further explained. "Like his undying love for his little brother, because he doesn't seem like the type" said Rachel. "No, he's not the type" "That's the point", said Jonathan "I mean seriously look at their relationship, neither one acknowledges the other in that way." said Jonathan. His mind still piecing this almost overload of information together. "Now that I think about it, every single time Adrian was referring to Mr. Edwards he never said his name" "Adrian never once said his name" said Jonathan. Rachel still wasn't following just yet. "Adrian never said Kane's name….Ever!" "He has always referred to him, as he or him" said Jonathan. "I mean just think about it, he suffered third degree burns as a boy from a fire I'm willing to bet Mr. Edwards started!" "You said it yourself they had a huge sum of money coming their way once their parents were gone" said Jonathan. "Evil must start young in that family" "He probably grew up idolizing his brother and serving his every whim and need" "Now that they're grown men, Adrian still works for him and does his bidding like when they were kids" said Jonathan; leaning into Rachel's face more and more with each revealing thought that came bursting into his mind to shed new insight on what was going on. "Rachel, Adrian hates him!" shouted Jonathan. "I know he does!" said Jonathan. Rachel understood what Jonathan was saying but she looked as if she needed more convincing. "But he's like his right hand" she said. Think about it, how would you feel about someone who murdered your parents for money and used you as a slave and never acknowledged you as family?" Jonathan asked.

"But we don't really know that Mr. Edwards started that fire" she said. Jonathan stared at her letting his facial expressions say things that his mouth didn't know how to put into words. "Ok, so maybe you do have a point after all" said Rachel; coming from the realm of reasonable doubt to the land of common sense, where harsh realities love to roam the streets from time to time. She knew he was right, who else would have started the mystery fire and why was it a mystery in the first place? Mr. Edwards probably paid off someone to fudge up the evidence even back then he had access to insurmountable resources. The two of them could only imagine what happened to that lead investigator, his body could be in some floor board somewhere in an old abandoned house that no one would ever find. "So you're saying that Adrian would do what exactly?" Rachel asked. "I'm saying that he's his false positive, a weakness he dubs strength, a foe he calls a friend" said Jonathan. "With the right push he would betray him, I'm surprised he hasn't shot him in his sleep by now" Jonathan replied. "Adrian's like a house of cards that if touched the wrong way ever so slightly the whole thing will come tumbling down" said Jonathan. "Yea but Jonathan, I mean maybe he doesn't hate him like that", questioned Rachel; for the first time doubting herself. "He scarred that man physically and emotionally and turned him into some kind of harbinger of death" "He loathes him" said Jonathan. The two of them sat there on the couch in silence for a few minutes, Jonathan was feeling better about himself and this situation that he thought was impossible to escape. It didn't seem so impossible now; for once there was a light in Jonathan's eyes when he thought about what he had gotten himself into. He didn't have a smoking gun just yet but he had something real to go on. Jonathan wouldn't try to get him on things that Mr. Edwards had done while he was in the city simply because if Jonathan ratted on him he would be implicating himself as well. That wasn't a part of the plan; he wanted to leave Mr. Edwards drowning in his own misery and corruption, not join him. So he would have to find a way to prove all of this information from Mr. Edwards past to the police without room for doubt. He had theory and motive but he knew he needed that smoking gun. Although this time the smoking gun was more likely to be in the form of an actual person, Adrian. If he could prove that Mr. Edwards did all of this, then he could knock down the King Pin. He could leave Edge City or stay if he wanted because Mr. Edwards would be off the street. The bottom line is he would be free; he could go about his life and get back to going after his real dream, not this horrible nightmare of a facade that he ran into. As the two of them sat there next to each other, Rachel slid her way over to Jonathan and rested in his arms. He held her for a while, breathing in deep and taking in his options with each breath. Then as he laid there, the light scent of Rachel's hair dancing around his nose; propped himself up. Rachel inevitably came up with him since he was holding her; he was responding to the entrance of another important thought that came into his mind.

"Hey, when did you find all of this out?" asked Jonathan. "Between last night and this morning, I had some of my connections help and then I got what I could from some of the hospitals" "Also some deep digging in public records and some dot connecting" "Why?" asked Rachel; as Jonathan loosened his grip from her. He was thinking about the whole keeping tabs thing that Mr. Edwards was so good at. "Are you sure you weren't followed?" he asked. "It's just that if this information was so top secret wouldn't he have some way of being tipped off if someone was getting too warm on the trail?" asked Jonathan. Rachel looked up at him with those beautiful eyes, she was smart but Jonathan was learning to think ahead. "I don't know" she replied. Then without warning there was a very swift and loud THUNDEROUS CRACK that came from the door. It all happened quickly; the sounds of the door coming off the hinges, the mixture of sounds coming from different materials all played a collective beat that made its own rhythm. The sound of the wooden door cracking and splitting open, coupled with the nails and screws coming off and shooting into different directions all made for a frightening symphony. Rachel screamed and jumped like in a horror scene out of a scary movie. Her eyes told her fear as Jonathan looked back at the door in suspenseful dread. Her screams alone shot that wrongful fear into Jonathan's life yet again, but this time the fear seemed to come at him with a vengeance. It was like a violent wave smacked him hard with no cause for intrusion and no explanation, it was just there and it expected obedience. It demanded fear to come from whoever it came into contact with. Jonathan's eyes were trying to make the origin of where this entire vehement act of destruction was coming from. His mind knew it was the door; he was looking at it come undone by its side. His eyes stayed on what was going on even though his body wasn't really responding in the manner he wanted it to. He watched as the hulking figure behind this assault revealed itself, it was Percy. He had on a black suit this time; it was fitting for the occasion as he was probably there to deliver death to the both of them. It seemed like everything in the room was moving in slow motion, everything except Percy. He appeared to be moving at regular speed which was an intimidating sight to see. Rachel screamed again as Percy drew nearer, her scream was played out in slow motion but only for a few seconds. The high pitch of her cries scratched Jonathan's ears as they slapped him back into reality. Percy came from behind the couch where they were sitting. His 6'4" frame towered over them. He was a well-built man and had the height to go with the size. Jonathan lunged at him from behind the couch. Jonathan was young but with a 6'ft frame, he was better built than most guys his age unless they played sports. Though Percy just didn't have an advantage of height but his build was far more superior in every way. Percy carried with him what looked like years of weightlifting experience; you could see his muscles protruding from his suit. If you looked closely you could see his veins in his biceps showing through, he was built like an ancient gladiator ready for war. He didn't look like a man who was born but one who was created somewhere in a lab. He caught Jonathan by the throat in midair, wrapping his heavy hand almost completely around his neck. He slammed him down hard on the wooden floor. The living room was an open space flowing into the kitchen which is almost where Jonathan landed from the sheer force of Percy's throw. Jonathan slid a little bit on the floor before stopping. He now had a full view from the floor and looked at Percy's mountain size back. He wasn't like Adrian. Percy was a whole other creature. He was an intense storm brewing in the midst of ordinary people with his fierce gust of wind ripping apart anyone who dared to get too close. He was beyond the bronze, he was the gold like some ancient Greek warrior from the days of old whose life story was carved somewhere in timeworn stone. Jonathan could see Percy grab Rachel, she was screaming as he yanked her by her hair and held one of her arms. "Noooo!" hollered Jonathan. He got back up and charged at Percy again. He never thought he would have done something like this; go toe to toe with a force like Percy. Guess he had Mr. Edwards to thank for that, his time in the city matured him. Although, he would have preferred that the methods had been different, he did experience some change in himself and now it was time to use some of that change. He ran at Percy as fast as he could, he didn't have a lot of room to gain tons of momentum but he used what he had. He screamed as he ran into him, going low as if he were playing football he aimed at Percy's midsection, barely missing Rachel's fragile body that was dangling in front of him "Agh!" he screamed as he smashed up against Percy's iron clad wall of a body. Jonathan wrapped his arms around Percy's waist as quickly as he could, trying to subdue him and drive him backward. For a second Percy slightly stumbled back losing some of his footing as he continued to hold Rachel while she was kicking and screaming. At the same time Jonathan was trying to tackle him. Percy then let Rachel go by slinging her over the couch, unfortunately for Jonathan, this now meant Percy could focus directly on him. Jonathan felt something on Percy's waist pressing against the inside of his forearm as he was squeezing with all his might. Percy looked down, lifted his right arm in midair, and hurled it back downward with his fist crashing into Jonathan's back. "Ahh!" shouted Jonathan; the pain was immediate and sharp as a sword. He felt it so hard it was like the pain traveled from his back and passed through his stomach. It buckled Jonathan to his knees. Whatever was around Percy's waist, Jonathan felt it drop to the floor with him; he may not have seen it but he felt and heard it. The next thing he knew he felt two large hands pulling him up from the floor, it was clear that Percy wasn't finished. He pulled and straightened him up enough so he could do some more damage and damage he did. He fired off a hard left jab to Jonathan's stomach; his fist sinking in enough to make a solid thud sound. Percy followed through with the punch as if her were trying to reach for Jonathan's spine. Jonathan gasped as his knees buckled again but Percy wouldn't let him fall. He held him up and hit him again. The last blow being worse than the first as he kept swinging, giving him hard and steady blows to his stomach until Jonathan threw up. It didn't take long it was about three more hard knocks to the stomach that made everything that was in it come out. Jonathan was down; he couldn't breathe. "Ugh" was the only word Percy had uttered in disgust of Jonathan throwing up over some of his left arm and leg. Jonathan dropped to his knees still trying to breathe as he was fighting to get air but felt like he couldn't. Percy put his hand on Jonathan's head and pushed it to the side, so he would fall all the way over, this was his way of dismissing Jonathan's petty efforts of trying to stand in his way.

Jonathan could hear himself gasping and wheezing. He was

curled almost to a fetal position rocking back and forth on the floor. His body, craving for air as if it had forgotten what it was like to breathe. He was in so much pain. His ears heard more screaming while he caught a glimpse of Percy slapping Rachel across the face. Then he heard nothing. It was a wonder no one heard any of this going on. There were no neighbors to the rescue but then again it was in the middle of the day so most people were probably at work. Although, it was possible that someone did hear all of this going on but they were too scared to do anything. Either way, Jonathan was alone at the moment and needed serious assistance. He watched as Percy carried Rachel out. His hand pressed firmly against her mouth. Air was starting to make its way back into Jonathan's lungs but he still couldn't muster enough to speak. He tried to slightly crawl and get up as he moved his hand forward; he couldn't let it end like this. Percy was taking Rachel away and he instinctively knew that if he didn't do something, this was would be the last time Jonathan would see her alive. His hand moved up again as he was trying to get up, then he felt something hard under his palm, when he moved his hand to see what it was; his assistance had arrived. It was a gun, wrapped in a dark brown leather holster; it must have been what Jonathan was feeling against his arm. It had fallen during Percy and Jonathan's short lived tussle. Percy hadn't noticed it nor was he paying any more attention to Jonathan, he figured he was down for the count; beaten and defeated. Jonathan watched as Percy was walking while carrying Rachel past the doorway. He had a clear view of them when Jonathan grabbed the gun and pulled it out of the holster. With more air filling his lungs by the second; he mustered enough strength to bring himself to his knees. He slightly moved to the left as Percy was now just outside the door with Rachel in the hallway. For a second, Jonathan took a deep breath as he felt the rubber grip of the gun fit snuggly into his hand. He didn't want to kill Percy; he wasn't ready for that type of warfare. Although these men were playing for keeps, Jonathan knew he was better than them. He couldn't do what they would do; he had to do what they wouldn't do, so he aimed the best he could toward Percy's right leg. He squeezed the trigger and let the gun do the rest. He heard a loud bang and saw a minor flash come from the barrel of the gun. It was the first time Jonathan had fired a gun, so he wasn't prepared for the kickback it had which caused his arm to rise up as he fired the gun again. Two more shots were fired successfully into the intended target. One bullet had went clean through the back of Percy's calf; the other hitting him right above the back of the knee in the thigh.

Jonathan stood to his feet; he could breathe again adrenaline pulsing through his veins and could feel the blood pumping in rhythm with his heart. There were still some traces of vomit around his mouth as he wiped it off. He looked at Percy who was now faced down in the hall. Percy dropped Rachel just before he fell; this gave her a chance to get out of the way and also prevented him from falling on top of her. She had tears in her eyes and a little spot of blood in the corner of her mouth from when Percy hit her. She got up and ran to Jonathan as he walked toward her, he was still in a daze trying to figure out what just happened. She hit his chest at almost full speed slightly knocking him backward. She buried her face in his chest as he wrapped his arms around her. She was sobbing uncontrollably but Jonathan was surprisingly calm. By this point, it wasn't too surprising since he's seen his fair share of violence in the city. He kissed her on the forehead, he looked up and saw Percy was still moving which was good sign that meant he wasn't dead, but he was definitely out of the game for now. "Rachel" said Jonathan. She was still in a state of hysteria, and, still crying. "Rachel" Jonathan repeated. "Rachel!!" this time he said in a firmer voice as he pushed her away from his chest. "We have to go" he said, "Listen to me we can't stay here" he said; knowing that there at least had to be one other person who heard shots being fired. Rachel was teary eyed looking up at Jonathan but complied. He grabbed her as the two of them left, and the next thing he knew they were in the car. The way down was a blur as if they had teleported to the car, with the key already in the ignition and the doors closed. Jonathan pulled out of the parking deck with retribution on his mind. The gun was in Rachel's lap and all she could do was stare at it in silence. Jonathan pulled out of the building's parking deck and onto the street as the day was still beautiful. That was the trick of the city; it tries to destroy someone but at the same time shows them its beauty in an attempt to distract them. Jonathan's fury passed through his hands and got into the car's engine, it roared up in horsepower as if it was aware of the pressing situation at hand. It did want Jonathan wanted, when he wanted. "Where are we going?" asked Rachel, still in shock over what had all just happened. Jonathan said nothing, only staying focused on the road ahead as he heard sirens in the back of him at a distance. It was an ambulance escorted by a mirage of police vehicles, all the lights flashing behind him lit up his rearview mirror. But he remained calm as he watched them turn off on another street. He knew where they were going. They were responding to the shots fired in his building to assist the broken juggernaut that was lying in the hall outside of his door. "To finish this", said Jonathan.

Mr. Edwards lived in the Hillcrest Estates which was on the other side of the city's main bridge. It was a decent drive to get over there but Jonathan was going to cut the time in half. He was driving like he had just robbed a bank. He even ran the occasional red light. He had no idea as to whether the police were looking for him or not but he didn't want to take any chances. As he continued ripping through the streets, he finally made it to the bridge. He remembered passing over the bridge from last few times he had been there; each time he looked at the river as he drove by. This time was no exception; he looked upon the face of the water as it was like a painting of pretty blue with white reflective lights from the sun dancing on top of it. It was like a beautiful soiree between two old friends always meeting at the same time every day and never growing old of each other's company. Meanwhile Jonathan was headed toward his own little soiree but it wasn't the friendly kind. "Rachel, do you know the name of this River?" he asked. "Yea, Cidal Point" "Why?" asked Rachel. "Because it might be the last time I drive past it" said Jonathan. Rachel looked over at him; her eyes still red from the tears that had been flowing through them. She said nothing only looking at him with shock and disbelief as they passed the bridge leaving the city. When they arrived at Hillcrest's gates, he noticed the man at the security station wasn't there and the gate was open. This wasn't the norm for a high-end neighborhood such as this. That didn't give Jonathan the best feeling but then again it helped him out because now he didn't have to try to figure out a way to get past the guard. Although if push came to shove he would have just waved the gun in his face and made him open it but this way was easier. Either way it was a bit out of place and he had learned by now to expect the unexpected with this man. So he grabbed the gun from Rachel's lap and placed it in his. He sped up once he passed the gate speeding through the residential streets of this high-end neighborhood. When he arrived at Mr. Edwards' estate, he pulled in hard and fast and slammed on the breaks as if he were about to go off a cliff like in some summer action movie. "What are you going to do?" asked Rachel. Jonathan flung his door open "Stay here and leave the car running" he instructed. He marched to the front door with the gun in his hand. He grabbed the big door knob that sat on the front door; it was surprisingly open. Something was off but he didn't care he had his gun to correct any problems that might arise. He took one last look back at the car and could see Rachel sitting in the passenger seat with fear still lingering in her eyes. He kept quiet. He glanced back at her before turning his attention to the house. He closed the door behind him. "KANE!!!!!" shouted Jonathan. At this point he had passed all formalities with his rage all but ripping through his vocal cords. He held the gun up in the event of an unfriendly surprise. "KANE!!!!!" he shouted again; hearing his own echo bounce off the walls of the multi-million dollar mansion. Suddenly Mr. Edwards's voice came over the intercom "There's no need to shout boy" "I'm in my study located on the same floor that you're on right now" he replied. "I trust you remember where it is" Jonathan headed over to the study; he remembered exactly where it was. When he got there he saw that the door was open. He leaned up against the wall with his gun drawn like some renegade cop ready for action. He paused for a minute then quickly turned, stopping in the middle of the doorway pointing the gun. On the other end of the barrel was his intended target leaning against his large wooden desk smoking a cigar with a glass of something expensive resting next to him. He was accompanied by a surprise guest as well; Adrian. Mr. Edwards took the cigar out of his mouth, "So I see we're on a first name basis now" said Mr. Edwards. "Yea you know I thought it was a bit more fitting since that name suits you." said Jonathan; walking toward him directly pointing the gun toward his head. "But that's no way to talk to your employer" said Mr. Edwards. "Well in case you haven't figured it out by now; I quit!" said Jonathan. "You know a part of me is proud of you, Jonathan…" said Mr. Edwards. "SHUT UP!" Jonathan shouted. "Enough with the mind games!" he belted out. "But I'm still going to have to discipline you" Mr. Edwards continued. Jonathan was too angry and busy screaming to allow Mr. Edwards to make any last remarks.

"I got your number, the jig is up you deceitful son-of-a-bitch!!" screamed Jonathan. "I know all about you and your little brother Carl over here" Jonathan confessed. He looked at Adrian for moment to see if he saw any humanity left behind those cold eyes. Adrian looked at Jonathan and then looked away. It wasn't all what Jonathan wanted but it was enough to let him know there was something there in Adrian; he wasn't completely dead if he could still show a sign of guilt or remorse. "I know what you did, I know about how you killed your parents in that fire!" "I'm sure you probably killed that lead investigator, just like you had Percy trash Rachel's house!" "Just like you tried to send him to break into my house and kill Rachel!" "Just like you had me beaten almost to a pulp in that parking garage!" "Just like you planted blackmailing evidence in the Mayor's house!" said Jonathan. "But you see, you forgot one thing!" "I know all of your dirty little secrets and I'll sing like a canary when the police get here, if I don't shoot you first!" "The one thing that I still don't understand is why Mr. Carl over here changed his name?" asked Jonathan. After he was done talking the room got quiet. Mr. Edwards took a sip from his glass and a puff of his cigar. He blew smoke out of his mouth almost making his face invisible to Jonathan. "Oh there's a lot you don't understand" slyly replied Mr. Edwards, still speaking through a cloud of smoke. "Well, for starters Adrian tried to forget who he was so he changed his name" "But I'll tell you the same thing I told him a long time ago, his name can change, but not his blood" "So if a simple swapping of the monikers made him feel better, than so be it" "Oh and as for the police, you were right about one thing, they are indeed on the way" Mr. Edwards continued. "But they're not coming for me, they're coming for YOU" said Mr. Edwards; the smoke was beginning to clear "They're coming to arrest the man who embezzled a million dollars from my company" said Mr. Edwards. Jonathan almost loosened his grip on the gun, when it hit him; the money that had mysteriously been placed in his account. "Wait, what?" asked Jonathan. It was starting to come into focus as Jonathan thought about it more and more. "See lets back up, I was looking forward to our partnership" said Mr. Edwards. "Then you're pretty little girlfriend had to rub her nose where it certainly didn't belong" "So she forced my hand and my people alerted me as to where she was and where she was headed, so I sent Mr. Percy to handle the matter." "But to my surprise, I get a phone call from Mr. Percy while he was bleeding in the hallway right outside your door, explaining to me how you managed to make a of mess of things" Mr. Edwards continued to explain. "I'll admit, that wasn't his finest hour but it certainly wasn't yours either" Now Jonathan started to think back to the comment Mr. Edwards made the last time they had spoken face to face. He said something about the money being for insurance; now unfortunately Jonathan was starting to understand what that meant. "But you gave that money to me; it'll show that the transfer was made to my account" Jonathan disputed. Mr. Edwards smiled "Oh no son, it won't; do you remember when you first joined the company you were given a login username and password to access the company's server" inquired Mr. Edwards. "Well, I had one of my I.T. guys make it look like you were stupid enough to use your username when you logged in and got access to the corporate account by using Ron Perkins' computer", Mr. Edwards cleverly answered. "You do remember Ron Perkins don't you? He's the CFO of the company; he has complete access to all of the company's corporate accounts." "He's also the man who your little girlfriend works directly under." "She's his Assistant remember?" asked Mr. Edwards. "Really Mr. Cross, you should pay more attention to who you're dating" he said. "I'll take her down with you and tell the police that she helped you get access to Perkin's computer so the two of you could steal his passwords for the accounts" "Like I said, you forced my hand" said Mr. Edwards, as he took another sip of alcohol. "Oh and not to mention that once I found this information out I sent one of my associates to go talk to you about it and you shot him" "That's my favorite part… Attempted Murder" said Mr. Edwards. "And as for the minor fact that he broke your door down, well yea it was forced entry" "But that's because Percy just felt so upset that you would take advantage of me after I'd taken you under my wing so to speak" "I promoted you and everything" "It's a shame really Officer I thought he was such a bright young man" "I really did have high hopes for him" concluded Mr. Edwards.

Jonathan stood there speechless; he had been completely set up he didn't know what to say. There was nothing for him to say really. "You tried boy, but you came up short" "You're playing checkers with a chess player, and it's my move" said Mr. Edwards. "And I'd have to say that this last move was indeed a CHECK MATE!" said Mr. Edwards. Jonathan blinked slowly. He knew he was right; Mr. Edwards had him all along. "I wasn't going to make this play but then you shot Percy, and I knew you'd probably do yet another idiotic move and probably try to come after me" Mr. Edwards further explained. "And I don't have time for all this kind of foolishness Mr. Cross I'm getting a little too old for it I suppose" Jonathan still stood silent pointing the gun, ready to shoot but he wouldn't… he couldn't he wasn't a killer. Suddenly the faint sound of sirens entered the room. "Ohh here comes your ride now" said Mr. Edwards. In that moment Jonathan knew what he had to do, although he hated to admit it he had no other choice. He put the gun down; he looked silently at the two of them with the scent of defeat hanging around in the air. He paused for a moment as the harsh reality continued to wrap itself around him. He then made a mad dash for the front door, he ran as hard as he could. He flung it open and ran to the car. He saw that Rachel was still inside as he reached for the car door. He flung it open and placed the gun in the back seat. "What did you do?" she asked with a worried and panicked look on her face. "I didn't kill him" he answered. "But he's trying to kill us" he said. He pressed on the gas launching out of the giant circular driveway as fast as the car would allow him. He happened to look in the rearview mirror and watched as Mr. Edwards and Adrian stood in front of the door as Mr. Edwards lifted his glass to Jonathan, making a toast. Jonathan began to explain to Rachel what all had happened and told her what it meant for the two of them. He was now a wanted man, a fugitive, with multiple charges to his name, and so was she if she decided to come with him. He offered to stop the car somewhere down the road once they were safely outside the city. She refused, she was sticking with the man who just saved her life; she wasn't going to abandon him. As he sped out of the gated community he passed a small army of police vehicles that were coming for him. They didn't expect to see him flying passed them, so they weren't able to stop in time as they slammed on their brakes. Rachel felt tears slide down her face, as Jonathan blazed through the streets with the police not far behind him. As he swerved in and out of lanes dodging cars he thought to himself about how he lost this battle; but he insisted that the war wasn't over. What Mr. Edwards failed to realize is that he did in fact succeed in changing who Jonathan was but not in the way he had hoped. Through the pain and the trials, Jonathan had become something he wasn't when he first came to Edge City; a Man. He learned about himself and what that animal really was that Mr. Edwards referred to. It in fact had a name it was called will; it was Jonathan's inner willpower that made him special. He had learned how to use it and would continue to perfect it along the way. He vowed that he would defeat Mr. Edwards and wouldn't stop until that man was rotting away behind bars. He resolved within himself that he'd be like a phoenix and rise back with a mighty vengeance. He would clear his name and Rachel's; his mission was now clearly defined. He wasn't going to stop until every wrong was made right. He refused to let it end like this. No, his life would not end here because this wasn't the end of Jonathan Cross; it was the beginning…

www.ingramcontent.com/pod-product-compliance
Lightning Source LLC
Chambersburg PA
CBHW061035120726
47910CB00006B/2258